DARK WARRIOR MINE

THE CHILDREN OF THE GODS BOOK 7

I. T. LUCAS

NOTE FROM THE AUTHOR:

Dark Warrior Mine is a work of fiction!

Names, characters, places and incidents are products of the
author's imagination or are used fictitiously and are not to
be construed as real. Any similarity to actual persons,
organizations and/or events is purely coincidental.

PROLOGUE

Harvard-Westlake High school
Studio City, California
13 years ago.

"*H*i, Nathalie." Leaning his hip against the metal door of his locker, Luke Bruoker produced his seductive smile. For her.

Walk away, the voice in her head commanded.

Shut up, Nathalie thought back.

Just do it. You know what he's thinking.

As if she needed Tut to freaking tell her what was on Luke's mind as he flashed her, *Nutty Nattie,* the perfect set of teeth that had all the other girls wetting their designer panties. With his good looks and rich daddy, Luke was one of the most popular guys in school, and for giving her the time of day, he probably expected her to fall at his feet in gratitude.

Not this girl, not going to happen, buddy.

Trying to ignore her too handsome and too full of

himself locker neighbor, Nathalie stuffed the books she came to retrieve in her backpack.

But what if she was wrong? What if Luke was just being nice? And anyway, even if he wasn't, she didn't want to be rude.

"Hi, Luke." Nathalie lifted the corners of her lips in a tight smile and waved goodbye.

You're not wrong, Tut snickered. *But if it's any consolation, he thinks you're hot.*

It's not.

Unfortunately, there was no way to hide things from the stowaway sharing her cranium space.

You're such a liar. Tut's laugh echoed in her head before slowly fading away.

Well, what did he expect? She was only human and couldn't help but feel flattered.

He was such a pain, but if she was lucky, for the next few hours he'd leave her alone. Tut, or *tutor,* as he'd introduced himself after chasing all the other voices away, hated math class. In fact, the ghost in her head didn't like school, or homework, or tests—which was probably the main reason she was such a good student. The only time Nathalie could be alone in her own skull was while studying.

Tut claimed to be teaching her about life.

Yeah, right, more like ruining it.

Watching TV with him was a nightmare. He wouldn't shut up for a moment with his nonstop derisive commentary about everyone and everything. And hanging out with friends or going to the mall was more of the same.

Who was she kidding? As if anyone wanted to hang out with Nutty Nattie—the girl who talked to herself.

Nathalie pulled on the straps of her heavy backpack, hitching it higher on her back as she walked faster—

pretending to rush so no one would notice that she always walked alone.

Mostly, she felt invisible. No one would look at her, except maybe for some of the nicer girls who would occasionally give her a pitying smile—as if she was retarded or deformed. The best she could hope for was to be regarded as the crazy genius. Unfortunately, even though she was smart and worked harder than most, she deserved only the first part of the title.

But at least her hard work had gotten her accepted into this overpriced private high school. Trouble was, her parents couldn't really afford it—not even with the generous financial aid they'd been awarded—and she knew for a fact that they were dipping into their equity line to finance the difference. The school called the discount a scholarship, but it wasn't. None of the rich kids were getting it, not even those who were excellent students.

Still, it wasn't as if anyone was privy to that information, but it wasn't hard to guess either. Her classmates arrived at school in Mercedes and BMWs while she drove a three-year-old Toyota Corolla hatchback.

Not that she was complaining, her car was great—the previous owner had hardly driven her, and she was almost as good as new. Besides, this was the best her parents could afford. God knew they had always given her everything they could, and probably more than they should—spoiling their only child.

When she was younger, she'd thought it was her due, but lately, it was making her feel guilty. It seemed as if by giving her all of their love, her parents were left with nothing for each other.

In fact, this morning, her mother told her that she'd filed for a divorce.

Oh, God, what is Papi going to do?

The coffee shop wasn't making much, and they would not have been able to afford much of anything without her mother's government pension.

How is Papi going to survive without it?

Thank God, it was her last year of high school, so at least this expense would be gone. And since she'd gotten a full-ride scholarship to the University of Virginia, college wouldn't cost her parents anything.

But savings aside, it meant that her father would be all alone once she left.

At sixty, her mother was still a knockout, while Papi, two years her junior, looked like a grandpa. It had to do with his love of baking—and eating. He was at least fifty pounds overweight and almost bald. But he was the sweetest guy. Which was probably why his business wasn't doing so well. He had never turned away anyone who was hungry, regardless of their ability to pay.

Not fair.

The God her father believed in so earnestly should've smiled upon a man like him, rewarded him for his good heart and generosity. But instead, his beloved coffee shop was barely staying afloat, and his beautiful wife was leaving him.

Nathalie had a feeling that her mother had just been waiting for her to finish school and go to college to make her move. Eva hadn't been happy for years—even when Papi had been much thinner and still had hair. She always looked troubled, almost fearful, though Nathalie couldn't figure out why.

Maybe her mother suffered from some mental disease —like Nathalie did. Though instead of hearing voices of dead people in her head, Eva might've been anxious or depressed.

It was about time she talked with her mother and

cleared things up. She was definitely old enough for a grownup conversation. Perhaps they both could benefit from psychiatric help. And maybe, just maybe, with treatment, Eva might change her mind about leaving.

But even if she wouldn't, to be rid of Tut, it was worth a try.

Problem was, psychiatrists were expensive.

Maybe that was why her parents had never taken her to one, even though they must've known that her so-called imaginary friends had been very different than those of other kids.

But Papi had said that it was harmless, nothing to worry about, and her mother had agreed. They'd cautioned her that it was okay to play pretend at home, but she shouldn't be talking to herself in public.

Nathalie had tried.

As she had grown older, she'd realized that it wasn't normal and that the people talking to her in her head were probably just elaborate hallucinations. A mental disorder and not ghosts. She'd stopped telling even her parents about it.

But here and there, she would forget herself and respond out loud—hence the damn nickname. *Nutty Nattie.*

ANDREW

I've just landed, taxiing in, I can be at your place in an hour. Andrew texted Bridget as soon as it was okay to turn cell phones on.

She answered. *Waiting impatiently* (ʔ~ʔ)

It took him a few seconds to decipher the meaning.

Cute.

For an immortal, who was born God knew when, she was surprisingly well versed in current texting lingo and etiquette. Better than he was. He'd never asked Bridget how old she was, in part because he felt it was impolite, and in part because he was afraid to find out. For a forty-year-old man, it would've been beyond weird to know that his girlfriend was hundreds of years old.

Andrew wondered how Syssi dealt with her husband's age. His baby sister, thirteen years his junior, had fallen in love with Kian before finding out that her Greek-god-lookalike boyfriend was so ancient.

The few clan members Andrew had gotten to know since he'd been sucked into their world ranged in age from nearly two thousand, like his new brother-in-law, to Amanda, who was over two hundred. Not to mention their mother, the goddess, who was over five thousand years old or more.

This was another lady who Andrew would never dare ask for her age. He was an adrenaline junkie, but he wasn't stupid enough to court certain death.

After a day of endless meetings, followed by a five-hour flight from Washington back to L.A., Andrew would've preferred for Bridget to come over to his place. Trouble was, whatever was in the fridge had probably spoiled over the two weeks he'd been gone.

True, he could've ordered takeout, but there was also the issue of his bed being messy, and probably not quite fresh smelling. He couldn't remember the last time he'd changed the linens. Not that they were all the way into the gross category, but Bridget deserved better.

He'd thought about buying her a present in D.C. but eventually had given up on the idea. First of all, Bridget was loaded, just like all other clan members, and what Andrew defined as a reasonably-priced gift, she might consider trash. Secondly, he had no idea what to buy for a woman in general and for this one in particular. Dr. Bridget's tastes gravitated toward the practical.

Except, she had a thing for red.

Damn, just thinking about those spiky red heels of hers was enough to get him hard. But it wasn't as if he could buy her shoes. And even if he were one of those guys who could guess a woman's shoe size, hers were probably the kind that cost over a thousand bucks—not something he could afford on his government salary.

So yeah, the only things he felt confident buying for a woman were chocolates and flowers.

But at least he wasn't as clueless as Bhathian, who

didn't even know how to behave around one, or what to say.

The guy had been terrified of going to see the long-lost daughter Andrew had found for him. So much so that he'd asked Andrew to accompany him to her coffee shop, just so they could sit there, pretending to be customers. It hadn't been a good feeling to bail on the guy, but Andrew had had no choice. Her place had been closed on the evening he'd delivered the news of her existence, and the next day he'd been told to pack up a suitcase and hop on a plane to Washington.

The trip had been a total waste of time. He'd spent two fucking weeks in Homeland Security headquarters—stuck in boring meetings, listening to bureaucrats who believed they knew best how to devise a plan of action that could've been condensed into five paragraphs on one yellow-pad page. Actually, it was exactly what he'd brought back.

One fucking page.

They could've bloody emailed him. Anyway, no one had listened to what he'd had to say.

Fuck, he hoped Bhathian hadn't waited for him to go see the girl—correction, woman; earlier this year the guy's daughter had turned thirty.

An hour later, Andrew knocked on Bridget's door. Luckily, no one had hitched a ride with him on the elevator that had taken him from the clan's private parking level up to her floor. And by no one he meant Bhathian.

He planned to call the guy after his reunion with Bridget.

Andrew and the doctor had a lot of steam to release. The entire time he'd been away, he'd been preserving his energy for the insatiable immortal.

Today, he would show her staying power.

She opened the door, wearing a long white T-shirt,

spiky red heels, and nothing else. "Andrew, you have no idea how happy I am to see you," she purred.

"Not as happy as I am." He lifted her up for a kiss, kicking the door closed behind him. She wrapped her legs around his hips.

Bridget was naked under that semi-sheer thing, every curve and shade of her generous breasts and aroused nipples clearly visible, and the bedroom was too far away.

Turning around, he pinned her against the nearest wall. "I can't wait," he groaned, holding her up with one hand and going for his belt buckle with the other.

"Let me." She pushed his hand away and opened things up for him. Freeing his shaft, she guided it into her moist heat. Bridget was drenched. He hesitated, but only for a split second, before ramming inside her with one powerful thrust.

On a groan, her head hit the wall behind her.

With the wall holding part of her weight and her thighs locked in a tight grip around his hips, he needed only one hand on her ass to keep going, and he put the other one to good use, pushing her shirt up and palming a breast.

Bridget did one better, pulling the thing over her head and tossing it on the floor. Now, she was completely bare save for the shoes.

They could stay on.

Damn, this was so fucking hot.

Thumbing one perky nipple, he pinched and tugged, taking turns and giving each the same loving attention.

Bridget's hands shot into his short hair, and she gripped his skull, bringing his head closer for a hungry kiss. As their tongues and teeth dueled, her sharp incisors were winning, and as she bit down on his lower lip, she drew blood.

Feisty immortal.

He brought his hand down on her butt with a loud slap, then gripped both cheeks and began pounding with gusto.

"Yes! Oh, dear Fates, yes!" Bridget seemed oblivious to the fact that she was being banged into the wall with such force that the plaster was cracking, and small particles of paint were flying in the air.

If she were mortal, she would've bruised badly.

Liberated by her resilience, Andrew kept going hard.

It was so fucking good to feel vital, strong, male. But as he neared his completion, Andrew had the passing thought that as amazing as this was, something was still missing.

"Now," Bridget hissed.

He obeyed her command, synchronizing his climax with hers and coming hard inside her—his shaft milked by the convulsing muscles in her sheath gripping him harder than any fist.

"God, Bridget..." He fumbled for words as he lowered her.

Her thighs trembled a little, but as her feet touched the floor, she was steady. "Come to bed." She bent and pulled his pants up but left them unzipped. "I don't want you to trip on the way. I still have a use for you." She winked and walked away.

To his relief, he saw that although her back was slightly reddened, the skin looked intact. But as she sauntered ahead of him, he noticed that one of her curvy butt cheeks still bore a faint outline of his handprint. That one, he didn't mind. Not at all.

In fact, he felt his shaft give a twitch. Good, the abstinence was paying off. Tonight, he would be able to last, hopefully for as long as it would take to satisfy the lustful immortal.

Two hours later, a Victoria's Secret lineup naked parade wouldn't have gotten a rise out of him. And if tongues could get sprains, his would've been sporting a brace.

The merry tune Bridget was whistling in the kitchen was like a slap to his manhood. She was going to kill him, pleasurably, but he'd be dead nonetheless.

Andrew closed his eyes and inhaled deeply. One didn't need an immortal's superior nose to smell the thick scent of sex on the bedding, and if he had an ounce of energy left in him, he would've gotten all domestic and taken them off for her.

Still naked, Bridget sauntered into the bedroom with a loaded tray and placed it on the side table. "Sit up. I'm going to nourish you. You look pale."

"I wonder why?" he said as he propped himself up on the pillows and took the coffee mug she'd handed him.

"Poor baby. Too much for you?"

Now, that was mean.

"Not at all. Give me an hour and I'm back up." *Not if my life depended on it...*

"Aha. Sure. Whatever you say." She handed him a pastry.

As he chewed, he was reminded of the call he still owed Bhathian. It would have to wait until he could move.

"This is good. Where did you get it?"

"I was on Fairfax earlier today, and the smells lured me into this new bakery. I don't remember the name, but it's on the box if you want to write it down. I bought an assortment to try it out, but I'm afraid this is the only one left." She smiled sheepishly.

"Oh, yeah? Who ate all the rest?"

"I did."

"How many?"

"Eleven. There were twelve in the box."

And here he'd thought that Bridget only ate veggies.

With an appetite like this for baked goods, it was a miracle she wasn't fat.

He appraised her lean midsection. "Where do you pack it all?"

"Breasts and butt." She patted the aforementioned parts.

"Then by all means, eat more. I love your curves."

A sad shadow clouded her eyes, but only momentarily. She shook it off so fast Andrew wasn't sure if it had really been there or if he'd just imagined it.

She grinned. "You and the construction workers renovating that old office building on Olive. Every time I pass by, they whistle and comment."

"Want me to beat them up for you?"

She laughed. "Why on earth would I want that?"

"Some women find it offensive." He shrugged.

"I don't mind the whistling, but the comments they think I can't hear…"

"My offer is still on the table."

She leaned and kissed his cheek. "You're so sweet."

"What is it with immortal females and calling me sweet? Even my own mother never called me that."

She kissed him again, on the lips this time. "What's the matter? Your machismo got hurt?"

He crossed his arms over his chest. "Yes."

Bridget refilled his coffee mug and handed him a piece of an apple as a peace offering.

"Can you stay the night?"

And prove himself a liar when even three hours later he would remain as limp as a noodle? No way. "I wish I could, but I got to talk to Bhathian. There is something I'd promised him to do, and I didn't have a chance because of that damn useless conference my boss sent me on with barely any notice."

"You could come back later…I'm flying out to Baltimore tomorrow…"

"I thought Julian's graduation was next week."

"It is, but I wanted to spend some time with him, and he made plans with his roommates for a road trip after the graduation."

Damn, he hated to disappoint her, but he hated the prospect of staying even more. His suitcase was still in his car because he'd come here straight from the airport, and tomorrow was another long workday. He needed to go home.

Andrew pulled her into his arms and kissed her lips gently. "I'm sorry, but I just have to go home and unpack, check what alien life forms are growing in my fridge…" He tried for humor, and it worked.

She smiled. "Fascinating, save some samples for me."

"I promise to save something better than disgusting growth for you to play with."

"And what might that be?"

"Life force? Energy?" He made a face.

Bridget laughed. "After another ten days of nada, you'll need it."

"I know."

SEBASTIAN

*S*tanding on top of the old monastery's newly added third-floor balcony, Sebastian leaned over the railing and glared at the cars parked outside. A damned parking lot was one more thing Sebastian realized he had neglected to plan for his new base of operation in the picturesque Ojai.

The front of the building looked like a junkyard, and in the daytime it was even worse.

From his balcony, he should be gazing at a grassy lawn and flowerbeds, not a bunch of used cars scattered on top of packed dirt.

A paved circular driveway and a fountain with a statue at its center, surrounded by rose bushes, would have made the place look grand.

But hiring workers now that the warriors were all in residence was problematic. Training would have to be suspended, and the guys would have to make themselves scarce.

The men hardly matched what one would expect of those visiting a restful *spiritual retreat*.

There was no helping the cars, though. The men needed vehicles to transport themselves to and from the clubs they were now scoping nightly in search of male clan members. Tom and Robert had gone shopping, and in a few days had managed to fill the lot with a bunch of used cars. Sebastian would've preferred to go into a dealership and lease a fleet, but Tom had insisted that buying from private owners was more discreet.

All in all, they now had twenty-nine vehicles at their disposal.

One was a big truck, for just in case, and the rest an assortment of minivans and SUVs. While the troops shared the used cars at a ratio of three to one, Sebastian had insisted that he and his two assistants each had their own brand new vehicle.

For obvious reasons, all had darkened windows.

The cars were serving dual purposes. The obvious one was transportation, but also, when needed, the back seats could be folded to provide a place for a quick fuck.

With his basement brothel's low occupancy rate, his troop's needs had to be satisfied off base.

Over the last two weeks, Sebastian had been able to find only five girls for his brothel. Not enough to take care of seventy-five immortal warriors, two assistants, and one sadist. But there was only so much he could do in a day, and snagging the right females required investigative work that took time.

Most hadn't been the right fit.

Which reminded him that there was another issue he hadn't accounted for. Human females required sunlight and fresh air to stay healthy and in a good mood. Thralling was not enough to counteract the underlying depression the lack of natural light and tiny jail rooms were causing.

He'd come to the conclusion that he couldn't keep them cooped up in the basement twenty-four hours a day.

On Pleasure Island, the women enjoyed several swimming pools, above-ground bars and restaurants, and the beautiful, tropical ocean. It was a gross oversight on his part to not realize the importance of those amenities.

Sebastian should have known that the exalted leader of *The Devout Order Of Mordth*, Lord Navuh, never did anything without a good reason. If Navuh had chosen to provide his whores with outdoor recreation, it had been only because it was crucial for the women's health and their ability to provide the exceptional services his secret island was known for.

Sebastian pulled out his phone and selected Robert's number. "Grab Tom and meet me outside."

"Yes, sir."

Sebastian rolled his eyes but didn't say anything. Robert was a lost cause. Jogging down the stairs, he glanced at the spacious recreation room. The men were done with their chores for the day, and several were taking a break playing pool or watching a movie before going to their rooms to get ready for the nightly club patrols.

There had been a lot of grumbling about the domestic chores they'd been assigned, but he had no intention of getting more humans on the premises to perform the cooking and housekeeping duties. Perhaps once the basement rooms were all filled, he would divert his attention to finding at least a decent cook. He was sick of the barbecued steaks and hamburgers the men were taking turns preparing.

Other than that, the lazy fuckers could keep on doing laundry, sweeping floors, and cleaning toilets. It wasn't as if they had that much to do during the day. Five hours of training was enough to keep them in shape, and the rest of their work was done at night.

Outside, the mountain air was crisp and cool, and other than the rumbling voices of the men inside, he could hear only the chirping of crickets and the hooting of the occasional owl. Even the coyotes didn't dare go anywhere near the compound.

"You wanted to see us, boss?" Tom said from behind him.

"Yes, I want to do something about the grounds." He waved his hand at the vehicles. In the weak moonlight, their colors were faded, all looking like different shades of gray and black. "I don't want to see this out of my window."

Robert glanced around at the gentle hills surrounding the former monastery. "This is the only flat area."

The problem with subordinates who were good at taking orders was that they didn't think independently, you had to chew everything for them.

"What do you have in mind?" Tom asked.

"I want the parking lot to be moved over there." Sebastian pointed to the side of the building. "And I want a circular driveway with a fountain in the center. The rest of the grounds need planting; grass, flowers, trees, the works." Sebastian began walking. "Come with me." He motioned for them to follow.

At some point, the back of the property had had grassy lawns with gravel paths meandering through them, but now there was nothing besides overgrown weeds and construction debris that hadn't been taken care of yet.

"I'm thinking of putting in a swimming pool over there, and an outdoor bar with shaded trellises on that side. We'll need to bring in large, mature trees to create a green canopy around the whole thing. Girls lounging in bikinis are not exactly what one expects to find in an 'Interfaith Spiritual Retreat'."

Robert looked intrigued.

"And how do you suggest we do it?" Tom asked.

"That's what I need to figure out. If it were only planting, I would've had the men do it, but for the pool and hardscaping we need a contractor with heavy equipment."

Robert crossed his arms over his chest and started pacing back and forth. "Curfew," he uttered a few moments later. "We need to coordinate several contractors with large crews to come and be done in a few hours. We'll have the men on lockdown in the house while the construction is going on."

"What about the cars?" Tom asked.

"We park them in a line on the side of the road, one behind the other."

Sebastian clapped Robert's back. "Great idea, Robert. We could tell the contractors that there are guests in the retreat and work needs to be confined to a predetermined number of hours a day. This will also explain the cars."

The guy, who was tall to begin with, seemed to grow a few inches. "Thank you, Sebastian," he said without stuttering or mumbling for the first time.

Clap, clap, clap. "Finally," Tom said.

ANDREW

I'm back and here in the building. Want to meet me downstairs? Andrew texted Bhathian.

Come to my place. 37 floor, #4.

I'm on my way.

Bridget's apartment was just one floor above Bhathian's, and Andrew opted to take the emergency stairs down.

They had already said their goodbyes. He'd offered to come get her and drive her to the airport, but she'd declined. Her flight was leaving in the afternoon, and she'd said that she saw no reason for him to take time off work. A taxi would do.

To his shame, he'd felt relieved. There was a big pile of files waiting for him in the office, and to catch up, he would need to not only work through his lunch break but stay overtime. His damn bosses still expected him to deliver a report despite sending him on that useless trip.

Andrew rapped his knuckles on the door and waited.

After a moment, Bhathian opened it. "Hey, my man, come in. How was your trip?" He clasped Andrew's hand.

"A waste of time." Andrew shook it then followed him inside.

The layout and furnishings were similar to Bridget's. But where hers had been personalized with all kinds of knickknacks, and everything was nice and tidy, the guy's place was typical of what one would expect to find in a bachelor's apartment.

There was an opened box of pizza on the dining table, and empty beer bottles littered every surface. It seemed that Bhathian had appropriated all that had been left from Kian's bachelor party because most of them were Snake's Venom, the expensive, super potent Scottish beer Anandur had bought for the occasion.

Bhathian followed his gaze. "Want one? I have plenty."

"Sure, why not?'

The guy ducked into the kitchen and returned with two cold ones.

Andrew took one. "I'm surprised so many were left. I thought we demolished all of them."

"There were none. But they were good, so the next day I went and bought two cases for myself."

"I thought they were pricey."

Bhathian shrugged his massive shoulders and planted his butt in a chair across from Andrew. "I have plenty of money and nothing to spend it on."

"You didn't go to see her." There was no need to specify which her he was talking about.

Bhathian winced. "The farthest I got was to stand outside her shop, but I didn't have the guts to go in."

"I'm sorry that I bailed on you."

"Not your fault."

"Do you want to go tomorrow?"

"If you can come, then yes."

"So, did you get a peek?"

Bhathian nodded. "She looks like her mother."

"Oh, yeah?"

"Beautiful." There was a definite note of pride in Bhathian's voice.

"Does she have anything from you?"

"Luckily for her, not much." Bhathian grimaced. "She has my thick eyebrows. Though, hers are pretty, not bushy like mine."

Andrew tried to picture a woman with Eva's exotic beauty and Bhathian's surly expression and came up blank.

Bhathian took a swig from his beer. "I need to find out what happened to Eva. Any idea how?"

Good question. The fact that the police hadn't found anything didn't mean much. Their investigation had probably been superficial at best.

"We can start by following the money trail. The government is still depositing her monthly pension checks into her bank account, and if she's still alive, I'm sure she is accessing it."

"And you can find out where she's making withdrawals?"

"Not easily, but yes. Unless the money is funneled through a Swiss bank. Then it's next to impossible."

Bhathian shook his head. "Just so you know, I'm forever in your debt. Whatever you need, whenever, just say the word."

"I appreciate it, but save your gratitude for when I actually find something."

"You already found my daughter, and for this alone I owe you big time. I'm not just blowing smoke up your ass, I mean it. Whatever, whenever."

"Okay, I got it, but it's really not necessary. If the roles were reversed, I'm sure you would've done the same for me." It seemed like the right thing to say, even though

Andrew wasn't sure it was true. He was an outsider, tolerated only because his sister was married to the regent.

But Bhathian nodded solemnly, and leaned forward, extending his hand with the bottle. "That's what family is for."

Okay, so he might have been wrong. It seemed that Bhathian had really accepted Andrew as one of the clan. "To family." He clinked bottles with the guy.

"To family," Bhathian echoed.

Andrew emptied his bottle of Snake's Venom and put the empty on the coffee table before pushing up to his feet.

Damn, the thing must've gone to his head because he had a moment of vertigo. But it passed almost as soon as it started. It was probably only the fatigue catching up to him. "Tomorrow after work I'll come to get you, and we'll drive to Glendale. Seven okay?"

Bhathian got up and escorted him to the door. "Whatever works for you." The guy pulled Andrew into a crushing bear hug and clapped his back.

"Careful, my man. I'm still only a fragile human."

A rare smile brightening his gloomy features, Bhathian let go. "You might be a human, but from what I hear there is nothing fragile about you, tough guy."

And wasn't that good to hear.

On his way home, as he drove through the deserted streets of downtown L.A., Andrew reflected on his conversation with Bhathian.

Family.

For better or worse, the clan was now his family—independent of his decision regarding chancing the transition or not. They'd accepted him as is—the first human ever to be admitted into their tight, secret community.

He wondered if things would've been different if he hadn't brought all that he had to the table. If he were just an average Joe, with an average job, would they have entrusted him with their secrets?

Probably not.

The truth was that the clan needed him. Not that it was a bad thing necessarily, being needed was just as important as being accepted, maybe even more. Especially for a proud son-of-a-gun like him.

Which made him think of Dalhu.

The dude had done the impossible. His acceptance by the clan, however, had come at an unimaginable price. Andrew could not think of a single male that could've taken the torment Dalhu had gone through—not with the dignity and unparalleled willpower the guy had displayed.

One thing was for sure, if Andrew ever needed someone to fight by his side, Dalhu would be his first choice. Not that there was a chance the guy would be allowed to fight anytime soon. For all intents and purposes, Dalhu was still under house arrest—during his probation period as Kian had called it. True, he was no longer confined to the dungeon, and was sharing Amanda's spacious penthouse, but he wasn't allowed to leave.

The guy must be going crazy.

For a warrior to be cooped up in an apartment without the ability to release some steam must be hard. And it didn't matter that he was living in the lap of luxury with the love of his life.

Maybe Andrew should go spend some time with the dude, invite him for a sparring contest down in the gym.

Right.

Who was he kidding? As if he could offer any kind of a challenge to the powerful immortal. Even among the Guardians, Andrew suspected that only Anandur, or perhaps Yamanu, stood a chance against the ex-Doomer.

Amanda had gotten herself one hell of a protector.

Damn, it still stung.

Losing to the other guy hadn't been good for Andrew's ego. But he had to concede that despite his initial opinion of the guy, Dalhu had turned out to be the better man for Amanda.

God knew that with the kind of trouble the woman courted, Dalhu was probably the only male on earth capable of keeping her safe.

SYSSI

"*C*ome here." Kian swiveled his chair and spread his knees in invitation.

It had been like this since the first day she had joined him in the office. The moment Shai would leave, Kian would turn his chair around and invite her for a kiss that would often end in nookie.

As it turned out, she was more of an impediment than help.

The only thing she'd managed to achieve so far, apart from keeping her hubby happy, was to reorganize one small section of the filing cabinet. One at a time, she replaced the old, worn files with new ones and created an electronic version, including making detailed spreadsheets and scanning the supporting documents. Since Kian and Shai were such old farts they were still doing things the old fashioned way, meaning like before the Industrial Revolution, her help was invaluable. Problem was, Kian and she were too busy necking to accomplish much.

"I'm waiting..." he growled.

Syssi rolled her eyes and punched one last number into the spreadsheet before obeying his command.

"Yes, sir." She pushed out of her chair and got between his spread thighs.

"That's what I like to hear." He closed his arms around her, pulling her in and kissing her, hungrily, as if they hadn't kissed just five minutes ago.

"You know, I was supposed to be helping you, but I don't think you're getting any work done." She moved to sit on one muscular thigh.

His hand snaked under her shirt, and he thumbed her nipple over her bra. "Yes, I love coming to work now. I didn't before."

He had a point there. Well, not really, but who could think straight with arousal short circuiting cognition?

"I don't want to be responsible for your conglomerate's demise...Oh, God..." she breathed as he snapped her bra open and tugged on the other nipple.

"Nonsense, you're providing an invaluable service." He pushed her shirt up and licked the engorged peak before closing his lips around it and sucking it in.

"Fuck..." she exclaimed.

Oh no... they had a rule about her using that kind of language. Because it wasn't part of her usual vocabulary, it had become an invitation to a game that she preferred to play in the privacy of their bedroom, and not in the office where anyone could walk in at any moment. And besides, the freaking place had glass doors, so anyone passing by could see what was going on inside. Never mind that she was already half naked. But for some reason, it wasn't as embarrassing as what was coming next.

As Kian lifted his head up from her breast, he had the wickedest smile on his handsome as sin face. "My sweet, naughty girl just earned herself a spanking."

"Not here," she whispered, feeling herself blush. But this wasn't the only heat that was spreading all over her body...

"Yes, here." In a heartbeat, she found herself face down over his other knee with her jeans yanked down and her butt exposed.

"Someone might come in," she hissed, struggling to get up without much success. Even with her new strength, the arm holding her pinned to his body was as unyielding as an iron band.

"Don't worry, no one is coming, and I'll hear if anyone is out in the corridor." With a loud crack, the first slap landed on her exposed behind.

As if he can hear anything over that...

But as the second and third fell in quick succession, she stopped thinking and stopped struggling and just gave in to the sensation. By the time Kian had delivered the tenth and last, she was so close to climax she was contemplating using another f-bomb to have him start over. There was no need, though. Thirty seconds later, as Kian penetrated her soaking sheath with two fingers and then added a thumb over her most sensitive part, she came all over his hand. And his jeans.

He lifted her limp, spent body and cradled her in his lap. "I love you so much." He kissed her lips.

"I'm going to sue my boss for sexual harassment," she croaked.

"Oh, yeah? And who is that wicked boss? You can't sue yourself, you know."

"So now I'm the boss?"

"Of course, you are."

"Didn't feel like it a moment ago when you were spanking me."

"Just fulfilling my matrimonial duties as promised."

She shifted up and kissed his lips. "I love you too. But seriously, now I need to go up and change underwear. Again. And you must be really uncomfortable." She wiggled her butt over his shaft.

"No problem. I'll accompany you upstairs, and we'll continue where we left off."

"For the second time today. This can't go on, Kian. We are like a couple of horny teenagers who can't keep their hands off each other."

"What's wrong with that? I think it's great."

"Because you have important work to do, you big lug. And frankly, although playing nookie with you is super fun, I'm wasting my time here. Anyone with basic computer skills could be doing my job."

"Don't you dare quit on me. For the first time that I can remember, I'm looking forward to my workday."

"What workday? You are not doing any work. Admit it, even when Shai is here, all you do is think about the next time he leaves so you can have your hands on me."

Kian ran his fingers through his chin-length hair, brushing it back. "I can't help it. Having you near me all day long is a temptation I can't resist. I'm just a simple man with simple needs. In fact, just one, you."

He was so sweet. "I love you, and I feel the same. But we are both adults with adult responsibilities. My time would be better spent helping Amanda find more Dormants. And you could actually accomplish something during the hours you spend here."

"I don't want to." He crossed his arms over his chest, pouting like a toddler.

She caressed his cheek. "I know, my love. How about this, you bring in another assistant, someone young who will modernize your ancient record keeping and help you finish your work in less time. I'll work with Amanda, but only until four in the afternoon. That way we'll still have plenty of time to spend with each other."

"What about the other stuff I need to do, besides office work? Like showing my face at meetings and classes, and visiting with people in my official capacity."

"I'll come with you to those."

"Okay, you won. But I don't like it."

"I know, neither do I. But it's for the best. Besides, it's not like it's carved in stone. If it doesn't work, we can reevaluate and make changes. Now let me go so I can pull my pants up. I've been sitting here bare-assed for far too long."

Kian helped her up and tugged her jeans back into place.

"Yikes, I hate wearing wet panties."

His smile was conceited. "Let's go. You can take them off in our private elevator. We have some unfinished business to take care of."

5

AMANDA

"So, what do you think?" Amanda crossed her arms over her chest.

"This bedroom is definitely better than the one facing the side of the building." Ingrid pushed the second layer of drapery aside. "If we position the easel next to the window, our resident artist will have plenty of natural light to draw by. We can knock out the dividing wall between this and the adjoining room, to give him more space."

Dalhu was in need of a studio, or rather Amanda was.

Her living room was a mess. With all kinds of drawings, completed and in various stages of progress, propped against the walls and couches and the coffee table. Soon, Dalhu would be spilling his mess into the dining room. Not to mention that there had been charcoal smears on her designer throw pillows before Onidu had rushed to hide the evidence, somehow managing to remove the stains and return her beautiful pillows to their previous pristine condition.

It seemed that her emotionless butler had taken a liking to Dalhu.

Figures, even a biomechanical creation and an ex-Doomer were doing the male bonding thing.

But the mess and the charcoal dust weren't the worst of it. A number of her clansmen were waiting in line for Dalhu to draw their portraits, and some had requested a full body nude. Well, just one. Anandur.

At first, she'd thought he was joking, but he'd kept nagging about it, and today he came over, thankfully posing only half naked. She could deal with him shirtless, but she drew the line there. Anandur's junk on full display wasn't something she wanted to see, which would be hard to avoid with Anandur posing for Dalhu in the middle of her living room.

Our living room...

Damn, after almost two centuries of living practically alone, it was one hell of an adjustment to live with someone other than Onidu. Having to be considerate, accommodating...

To keep the façade going twenty-four-seven.

It was such an ingrained habit that she just couldn't drop it no matter how hard she tried.

She kept telling herself that it wasn't needed, that Dalhu loved her unconditionally, and that he didn't expect her to act upbeat and smile all of the time. But it was no use. Wherever she had an audience, even if only of one, Amanda felt compelled to put on a performance.

She sighed. Small steps, one little thing at a time.

"What else do we need here?"

"Shouldn't you ask Dalhu what he wants?"

"Nah, he wouldn't know. It's not as if he has ever set foot into an art studio. And anyway, I want it to be a surprise."

"I was wondering where he was. What have you done with him?"

31

"I had Anandur take him down to the gym for a workout. After all, we can't have all those amazing muscles atrophy, can we?" She winked at Ingrid.

"Certainly not. The guy is such eye candy…"

"Watch it." Amanda pointed her finger at the covetous designer. "He is mine. Eyes and hands off."

Ingrid laughed. "Yes, ma'am. But you need to hurry up and find more male Dormants for us because there is talk among the girls of going down to the catacombs and reviving us some Doomers."

"You are joking, right?"

"Give it a little time and the joking will turn into doing. I'm not kidding. Some of us are green with envy."

"Listen, Ingrid, tell your horny friends to forget about it. Dalhu is the one and probably only exception to what we know is a typical Doomer. Should I remind you what we are dealing with? Brainwashed murderers who thrive on death and suffering. Minions of evil who will target a preschool and laugh with glee when children are blown up. That's what Doomers are. Tell them."

Damn, her outburst had gotten her so worked up that she needed a drink to calm down. "I'm going to make myself a margarita, do you want one too? Or are you in the mood for something stronger?"

"A margarita is fine." Ingrid followed her to the living room. "I'll send a couple of guys to clear that bedroom. Just tell me when is a good time."

Amanda mixed the two drinks and handed Ingrid hers. "Tomorrow, same time. I convinced Anandur that he needs to take Dalhu to the gym every day. My guy will go crazy if he stays cooped up here."

"Good deal. I'm going to do a little Internet search to see what he needs. Do you want me to run it by you? Or are you okay with me just going ahead and ordering whatever I see fit?"

"I don't want to waste time, just pick the most expensive stuff. You can't go wrong with that."

"Sweet, I like an open-ended budget." Ingrid took her drink for a walkabout to check out Dalhu's various creations. She stopped in front of the large canvas Dalhu was currently working on as a wedding present for Syssi and Kian. "Oh, wow. This is gorgeous. I didn't know Syssi posed for him in her wedding dress."

Amanda snorted. "Right, as if Kian would have been okay with her posing for a *Doomer*. Heck, the Doomer thing is secondary. He wouldn't want any male looking at her for a prolonged period of time let alone drawing her. Dalhu is using one of the wedding photos. His next one will be of them together at the altar with Annani presiding over the ceremony. Here, let me show you."

Amanda walked over to the media cabinet and pulled out a small wedding album, one of the hundreds that had been sent to every guest at the wedding. She flipped to the right page and showed it to Ingrid.

Ingrid sighed and put a hand over her chest. "They are so in love. Just look at how they gaze at each other as if nothing else exists. I want that."

"I'm working on it." *Not really.* For some reason, Amanda was reluctant to go back to the paranormal research without Syssi, the traitor who had abandoned her to go work for Kian. And anyway, Amanda was so behind on her formal research that she'd decided it was more important to catch up on that and not stress herself out by trying to do too much at once.

And as to working overtime? Forget it. She wasn't about to stay longer than was absolutely necessary when there was a hunk of a man waiting for her at home.

Priorities, priorities. Amanda first, the rest of the world second.

"What are you going to do with Syssi and Kian's portraits?"

"They are a present from Dalhu to Kian. A thank you for not making too much of a fuss over us moving up here. We were expecting a war when Kian came back from his honeymoon, but, apparently, the vacation had done him good, and he was in an uncharacteristically agreeable mood. Or perhaps it was all the sex. But in any case, all we got was a frown. And a cuff. William engineered a special contraption for Dalhu."

"I'm almost afraid to ask. Is it some kind of detonation device that is triggered if Dalhu tries to leave the building?"

Ingrid was such a weirdo.

"No, silly, you read too many suspense novels. There are no explosives in the cuff, but there is a transmitter that interferes with cellular signal. Dalhu can only use a landline, and as you know, all of them go through security."

Ingrid looked disappointed. "Oh."

"Of course, Dalhu couldn't care less. It's not like he has anyone he wants to call."

Well, it wasn't entirely true. He called her at work, about every thirty minutes—to tell her how much he loved her.

6

ANDREW

*a*fter work, Andrew headed to the keep—but picking Bhathian up to go see his daughter would have to wait. Kian had called for a meeting to discuss what to do about Alex.

Fuck this goddamned traffic.

He was supposed to be there at quarter to six, but with the offices occupying most of the real estate in the less than six square mile area spewing out their employees at this time of day, downtown Los Angeles was one big fucking parking lot.

For some reason, it brought to mind an image of a flooded giant anthill evacuating tens of thousands of its little workers. Except, in this case, each ant was driving away in its own car.

Damn, why the hell had Kian picked the worst neighborhood, as far as traffic jams that is, for his fucking keep?

And it wasn't as if there were great views or anything else for that matter to recommend the place.

Just a concrete jungle, and a small one at that.

He could never understand the rich idiots who spent

millions of dollars to live in a crappy Manhattan apartment with windows overlooking the next high rise building. Andrew's home had cost just a couple of hundred thousand dollars when he'd bought it, had a large yard, and the windows were not looking into his neighbors' homes.

As he finally made it down into the building's parking structure, he wished there was a valet he could leave the car with, but, of course, there was no such thing. Andrew cursed as he drove in circles down to the clan's private level. When he got all the way down, the bloody garage door blocking the entrance took forever to open as he waited for the sensor to communicate with the sticker on his windshield. The only good news was that once it finally did, he found plenty of spots available.

Wheels squealing in protest, Andrew skidded into one, threw the gearshift into park, and got out. Slamming the door behind him, he practically ran all the way to Kian's office, hoping not to be the last one.

Damn, he hated to walk into a room full of people who he had kept waiting.

But as he got there, he saw through the glass doors that everyone was already there: Onegus, William, Anandur, and, of course, Kian.

He pushed inside. "Sorry, guys. I swear, one of these days that goddamned traffic is going to give me an aneurysm." He grabbed one of the chairs surrounding the conference table and brought it to face Kian's desk.

Rapping his fingers on its surface, Kian tilted his head and lifted one corner of his mouth in a sardonic smile. "There is an easy solution and a tough one. The easy one is you quit working for Uncle Sam and come work for us full time, therefore, no more nasty commute. The other is you grow a set and attempt the transition, after which heart attacks and aneurysms will no longer be a concern."

Andrew unbuttoned his blazer and sat down. "If I quit my government work, I will no longer have access to the shitloads of information you find so valuable. And if I go for the transition and end up dead, we both lose, again. I'd rather live with the traffic and take my chances with my fragile human heart."

At his age, going for the transition was an iffy proposition at best. The only two other examples the clan had of turning adult Dormants were Michael, who was no more than twenty years old and had handled it with no problem, and Syssi, who was not yet twenty-six and almost hadn't made it at all.

So yeah, he'd rather live out his short human life than reach for the pie in the sky and drop dead.

"Can't argue with your logic." Onegus grimaced and clapped Andrew's shoulder.

"I don't know." William shook his head and shifted in his chair, readjusting his bulk to get more comfortable. Andrew could've sworn that William had gotten fatter since the last time he'd seen him, which was just a little over two weeks ago. The guy needed to cut down on the amount of junk he was eating. "If it were me, I would go for it and the sooner the better. Every day you procrastinate is another day your body ages. It would only get worse."

"I concur." Anandur winked. "There are a number of ladies who'd be very happy to get their hands on a new immortal male. You're missing out, buddy."

Anandur could stuff his opinion up his ass, but William had a point. Still, this meeting was supposed to be about Alex, and not about Andrew gaining immortality by attempting suicide.

"Okay, guys, that's enough about me. How 'bout we move on to the purpose of this chatty get-together."

"The private investigator that I hired to watch the boat has been scratching his balls for the past two weeks, observing absolutely nothing. The boat stays moored at Marina Del Rey, and Alex hasn't visited even once. His Russian crew comes and goes, but none of them bring any friends aboard, male or female. I think we need to come up with a new strategy. Unless, you think that we need to wait until something happens." Kian looked at Andrew, one brow cocked in question.

"Keep the private eye there. Stakeouts are never as exciting as they are portrayed in the movies. They take time, sometimes months, and are mostly about being bored out of your mind and eating too much pizza."

"Okay, I have no problem with that, but how about upping the ante?"

"I say we go after the Russians," Anandur said as he got up and walked over to the buffet. He grabbed a pastry from the tray that had been left there, most likely by Okidu, Kian's butler.

"Bring the whole thing over here." William waved his hand, practically salivating in anticipation. Though Andrew wondered why the guy hadn't helped himself to something before. Perhaps he was one of those overweight people who were embarrassed to eat in front of others.

Anandur stuffed the pastry into his mouth, holding it with his teeth as he grabbed the long tray by the handles and brought it over to Kian's desk.

Eh, what the hell, why not. Andrew snatched a cheese Danish.

"How do you suggest we go about that?" Kian asked.

Anandur finished chewing and wiped his mouth with the back of his hand. "Easy, seduce one of the bitches."

Onegus snorted. "You volunteer?"

Anandur shrugged. "Why not? I'll do it. I'm not too picky."

"Damn right," Onegus confirmed. "I've seen some of the skanks you've been picking up."

"As if you snag only beauty queens, you pompous bastard."

"Better looking than yours, that's for sure."

William looked uncomfortable and reached for a croissant.

"Can I go now?" Andrew asked, "I have better things to do than listening to who scores with whom."

Anandur looked like he wanted to fire up a retort, but all he did was open his mouth and then close it like a fish out of water.

Kian raised his hand. "So, let me get it straight. You are going to charm the pants off one of the Russians and pump her for information. Is that what you suggest?"

"Information and otherwise." Anandur winked.

William stuffed another pastry in his mouth.

Kian leaned forward and fixed his intense blue stare on Anandur. "How?"

"You know, I'll start with a light caress." He demonstrated on his own thigh. "Move on to a feathery kiss, right here." He tilted his head and pointed to a spot on his neck.

Andrew snorted. Onegus's shoulders shook with stifled laughter. William continued munching with gusto.

Kian didn't even blink. "I meant, where are you going to meet one of them? And how are you going to introduce yourself? Who are you going to say you are?"

"Deck cleaner." Anandur pumped out his chest and smiled. "Short, frayed shorts and no shirt, a bucket of sudsy water, and a sponge. Works for next to nothing too. You think there'll be a female in the vicinity who wouldn't want a piece of this?" His hand made a sweeping motion over his chest and lower.

Onegus groaned.

Kian nodded but then turned to Andrew. "What do you think?"

Andrew shrugged. "Worth a try."

"Then it's agreed. The Russians are yours, Anandur, do your worst. Next. William, what's the status with the surveillance?"

William swallowed the last piece of the pastry he'd been eating, licked his fingers clean, and then wiped his hands on his billowing Hawaiian shirt. "The team working on the drone will need another month at least. But if Anandur is going to infiltrate enemy territory, he can plant some listening devices for us."

Great idea. Andrew should've thought of it first, but, apparently, William's quick-thinking, brilliant mind wasn't restricted only to things related to computers and electronics.

"Do you need me to get you some? But this time, you'll have to pay for them. I can't keep supplying you with government stuff. As it is, I'm already afraid of accounting coming down on my ass for appropriating too many devices. And, potentially, they can involve internal affairs."

Kian looked irate. "Of course not. You should have said something before. You know money is no object."

"I know. At the time, it was just more expedient."

"It's all taken care of," William interjected. "After you planted that one in the Doomers' rented Beverly Hills mansion, I ordered a bunch, and I am working on modifications." He turned to Anandur. "Stop by my place tomorrow. I'll have a couple ready for you."

"By the way, Andrew, what's going on over there? Anything interesting?" Kian asked.

"Dalhu's team was sent home, and the place has been rented out again. Unfortunately, it was all done without providing us with any clues about their new center of operations. They probably communicated via email, which I failed to monitor. My bad."

"Water under the bridge. We move on."

7

NATHALIE

"*A* cappuccino for Melanie and a latte for Daphne!" Nathalie called out.

On their way to collect their drinks, the teenagers passed by her father and giggled, exchanging hand gestures that didn't require familiarity with the American sign language to interpret.

Nathalie sighed.

Today was a particularly bad day. Not that any of them were easy. Things were just getting worse as her father's dementia progressed. But most days, he just sat in his booth, the last one in the row, mumbling to himself quietly.

Since this morning, though, Fernando had taken a turn for the worse, or the bizarre as it may be. He was loud, arguing with what seemed like a group of imaginary people, waving his hands and pointing at the air around him.

It could've been worse. She shouldn't complain. The doctors had assured Nathalie that her father's dementia was eating up his brain at a much slower rate than the norm. She was lucky that he could still recognize her and was able to control his bodily functions, which was no less important.

She had no idea what she was going to do once this grace period ended. One day at a time, it was all she could manage. Stressing about the future was a luxury she didn't have energy or time for.

Right now, the only thing she could do to calm him down was to sit down beside him and talk to him, or rather at him. It was more the sound of her voice than the words themselves that usually did the trick.

Simple enough, but a tough one to pull off without someone to help with the customers. She was the only one here, taking orders, making coffees, preparing sandwiches, and washing the dishes. Not to mention that she'd been up since four in the morning, baking today's assortment of pastries.

Damn, where the hell was Tiffany?

At first, Nathalie had thought her one and only waitress had flaked out on her. Sometimes, Tiffany would get info about an audition and in her rush and excitement forget to call and let Nathalie know.

But when yet another day passed, and the girl hadn't shown up, Nathalie called her. The phone had ~~rang~~ ringing for a long time before going to Tiffany's voicemail.

Nathalie had left a message—an angry one.

A day later, Nathalie called again and left another message—a worried one this time. Perhaps, Tiffany had gotten offended, or scared by the scathing tone of her previous voicemail, and that was why she hadn't called back.

Still, she'd gotten no response.

Since then, she'd been calling every couple of hours, hoping to catch Tiffany before being sent to voicemail. She had even borrowed a customer's cell phone, hoping Tiffany would pick up a call from an unknown number thinking it was about one of her auditions.

She'd gotten the damn recording again.

Nathalie couldn't shake the feeling that something had happened to the girl. Tiffany's address was in her employee file, so potentially she could've driven there and asked the girl's roommates what was going on. Except, what would've been easy for most anyone else, would have required a Herculean effort from her, considering the fact that she would've had to schlep her father along because there was no one she could leave him with. And leaving him alone, even for a few minutes, was a big no-no.

Whenever she needed to spend more than a moment in the bathroom, Nathalie had to lock the door from the inside and hide the key. It seemed as if Fernando was just waiting for an opportunity to run away and wander the streets.

He reminded her of a cat she'd had when she was a kid. Fritz had been a house cat who'd unfortunately refused to accept his elevated status as a beloved pet, thinking of himself as a mighty mouse hunter instead. The cat would shoot out like a rocket the moment someone opened the door.

Poor Fritz had probably ended up as a coyote snack.

Fernando would just get lost. The dog tags she had him wear at all times meant that good people would bring him back, or call her to come get him. Problem was, not everyone was good, and there were plenty of coyotes of the human kind around.

You should've put him in a home a long time ago, Tut said inside her head.

She turned her back to the pastries display and hissed, "Stop saying it. I'm never going to do it. He'll die if I do."

I know, Tut said, sounding sad, then faded away.

This was surprising; she hadn't expected him to give up so easily, or to agree. He was way more contrary than this. And it wasn't as if she herself was convinced of the veracity of her statement. Maybe an institution that specialized in dementia and Alzheimer's could actually benefit her father. But in her bones, Nathalie knew that Fernando would wither and die if she were to abandon him to some institution. He was hanging in there and doing better than other patients afflicted with the same disease because he was with her, surrounded by the familiar smells of baked goods and seeing new faces every day.

So yeah, it was tough, and she didn't have much of a life, but she was all he had, and he was all she had.

Well, other than Tut.

She wondered where her ghost, or rather the figment of her own malfunctioning brain, went when he wasn't bugging her. Was there some other dimension where ghosts and figments hung out together?

He must be lonely if there wasn't.

The only good thing about her quitting college and coming back to take care of her father was her semi-liberation from Tut. Her cerebral roommate was bored out of existence—his words—with her new life. So much so that he didn't want to hang around. Much. Luckily, he still kept enough of a presence to keep the other voices at bay.

Thinking of what would've happened if Tut had left her permanently, Nathalie shuddered. As annoying as he was, having to endure just one voice was infinitely better than the onslaught she'd suffered before he'd come to her rescue and stayed, appointing himself the guardian of the gateway to her brain and holding back all the other voices clamoring to be heard.

You're welcome.

Don't let it get to your head. You're only the lesser evil, doesn't mean that you're good.

Everything in life is a compromise, my dear.

And in death?

She heard his laugh as he began fading. *Nice try, Nattie.*

Argh, she could've strangled him if he were real. The annoying jerk never answered any questions about the other side. Using that nickname had been his way of getting back at her for asking. He knew how much she detested it.

Nutty Nattie had been buried six feet under, together with all the other unpleasant memories from high school.

College had been good. No one had known her, and she had done her damnedest not to get caught talking to herself. Occasionally she'd still slipped, especially when Tut was goading her, talking nasty about any guy she'd found attractive. But she'd managed to hide it, always having a set of earphones in her ears as camouflage. If someone had seen her talking to no one, they'd assumed she was mouthing the words of a song she was listening to.

Cellphones and Bluetooth had been a godsend. Everyone looked as if they were nuts.

"Thank you. Goodbye." The teenagers waved and stepped outside, the small bells she'd hung on the door clanging when it opened and then again as it closed. It was a precaution, in case her father tried to sneak out behind her back.

Damn, what was she, the Bermuda Triangle that people around her kept disappearing?

Her mother had been missing for six long years. But

despite the pitying looks from the police detective who had been assigned to the case, Nathalie refused to accept that Eva was dead. She had to believe her mother was alive somewhere and had a damn good reason for not getting in touch with her only daughter or at least letting her know that she was alive. Though the only excuse Nathalie would find acceptable was that Eva had been suffering from amnesia.

And now Tiffany. But Nathalie didn't dare file another missing person's report. First of all, the girl might be perfectly fine and had just quit without notice. And second, if she reported another person missing, the police might start suspecting her of foul play.

Nathalie chuckled. They'd think she was doing away with people.

She noticed it had become quiet in the shop and glanced at her father. He'd stopped arguing with his phantoms and was conducting a quiet and civilized conversation with just one.

Funny, how she could relate. Though, in her case, she couldn't blame dementia. When Fernando had first started showing signs of hallucinating, she'd been sure that he was suffering from the same thing she did, and even tried to find out more about his apparitions. But she'd soon realized that what he was seeing and hearing was very different. His imaginary people had no names and didn't stick around—just random phantoms.

At the moment, they were alone in the coffee shop, and she walked over to his booth and sat down.

"Hello, my love." Fernando leaned and kissed her cheek. "You are as beautiful as ever."

It took her a second to realize he thought she was Eva. She took his hand. "It's me, Papi, Nathalie."

The fog clouding his eyes receded, and for a moment,

they looked lucid as he regarded her. "Yes, of course you are, my Nathalie. Who else has a voice of an angel?"

She smiled at him through the tears prickling the back of her eyes. "Nobody, only your Nathalie." It was the answer she'd been giving him since she learned how to talk.

"That's right, my sweet little girl, Nathalie."

8

BHATHIAN

*F*or a guy who was rarely motivated to look at his own reflection, Bhathian was spending a hell of a lot of time in front of his fucking bathroom mirror.

Not that what was staring back at him showed much improvement, despite his best efforts.

After his morning workout, he'd stopped by Anandur's barber and had gotten a trim and a good shave. Regrettably, the change was marginal.

He looked like a surly son of a bitch. Or worse.

People still crossed over to the other side of the street when they got a gander of him, and he could still clear a supermarket's aisle faster than an announcement of a free giveaway at the checkout counter. You'd think he was an ogre who ate babies for breakfast or something.

Not a charmer, that was for sure, but he wasn't all that bad either. In fact, he was a pretty decent guy, if he did say so himself.

Trouble was, he brooded—he was the-glass-is-half-empty kind of guy. Hell, the thing was more like three-quarters empty.

He couldn't understand all those bloody optimists who pretended not to see the crap around them, supergluing pink-colored shades on top of their upturned noses to obscure reality. As if everything was going to be okay with the world because they believed it, and if they didn't see the crap it didn't exist.

Lucky bastards.

He wished he could pretend like shit didn't happen. But as someone who had to swim in it time and again to fix the mess, he couldn't.

The lingering foul smell wouldn't let him.

The humans, he could understand. Their lives were short and their memories even shorter. Atrocities that had happened more than twenty years ago were a distant memory that didn't impact them emotionally, and those committed a century or more ago were completely forgotten.

Turning blind eyes and deaf ears to shit that wasn't promoted by the media was so damn easy. If it wasn't shoved down their throats because it served the agenda of someone who was willing to pay to have it in the spotlight, they had no reason to look elsewhere for much more disturbing crap.

Obliviousness was bliss.

But the same couldn't be said about his fellow near immortals, most of whom were on the-glass-is-half-full team. And the one with the biggest fucking set of pink-colored glasses was none other than their clan mother, the only surviving full-blooded goddess, Annani. How the hell could someone as ancient as she remain the quintessential optimist after all she'd been through? Annani had not only witnessed humanity's bloody history first hand, but had had the love of her life murdered by a fellow god, the insane Mordth. And if that hadn't been enough to crush her spirit for good, the fucker had launched a nuclear attack against the other gods in order to avoid prosecution for his crime, wiping out all of her people including, unintentionally, himself.

And yet, if you asked her, things were getting better. There were the occasional setbacks caused by Mordth's vengeful followers, like a Dark Age or two, but the overall trajectory was positive. Annani was convinced that her clan and their positive influence on humanity's progress was winning the long-term war against the destructive power of the *Devout Order Of Mordth*.

Bhathian suspected that Mordth's son and successor, Navuh, had a different view of things. The Doomers' fucking leader had managed to breed an army of immortal warriors that was ten thousand strong. Not to mention his *little* side business that was helping finance his nefarious activities—the brothel he'd built on some godforsaken island in the Indian Ocean.

Fuck, now he had gotten himself all worked up, and the face staring back at him from the mirror looked like it belonged to a serial killer. Bhathian wondered if it was too late to ask Kri or Bridget to do something about his bushy brows.

Perhaps, with the unibrow tamed by a pair of scissors, he could look less threatening.

Or better yet, he could try to get rid of the frown.

His phone buzzed, and he pulled it out of his pocket.

"You're coming up, or I'm coming down?" he asked Andrew.

"I've just finished with Kian. Come down to the parking garage."

"On my way." He clicked off and stuffed the thing back in his pocket.

Standing in front of the mirrored wall of the elevator, he practiced releasing the frown and even tried to smile. He better not. Instead of just a normal, run-of-the-mill killer, the fake smile made him look like an insane one.

He shrugged and adjusted the collar of his white button-down, then re-tucked it in his jeans. Should he keep the second button open? Or close it?

Why was he obsessing? It wasn't important. It wasn't as if he was going to go up to his daughter and introduce himself. All he planned to do was sit somewhere in her coffee shop where he could look at her without her noticing it and listen to her voice as she interacted with her customers. Andrew would provide the cover, pretending to talk to him from time to time so she wouldn't grow suspicious.

When the ping announced that he'd reached the parking level, Bhathian closed his eyes and took a deep breath.

Man up, asshole. You were stressing less heading out to battle.

As he got out, Andrew was waiting by his car. "Nice shirt. You look good." He offered his hand.

"Yeah, I bet." Bhathian shook what was offered.

"How about presentable, better?"

"At least it sounds as if it could be honest. I don't need a pep talk."

"Wasn't giving any." Andrew opened the door to his Ford Explorer and got behind the wheel.

As Bhathian walked over to the other side and folded himself into the passenger seat, he couldn't help but notice that unlike his own car, which was littered with empty In-n-out paper bags, crushed coke cans, and ripped candy bar wrappers, this one was spotless. The car's interior looked like it was brand new or had very recently gone through a detailing service.

"Your government provides car-washing services?"

"No, I do." Andrew backed up the car and drove up to the garage door which began sliding open.

"Impressive."

Andrew cast him a sidelong glance. "I like to keep it clean."

"As I said, impressive. Mine looks like a pigsty."

"Oh, yeah? What do you do when you need to pick up a lady friend to go on a date?"

Bhathian snorted. "What lady friend?"

"I thought all of you immortals needed lots of sex."

"We do, but it has nothing to do with ladies or friends."

Andrew rolled his eyes as he waited for a car to pass him by so he could pull into traffic. "And to think they let you teach the sex-ed class."

What the hell was that supposed to mean? Bhathian rubbed his clean-shaven chin. "Did I say something wrong?"

Andrew sighed as if he was explaining things to a clueless teenager. "Every woman who you hook up with, even if it is for only one night, deserves to be called a lady friend. Not a piece of ass, not a pussy, or any of the other creative substitutes men use. Language has power, and to think in these terms erodes your respect for women. True?"

Bhathian crossed his arms over his chest. "You keep forgetting how old I am; that's why you got it all wrong. When you say a lady, I see in my head a British matron fanning herself because she's stuffed into a too-tight corset and can't breathe. Fates know I've never hooked up with one of those. And as to friends, I'm very picky about who I regard as one."

"My apologies. I hope you still think of me as a friend."

Bhathian put a hand over his heart as he turned to look at Andrew. "For as long as I have breath in my lungs and blood in my veins."

Andrew seemed taken aback. "It sounds like a pledge."

"It is, and I do not offer it lightly."

9

ANDREW

*T*ouching, but he hadn't done enough to deserve the guy's unending gratitude. The few hours of work he had dedicated to the search were a far cry from the kind of service that qualified for such a solemn pledge. After all, he hadn't sacrificed anything for Bhathian or rescued some relative of his from certain death.

But he wasn't about to tell the guy that finding his daughter wasn't enough of a big deal to warrant his heartfelt thanks. Obviously, for Bhathian it was.

When Andrew got off the freeway, Bhathian turned to him. "I forgot to ask you the name of her place."

"Fernando's Bakery and Café."

"That's the name of her adoptive father?"

"Yeah. Keep an eye out for the sign, it should be somewhere around here." Andrew turned into South Jonson Street.

At seven in the evening, the various shops and Cafés were still open, and judging by the number of cars parked along the street business was good.

"That one is leaving." Bhathian pointed toward a white Honda.

Andrew got behind it and waited for the driver to ease into traffic.

"You ready?" He turned to Bhathian as he parked.

The guy nodded and wiped his hands on his jeans before reaching for the door handle.

Andrew locked things up, and they hit the pavement together, walking at a measured speed that was neither fast nor slow. It must have been a hell of an effort for Bhathian, who Andrew had no doubt itched to march ahead. But even at a casual stroll, the big man was attracting attention and not in a good way. Conversations halted, and people moved out of his way, their steps getting just a bit longer and faster as they tried not to be obvious about their unexplained urgency to increase their distance from him.

Casting a sidelong glance at his companion, Andrew wondered what was so scary about Bhathian that he was provoking such strong reactions. He was well dressed, with his plain white dress shirt tucked into jeans that weren't drooping. And the guy had no tattoos or piercings. True, he was a big guy, about six four or five, with the body build of a professional wrestler, but so was Dwayne Johnson and yet people loved him. If the ex-wrestler turned movie star were to show up on the street, there would be a stampede of girls trying to get to him and not away from him. But the big difference between The Rock and Bhathian was Dwayne's big, friendly smile, as opposed to the immortal's angry scowl.

Andrew couldn't blame people for wanting to get away from a surly son of a bitch who looked like he could lift cars. A guy this size in a bad mood was bad news.

"You should try to smile more."

"Sure about that?" The dude's grimace of a smile was way worse than his scowl.

"Maybe not."

Andrew shook his head. He'd thought that accompanying Bhathian would soften the guy's impact, but it wasn't working. Probably because Andrew's presence didn't provide a strong enough contrast. True, he was shorter and less muscular than the hulking guy, but he was still over six feet tall and far from harmless. The scars on his face, although old and faded, betokened a life of violence.

Fuck, they'd better cut their visit short. With the two of them sitting in her café and scaring customers away, Nathalie would lose sales she couldn't afford to.

"Ready?" he asked Bhathian as they reached the place.

"Yeah, but you better do all the talking. I'm not good at that."

"Sure thing."

Andrew pushed the door open, and the jingling of the little bells hanging over it on the inside announced their arrival. As the few customers sitting inside the café glanced their way, their expressions changed from mild curiosity to alarm.

A moment later Nathalie emerged from what must have been the kitchen with a tray of freshly baked croissants.

The resemblance to her mother was striking. Hell, everything about her was. Andrew, who was supposed to do the talking, was rendered momentarily mute.

She put the tray down and took off the oven mitts before taking her place behind the counter.

She smiled at Bhathian and him, her lovely face showing none of the alarm her customers displayed. "Hello, what could I interest you in, gentlemen?"

Oh, boy, that deep and smooth voice of hers was doing

unseemly things to his male anatomy, which was doubly embarrassing since he was standing next to her father. Mercifully, he'd headed to the keep straight from the office and hadn't changed out of what he'd worn to work—his reaction was well hidden under his blazer.

And yet, even though he knew better, he had the absurd impulse to reply *you*. Instead, he tugged at his necktie that suddenly felt too tight, then blurted out, "Coffee, two, for me and my friend."

She entered their order on her register. "Anything to go with your coffees? I've just taken this batch of chocolate croissants out of the oven." She pointed to the tray she'd put on top of the counter to take their order. "There is nothing like eating them when they are hot—when the chocolate is still melted, and the crust is so flaky that it melts in your mouth." Her tone turned husky and suggestive as if she was talking about something completely different, and yet he was certain that it wasn't intentional. For some reason, Nathalie projected an innocence befitting someone much younger.

"Sure," he said, though she could've offered him yesterday's stale donuts and he would've responded the same.

She smiled again, and he noticed that her teeth were incredibly white. "How many would you like?

"I'll have three." Bhathian found his voice.

Her smile got even wider. "And you?"

"The same."

Now her smile reached all the way to her beautiful brown eyes. "Big boys with big appetites. I like it." She leaned forward and whispered, "Not like all those health freaks who count every calorie." She winked, her incredibly long lashes fanning over her peach-colored cheek.

Up close, he saw that her perfect complexion wasn't the product of a clever makeup job, and the dark lashes outlining her almond-shaped eyes were not only long but also dense. If he weren't standing so close to her, he would've thought that they were fake—the kind some women glued on for special occasions. But hers were a gift from Mother Nature.

Regretfully, Nathalie's thick, dark hair was pulled back away from her face. Andrew wondered how long it was. He would've loved to see the thick waves cascading around her slim shoulders.

His question was answered when she turned and bent down to grab a pair of metal tongs from inside the display, and the heavy braid fell forward, almost brushing the floor. When loose, her hair probably reached her behind.

Using the tongs to lift the still steaming croissants from the tray, she put them on two small plates and handed them to Bhathian and him. "Here you go, and I'll bring your coffees to your table."

Andrew was very careful to take it without touching her hand, not because of some outdated notion of propriety, but because he was afraid of his reaction.

There was something special about Nathalie that affected him on a whole different level. Without her intent or even knowledge, she had planted her metaphorical hooks so deep inside him that frankly, he was weirded out.

10

NATHALIE

*T*here was something strange about these two, but she couldn't put her finger on what it was. Nothing alarming. On the contrary, they exuded strength and confidence in the same way firefighters did. Their presence was reassuring.

The very tall one looked to be in his late twenties or early thirties, but she had her eye on the older one, a sexy man in his late thirties. If she had to guess his occupation based on what he was wearing, he was either a real-estate agent or a police detective.

Hardly anyone else still wore a tie and blazer to work.

But given the small scar over his left brow and the one on his chin, the latter was more likely.

What was strange, though, was that Tut didn't come barging in with his nasty commentary the way he'd always done whenever she had naughty thoughts about a guy. And she was definitely having them about this one.

His lips in particular… and his hands…

God, to have a man like him kiss her with that cruel yet

soft looking mouth, to have him hold her to him with those strong, calloused hands...

Stop it! She needed to banish these thoughts, fast, before not only embarrassing herself by blushing like a ripe tomato but summoning the annoying voice in her head.

Perfecting her friendly yet uninterested act, she was often able to fool Tut along with the guys who flirted with her. It wasn't that she didn't want to respond, but she could never say yes, even to those she would have loved to—like this one. Because what was the point? It wasn't as if she could go on a date with anyone.

Mr. Sexy's younger friend was a huge man, with a pair of shoulders that had barely made it through her shop's front door, and a rugged face that was nevertheless very handsome.

She should have felt intimidated by his sheer size, but she wasn't. For some inexplicable reason, he made her feel safe. Not that she'd been fearful before—well, except the worry about what might have happened to Tiffany... and the old one about her mother. But as for herself, she had a sense that while this man was around, he wouldn't let anything bad happen to her. He was the kind of guy who you wanted by your side when shit happened.

It was almost palpable, the aura of a capable fighter, and one who she instinctively knew fought for the good side. Perhaps he was a Marine or a soldier in some other elite military unit. But one thing was for sure, despite his rough looks, he wasn't a thug.

Without asking how much, he pulled out a wallet from his back pocket and handed her a couple of twenties. But his friend stayed his hand.

"No, this time, it's my turn." He pulled out his own wallet and handed her a MasterCard.

She saw right through him. The only reason he offered to pay was that he wanted her to see his name on the card.

"Andrew Spivak," she read out loud and could've sworn that he blushed. But the slight flush had come and gone so fast she wasn't sure.

"Now that you know my name, could I have yours?"

Bingo. I was right.

"Nathalie Vega, very nice to meet you, Andrew." She extended her hand for a handshake.

For a split moment, he looked at her offered hand as if he didn't know what to do about it. But then, a determined expression slid over his handsome face, and he took it, closing his large calloused hand around hers.

"The pleasure is all mine, Nathalie."

As he clasped her hand for a long moment, his eyes holding hers captive, she felt something pass between them —a sort of subliminal communication that was electrifying and tantalizing.

Futile, because nothing could ever come of it.

She pulled out her hand from his grasp, and the loss of contact left her feeling bereft. "Please, choose any booth you like. It's self-seating. I'll brew you guys a fresh pot of coffee and bring it to your table once it's ready." She was well aware that she was talking too much and too fast, but she couldn't help it. She wanted him to go away so she could regain her equilibrium.

"Thank you," the other one said as Andrew just kept staring. "And if we're already doing introductions, I'm Bhathian." He extended a hand that was the size of her oven mitt.

"Nice to meet you, Bhathian." This time, as she shook the hand she was offered Nathalie only felt warmth and strength at the contact. He closed his huge hand around hers very gently, even though she had no doubt it was powerful enough to crush it with minimal effort.

"Bhathian, I've never heard the name before. Where is it from?"

He smiled and his chest inflated with pride. "Scottish." Bhathian exaggerated the accent. "It means ruler of army."

She could just imagine him in a kilt and hose, leading an army of Highlanders into battle. "Very fitting, it's perfect for you."

His smile broadened. "My mum thought so when she named me. She said I looked exactly like my father."

"Do you?"

"Do I what?"

"Look like your father?"

"Oh…" He rubbed his hand over his neck. "I don't know, never met the old bastard—" He slapped his forehead. "Forgive me, I forgot my manners."

It seemed Bhathian's embarrassed apology had shaken Andrew out from his trance, and he chuckled.

She laughed. "That's okay, I hear much worse in here on a daily basis." She leaned forward and whispered, "Sometimes, I even do it myself."

Bhathian looked relieved, even happy. "That's my gi…"—he stopped himself mid-word—"not that you are mine or anything, I just meant good for you."

"Come on." Andrew tugged on Bhathian's enormous bicep, "let's go before you put your foot in your mouth.'

The guy followed his friend. "Why the hell would I put a foot in my mouth?"

"It's just an expression, big guy."

Bhathian answered something, but she didn't hear what it was. The jingling bells were announcing the arrival of new customers she had to attend to.

11

ANDREW

Fuck, he handled the situation just great. It was a sad day for Andrew Spivak when Bhathian was doing all the talking because the amazing Andrew was fumbling for words.

Damn, this was the second time in his adult life when he'd felt like a stupid teenager again. The first had been when Syssi had introduced him to Amanda. It had taken him a while to get over the impact of her preternatural beauty. Andrew had felt overwhelmed, even intimidated, but eventually he'd recovered enough to conduct a decent conversation with his sister's stunning boss.

The second time was today.

Problem was, he was damn sure it wasn't going to get better any time soon with Nathalie, and once she delivered their coffees he would be rendered stupid again and would have nothing interesting or flirty to say.

Not that flirting with Bhathian's daughter was such a hot idea.

Fathers had peculiar attitudes about their grown

daughters. And aggravating someone who could crush him like a bug was not smart.

"You did good," he told the guy. "I was surprised. You've waited to see her for no good reason. You didn't need me after all."

"No, I'm glad I waited. I would have been too afraid of saying the wrong thing. I opened my mouth only because you were having trouble."

"Sorry, I don't know what happened to me."

Bhathian hiked one bushy brow. "Yes, you do. I know my Nathalie is beautiful, and you're just a human male. I understand, and it's fine by me."

"Really? So if I asked her out on a date, you wouldn't mind?"

"Nope. But no hands, or I break them like twigs." He pulled a straw out of the dispenser and demonstrated.

Was he joking? Or was he serious? It was hard to tell with the guy. Though Andrew had to admit that he'd never seen Bhathian in a better mood. So maybe he was joking.

"What if I marry her? What then? Don't you want to become a granddaddy?"

Bhathian grimaced, some of his good mood evaporating. "Hypothetically speaking, if you end up marrying my daughter, I will not ask questions I don't want to hear the answers to."

Andrew laughed. "This conversation stays between us. If anyone we know overheard us talking like a couple of teenage girls, we would become the laughing stock of the keep."

Bhathian frowned. "I don't get what's funny about it."

"For both of us, it's our first encounter with Nathalie, and here we are discussing a wedding, if not like teenagers then like a couple of yentas. I don't know if she even likes me."

"She likes you."

"How do you know? Your experience with ladies? Or assumptions about a daughter that you've just met."

"Shh... she's coming."

Andrew clamped his mouth shut and tilted his head toward the aisle. Bhathian must have heard something with that freaky immortal hearing of his, because sitting with his back to the front he couldn't have seen her coming out from behind the counter.

Watching her sashaying toward their table, holding a tray loaded with their coffees and a tall glass of orange juice, Andrew swallowed. The lady had booty and then some, flaring out from a tiny waist and gently tapering down into generous hips and shapely thighs. And as she walked, those fabulous assets swayed from side to side in a most enticing way.

She wasn't wearing the apron she'd had on before, and behind the tray she was carrying, he glimpsed part of a breast stretching her black T-shirt. Clearly, Nathalie wasn't as endowed on top as she was on the bottom. Not that it detracted from her attractiveness in any way—Andrew considered himself an ass man.

Besides, the woman was a knockout by any guy's standards.

She stopped next to another booth first and placed the juice glass together with a napkin and a magazine in front of its lone occupant. "Here you go, Papi. I brought juice and your newspaper," she said, her tone conveying affection.

So this is Fernando, her adoptive father.

"Thank you, my sweet Nathalie," the older man said.

"You're welcome." She patted his shoulder and turned toward them, her sad smile lingering for a moment before turning bright for them.

"Two freshly-brewed coffees for Mr. Bhathian and Mr. Andrew." She placed the cups in front of each one as she said his name, then glanced at their plates and frowned. "You guys better eat these croissants before they get cold." She removed from the tray two individually sized creamer containers and placed them next to the cups.

"Yes, ma'am." Andrew saluted with two fingers, then picked up one flakey croissant off his plate. The thing was still warm, and as he lifted it to his lips, Nathalie's eyes followed his hand, staying glued to his mouth while he took a bite and chewed.

Andrew wasn't faking his reaction when he closed his eyes and moaned. It was so good that it was decadent.

"This is amazing," he overlooked good manners as he mumbled with a full mouth.

The satisfied look on Nathalie's face was worth it.

"Try it." She motioned to Bhathian, and he quickly obeyed, lifting the pastry and biting off half of it in one go.

Nathalie waited patiently until he finished chewing and swallowed, then dabbed his lips with a napkin.

Surprisingly, the brute had table manners.

"The best I've ever tasted," he agreed with Andrew. "What time do you usually bake them? I plan on stopping by every day and buying a few, or a dozen, from now on."

Sly, sly, Bhathian.

Andrew would've never expected the guy to come up with the perfect excuse for hanging around Nathalie's shop on a daily basis. But this was so good that he jumped on it as well. "You got yourself two new loyal customers. I will be joining him."

Nathalie couldn't have looked happier if they had just told her that she'd won the lottery. "I'm glad. Though if you keep your promise, I'm going to have you sample some of the other pastries. These are not even my best."

Andrew faked shock. "Noo…it can't be…"

She laughed. "The only way to find out is to try. Do you guys live nearby?"

Okay, it was time to twist the truth a little, and Andrew signaled to Bhathian to leave it to up him. "No, but we work together on a project in the area."

She moved the tray to her other side and propped it on her hip. "Oh, yeah? What kind of project?"

Andrew winked and leaned closer. "If I told you, I'd have to kill you," he said in a whisper.

Nathalie seemed unfazed. "So I guessed right, you're a police detective."

Andrew pretended defeat. "What gave me away?"

"The tie and jacket…and the scars," she added the last part hesitantly. "Don't get me wrong, you're very handsome, and they are barely noticeable, it's just that they hint at a less than peaceful past."

She thinks I'm handsome—very handsome! Yes! As he stifled the urge to pump his fist, the rest of what she'd said barely registered.

"Thank you, I'm flattered."

She looked a little confused by his thanks. "Sure thing. Anyway, I'm open from eight in the morning till eight in the evening with an hour break from two to three. I bake most of the stuff early in the morning, so the best time to come is breakfast. Today was an exception. I was running low on everything and had to bake another batch."

Poor Nathalie, at this rate she would work herself into an early grave.

"Breakfast it is, consider it a date." The double entendre was intentional, and he offered his hand to seal the deal.

She smiled and shook it, sending another electric shock straight to his groin. "It's a deal. I'm about to close, so hurry up and finish your croissants. Unless you want them to go?"

Bhathian turned to look at the display up front. "What are you going to do with those?"

"There isn't much left, but I can't serve it tomorrow, so it'll go to the trash. I have a reputation of everything freshly baked."

"Then we'll take everything you have to go. The guys back at the office will love it."

She looked horrified. "I don't want you to bring these to work tomorrow—they will not be fresh anymore."

Bhathian snorted. "Don't worry about it. When I get it to the guys, they'll demolish everything in under two minutes. There won't be even a crumb left for tomorrow. We have a bunch of piranhas back there."

She nodded. "A night shift, eh?"

Bhathian shifted in his seat. "Yeah, something like that."

"Great, let me load whatever is left into a box for you."

Aside from Fernando, they were the only ones there. Quickly devouring the remaining chocolate delicacies, Andrew washed them down with the rest of the coffee. When they got up to leave, she handed Bhathian the box.

"How much do we owe you for these?" Andrew asked.

She waved her hand. "Nothing, I was just going to throw them away."

Bhathian's face went red as he handed the box to Andrew and pulled out his wallet, placing a Benjamin on the counter. "Don't even think to argue about this." He pointed a finger at her when she opened her mouth to protest.

"Yes, sir." She saluted.

Smart girl.

"Goodnight, Nathalie, we will see you tomorrow." Andrew opened the door and waited for Bhathian, who looked like he was desperate to embrace his daughter. In the end, he just stuffed his hands in his pockets.

"Goodnight, and lock the door behind us," he said as he stepped outside.

"I will. Goodnight, guys. It was really nice to meet you. I'm glad that you stumbled upon my humble establishment." She closed the door, and they both waited to hear the lock engage.

"That went surprisingly well," Andrew said when they were some distance away from the café.

"Yeah. She even seemed to like me."

Come to think of it, Nathalie reacted to Bhathian as if he was the nicest guy and not an intimidating ogre. Perhaps she'd sensed a connection between them.

But more importantly, Andrew had a feeling that she'd been just as intensely aware of him as he'd been of her.

SYSSI

I need to talk to you. It wasn't late, but Syssi preferred to send a text instead of calling—just in case Amanda was busy.

After all, she and Dalhu had a lot of catch-up to do, and most of it was the kind of activity that precluded answering the phone.

A text could be easily ignored and returned later.

But she didn't have to wait long. Amanda's reply came almost immediately.

I can come over.

Syssi sent back an emoji of a thumbs up.

She had expected Amanda would rather meet at her and Kian's place. Ever since Dalhu had turned their living room into a studio, Amanda had stopped inviting people. Though come to think of it, that wasn't entirely true. Syssi had seen Anandur and some of the other Guardians come and go out of Amanda's penthouse, so maybe it was only her and Kian that Amanda didn't want to entertain.

Perhaps she was afraid that Kian would make Dalhu uncomfortable.

There was something to it. Kian no longer regarded Dalhu with outward hostility, but they were far from pals.

Though in Syssi's opinion, Amanda was making a mistake. Better to go through several uncomfortable get-togethers than perpetuate the status quo. Eventually, the men would realize that they weren't as different from each other as they believed they were, and a tentative friendship could ensue.

It could be so nice; living as they did across from each other, it wouldn't require much effort or planning for the four of them to spend time together, and the interaction would enrich their lives. It was less crucial for Amanda and her—they still hung out with each other and often also with Kri, Bridget, and Ingrid—but the men were terribly isolated. Neither had social interactions with people other than their mates.

Kian preferred it this way, claiming that the little off time he had he wanted to spend with her and nobody else, but it wasn't healthy, and she intended to remedy it. From what the guys who'd attended his surprise bachelor party had told her, Kian had had a great time and had even gotten a little drunk.

Her man needed more of that.

"Knock, knock," Amanda announced as she rapped her knuckles on the door she'd already pushed open.

"Come in. Kian is not here, so you don't need to bother with knocking."

"And where is your neglectful husband?"

Syssi chuckled. "Catching up on work that wasn't done during the day because he was too busy snogging with me."

With a pout, Amanda plopped down on the couch. "So I see you guys have oodles of fun working together."

"That's what I wanted to talk to you about. But first, can I offer you coffee? Or perhaps a drink?

"Coffee."

Syssi got busy with the new automatic coffee maker, pouring fresh coffee beans into the container. From there the thing did everything by itself. It was even hooked up to the water filter, so there was no need to fill it up with water.

"How are you enjoying your Nespresso machine?" she asked Amanda.

Amanda shrugged. "It's easy to use, which makes it perfect for me, and it makes decent coffee, but nothing compared to a commercial espresso machine."

"Let's see what you think about this one."

Syssi waited for a few more seconds until the contraption finished the grinding and the tamping and the brewing and spewed the final product into two small cups.

To go with their coffees, she grabbed from the fridge the fresh apple pie Okidu had made for dessert. There was just enough left for her and Amanda.

"Do you want ice cream with your apple pie?"

"No, I'll pass."

Syssi brought the loaded tray into the living room and put it down on the coffee table.

Amanda stirred a teaspoon of brown sugar into her coffee and took a sip.

"Well? What do you think?"

The grimace didn't bode well for the new coffee maker. "It's good, for homemade, but I miss real coffee, like what they serve at Gino's or Café Milano."

"Don't you go to Gino's for lunch anymore?"

Amanda put down her coffee and picked up the plate with the apple pie. "No, and to tell you the truth, I'm sick of eating candy bars from the vending machine for lunch."

"So busy, eh?"

"No, just not in the mood to go out by myself."

Syssi stirred in the sweetener and took a sip. It was good, Amanda was just finicky, that's all. "You used to do it all the time, what happened?"

"It's different now that I'm with Dalhu. All the attention I get from guys annoys me. I'm starting to understand why Yamanu hardly ever leaves the keep."

Syssi snorted. "You poor, gorgeous people, life is so hard for you."

"Well, I'm not complaining, but it's not always fun."

"What if I come with you to lunch at Gino's, would that make it better?"

"Of course, it would. But I can't expect you to drive there every day just so that I can eat a decent lunch. After all, I can have Onidu prepare something and bring it over. Though it could be fun if we can meet there for lunch at least once in a while."

Syssi smirked. "What if I don't have to drive there?"

Amanda arched a brow. "Skyping doesn't count as company."

Since when had Amanda become so dense?

"Not like that, silly. I'm trying to tell you that I'm coming back to work at the lab."

"Really? Oh, dear Fates, thank you." Amanda blew a kiss at the ceiling. "You've just made my day. Who am I kidding, you've just made my semester." Amanda jumped up and down in her seat.

Anticipating her next move, Syssi extended her arm, just in time to get her coffee cup out of the way before Amanda lunged to give her a hug.

When she let go, she asked, "But what happened? Don't you like working with Kian?"

"I love it, and so does he, too much. Instead of helping him get more done, I'm the reason he gets almost nothing done. All he wants to do is neck and play kinky games."

Shit, did she just say it out loud? *God*, she was so stupid. Telling Amanda something like this was like waving a red rag in front of a charging bull.

Amanda's eyes widened and then narrowed. "Oh, really? How exciting and naughty... Please, do tell."

Syssi felt the heat rising and engulfing her ears. "I'll do no such thing. Our love life is private, and the last person on earth who I want to talk about it with is Kian's sister. Well, perhaps not the last, that would be my dad, and next Andrew, but after them it's you."

Amanda lifted one corner of her mouth in a half smile. "At least I'm in good company. But have no doubt"—she pointed a finger at Syssi—"I'm going to find out one way or another."

"No, you're not. Because I'm never going to tell you, and you can forget about getting anything out of Kian."

"I have my ways." Amanda made an evil face.

Was she kidding, though? Probably. Because there was no way unless she planted a listening device in their bedroom, and Syssi didn't think even Amanda could pull this off.

"When can you be at the lab?"

Thank God, Amanda let go of that embarrassing subject.

"When do you want me?"

"Tomorrow."

"Okay."

Amanda looked surprised. "Really? I was expecting you to say something like next Monday, but I'm thrilled. Now we can put the search for Dormants back on track. I haven't done any paranormal research since I went back to work. It just wasn't the same without you."

She took Syssi's hand and gave it a squeeze. "I've gotten so accustomed to you running most of those that doing it myself somehow just didn't feel right. I kept telling myself that I need to put out an ad for more subjects, but never got around to actually doing it."

"Speaking of ads. I think we should expand beyond the limited pool of university students as subjects. We need to put out an ad, maybe even something on Facebook, that would attract people with paranormal abilities to come to us and submit to testing."

Amanda clapped her hands. "That's brilliant, Syssi. Could you do it? Come up with an idea for an ad?"

"I can try, though I've never written ad copy so I don't know if it will be any good."

"Talk to Brandon; he deals with media all of the time. I'm sure he'll have good tips for you."

Not a bad idea. "You're right. I will."

"Wonderful." Amanda pulled her in for another hug. "Welcome back."

13

SEBASTIAN

"*W*arriors, you have your assignments for tonight. Good hunting!" Sebastian sent the men off with the same words he'd been using every night.

For now, their spirits were still high, but he suspected this would change as time went by without their efforts producing results. The chance of them finding one of Annani's clansmen in the bars and clubs they were scoping nightly was slim.

He would have to come up with something else for them to do.

Unfortunately, none were capable of taking over any of his tasks, which were proving more challenging and time-consuming than he'd expected. And finding girls for his brothel was just one of many.

This morning's visit to the headquarters of Imagine Studios had been very educational. He would have to rethink his whole strategy as far as using Hollywood for his boss's agenda. Money still talked, that at least hadn't changed, but it was no longer the good-old-boys network it used to be, not exclusively. His impression was that women were running the show now.

Sebastian chuckled. It should be renamed the good-old-girls network.

And the few male executives that he'd talked with were either gay or didn't know what to do with all the pussy already available to them. So his idea of sexual bribes wasn't going to work.

Unless he could offer the kind of sex they could get nowhere else. After all, he wasn't the only one with unusual tastes. There was a wide variety of kinks to choose from, and he could arrange to provide most if not all.

If he could get his hands on enough girls, that is. Perhaps he could train his two assistants to help him out.

Sebastian cast a sidelong glance at Robert. *Nah*, this one was such a straight shooter that he barely deserved the designation of a Brother of the *Devout Order Of Mordth*. He was a good fighter, though, and not everyone in the organization had to be a cruel and underhanded bastard. After all, every commander needed someone he could trust.

That left Tom.

The guy was charming and intelligent but not handsome. Not ugly, but nothing women would drool over either. He was short, which was one of the reasons he was trained as an administrative assistant and not as a warrior, and the lack of vigorous military training meant that he wasn't muscular either. He had a good set of teeth, though, and a charming smile was sometimes all that was needed to lure a woman into a trap.

Besides, he had nothing to lose by giving Tom a chance. Worst case scenario, the guy would come back empty-handed or with a girl that wasn't all that attractive.

"Tom, a word." He motioned for the guy to follow as he headed for the stairs.

"Sure thing." Tom climbed behind him.

As they reached his upstairs study, Sebastian pointed to the chair facing his desk and closed the door.

"Is there something wrong?" There was a note of anxiety in the guy's question. Unusual, considering his otherwise flippant attitude.

Did Tom have something to hide?

Sebastian made a mental note to keep better tabs on the guy.

"Not at all." He took a seat behind the desk and steepled his hands in front of him. "I wanted to talk with you privately. I have a job for you that doesn't involve Robert or any of the other men."

Tom's face relaxed and his familiar smug smile returned. He straightened in his chair. "Whatever you want me to do, I'm on it. You know me, boss. I get things done."

"I know. That's why I chose you for this. I need help getting more girls."

For a moment, Tom looked stunned, but he recovered quickly. "Sure thing. And I appreciate that you thought of me for this, but isn't Robert a better choice? I mean, it's not like I have trouble getting myself a piece of ass, but Robert is like a chick magnet. He can do better."

Sebastian smiled. "It's not all about the size of a guy's biceps, Tom. We both know Robert. Do you think he can pull off something like this? Hell, if he were even half as devious as you, I would've at least paired you up. He could do the luring and you the catching. But the guy has no initiative and can't think on his feet. You'll have a better chance of catching flies on your own. Just use that charming smile of yours."

"You think my smile is charming? I don't know what to say, boss, I'm so flattered."

Sebastian rolled his eyes. *Give a guy one measly compliment and he thinks you love him.*

How did that human saying go? You can catch more flies with honey than with lemon? Or was it vinegar?

"Get over yourself and go get dressed. I'll meet you downstairs in twenty minutes."

"You want me to start tonight?" Suddenly, Tom's bravado went *poof.*

"The sooner, the better. I'll explain on the way. When we get to the club, I'll watch you go for it. If I think you need correction, I'll text you instructions, or if things are going real bad, I'll tell you to abort."

"Maybe I should have a bug on me, you know, so you can listen in and tell me if I'm saying the right things."

"No need. Don't worry; my hearing is excellent, and I'm going to stay close."

As Tom left to get ready, Sebastian went back downstairs and headed to the kitchen pantry, where Robert had carved a little space for himself to work. In addition to shelves loaded with canned and dry foods, it now contained a desk, a computer, and a chair.

Tom didn't mind working with background noise, and he either used the kitchen table or worked from the couch.

This was another thing Sebastian overlooked in his plans—a space for his assistants to do their jobs. Not that he'd had much choice. Most of the available space was turned into bedrooms for the warriors, and the rest was divided between the various storage and service facilities, a dining room spacious enough to serve the men in two shifts, and a large recreation room. The weapons were stored outside.

So given that his available options had been limited to stuffing three men instead of two in a room, giving up his luxurious third-floor apartment, or having his assistants work from the kitchen, he had chosen the third.

And besides, the pantry was spacious enough.

"Robert," he said as he entered the guy's domain.

"Yes, Sebastian?" Robert swiveled his chair around to face him.

"What's the status with the yard work?"

"The pool contractor is going to be here with two crews tomorrow at seven in the morning. He said he could be done in four days. And I ordered the planting material so it will arrive the day after he is done."

"What about the sprinkler system?"

"The pool contractor is going to take care of it. He needs to move pipes around to make room for the pool anyway."

"Good job." Sebastian clapped the man on the shoulder, "Tom and I are going out. You are in charge."

"Yes, sir. Any special instructions?"

"The usual. Check on the girls, see that they have everything they need, and make sure that the men who are on cleanup rotation do their job. I want to see and smell the clean when I come back."

"I'll make sure it is done to your satisfaction."

As he left the pantry and headed out, Sebastian thought about his girls. With only five available, using any of them for himself was out of the question. He couldn't have even one out of commission for the time it would take her to heal.

Regrettably, his lawyer was available no more than twice a week, which meant he'd been forced to use random subs at the club in between.

Blah, boring and predictable.

Sebastian sighed. Perhaps now that Tom was joining

the effort, he could devote time to finding something better for himself.

When he got to his car, Tom was already waiting by the Escalade. Sebastian clicked the thing open.

"Want me to drive?"

"Knock yourself out." He tossed the keys at his assistant, then got in on the passenger side.

Tom turned on the ignition, then adjusted the seat and mirrors to his smaller size. "So, boss, how do I go about choosing my victim?"

"You start by selecting ordinary girls with potential for improvement. Ignore the knockouts—they get too much attention and are hard to snare. Zero in on a suitable candidate, then continue with asking a lot of questions."

14

ANDREW

"*I*'ll see you tomorrow morning." As Andrew pulled into one of the vacant spots in the clan's private parking level, he shifted the transmission to park and cut the engine even though he was just dropping Bhathian off.

"What time?" Bhathian closed the passenger window and depressed the handle.

"I have to be at the office at nine, so right as she opens at eight. I'll meet you there."

"Good deal." He unfolded his frame and stepped out. "Thanks, man. I really appreciate what you're doing for me," he said, leaning into the cabin.

"Think nothing of it."

Bhathian gave a curt nod and pushed the door closed.

Sitting in his car, Andrew debated what to do next as he watched the guy open the heavy, reinforced door leading to the bank of elevators, then let it slam shut behind him.

It was still early, and the prospect of going home didn't particularly appeal to him. But Bridget was gone, and showing up uninvited at Syssi and Kian's, because he had nothing better to do, would spell 'pathetic' in big fucking neon lights.

So what were his options?

Hit *Barney's*?

Call Susanna?

Andrew shifted in his seat, pulling out the back of his blazer from under his butt so it wouldn't wrinkle.

Damn, even though what he had with Bridget was more or less the same arrangement he had with Susanna, it didn't feel right to call his co-worker while he was still seeing the doctor. Decency demanded that he at least keep it down to one casual friend with benefits at a time.

And then there was Nathalie.

True, there was nothing going on between them, yet, that he should feel guilty about. But he was more than tempted to give it a try. There was no doubt in his mind that he would flirt with her tomorrow, even at a risk of antagonizing Bhathian. After all, the guy owed him, and what's more, he didn't seem to be against the idea—in principle at least.

Not that Bhathian was okay with Andrew, or any other male for that matter, hooking up with his daughter, but he would be fine with a more meaningful relationship.

Question was, however, whether Andrew was fine with it.

There was something decidedly different about the way he'd reacted to Nathalie. Besides the attraction, she'd awakened a protective instinct in him that he hadn't felt for any of the other women in his life. Well, with the exception of Syssi, but she was his baby sister so that went without saying. But the women he'd dated had been capable of taking care of themselves and hadn't needed him for anything other than sex or, on occasion, his company.

It didn't make sense. Nathalie was a capable and independent woman, who was not only running a business on her own, but was also taking care of her ailing adoptive father.

And yet, deep down in his gut, he had this overwhelming need to protect her, keep her safe, make sure she was okay.

For some reason, it made him think of Dalhu. Amanda was capable and independent, and yet the guy was extremely protective of her, which given the circumstances —with Dalhu being a kept man, dependent on her for his support—didn't make much sense either.

He should go see the guy. In fact, he should've done it already. After the ordeal he'd undergone, Dalhu had needed time to recuperate, but almost a month had already gone by, and the guy deserved at least one friendly visit.

Trouble was, Andrew didn't have Amanda's number, and he didn't feel like going up and just knocking on the door. Then again, the guys manning the security desk in the lobby could make the call for him.

With that in mind, he got out of the car and headed for the elevators. He didn't bother to lock the thing, there was no need. The only ones with access to this level were clan members, and he doubted any of them would want to steal his car. It was crap compared to what was parked there.

As he got up to the lobby, one of the security guys recognized him from his previous visits.

"Mr. Andrew Spivak, how can I assist you this fine evening?"

"What's up?" He clasped hands with the guy.

"Nothing exciting, I'm happy to report."

"Excellent. No news is good news, right?"

"You got it."

"Could you please check if Dr. Dokani is home? She is

not expecting me, but I just dropped off a friend and thought to go up and say hi."

"Let me check." The guy tried the penthouse, but there was no answer, and he called her cellphone next.

"She wants to talk to you." He handed Andrew the phone.

"Hi, Amanda, sorry to interrupt whatever you're doing, but I wanted to come see Dalhu, and I don't have your home number. "

"You're not interrupting, Andrew, never. I'm over at Syssi's, but I'll call Dalhu and let him know you're coming. I'm sure he'll be very pleased to see you. Oh, and Syssi says that she wants to treat you to a cappuccino from her new machine. So come over here after you're done with Dalhu. On second thought, grab him and get him to come as well. He needs to taste the difference between this and our Nespresso. And anyway, he should take a break from drawing all day long."

Andrew chuckled. "Are any of you getting any sleep with all that coffee? You sound a little hyper."

"Yeah, I am. But I'll tell you about it later." She snorted. "Over coffee."

"Good deal."

He handed the phone back to the guard and stayed a couple more minutes to chit chat with the guys about the security measures in the lobby, which were impressive, to say the least, then headed up to Amanda's penthouse.

The door was open, and he rapped his knuckles on it before walking in.

The place was a mess. What had used to be an elegant and luxurious living room was now a painter's workshop, and stunk from oil paint and paint thinners and other things he didn't recognize.

Several tall easels held portraits in various stages of

completion. One was of Anandur—with no clothes on. Thank God, so far Dalhu had done only the upper body.

"I see you've been busy," he said as Dalhu walked in from what looked like washing his hands. The guy needed to clean more than just those, though. There were paint smudges all over his clothes and even some on his face.

Messy.

Dalhu came closer, and as they shook hands, Andrew observed that he hadn't regained his full strength yet. The guy was thinner than he used to be, and there was still a gray overtone to his naturally tanned skin color.

"Yeah, it seems my services are in high demand. I have a waiting list of portraits."

Andrew smiled. "How much do you charge for one?"

Dalhu looked surprised by the question. "Nothing, why would I charge for something I enjoy doing? It's a hobby, not a job."

The guy needed a reality readjustment. He was never going back to his old job, and the sooner he realized it, the better.

Andrew walked over to the bar and poured himself a glass of Lagavulin.

"Care to join me for a drink? Perhaps a light beer?"

"I'll have what you're having."

"You sure it's okay? Did the doctor clear you for alcohol?"

Dalhu shrugged. "I don't need medical assessment. I'm fine."

"You don't look fine." Andrew poured the second glass.

Dalhu chuckled. "You should've seen me right after. I looked like the walking dead." He waved a hand over his face. "This is a vast improvement."

Andrew handed Dalhu the drink and walked over to the only couch that wasn't littered with various art supplies. "Amanda must've been distraught to see you like that."

"Yeah, it wasn't pretty." Dalhu lifted a wrapped pack of three canvases from one of the chairs and put it on the floor, then sat down.

"So, how are you feeling?"

"Great." Dalhu took a swig. "I started a weight lifting regimen. Anandur is helping me get back in shape. The loss of muscle was surprising. I had no idea one week of stasis could do so much damage. It's creepy to think what the others would look like after all this time."

"I bet they look like walking skeletons."

Dalhu shook his head. "If they are ever awakened, I doubt they will be able to move at all, let alone walk. Anandur and Brundar had to practically carry me here. It took me a good full day to regain enough strength to use the facilities on my own."

Poor schmuck. Must've been a hell of a blow to his ego to have Amanda help him to the toilet. Not a pleasant thought, that was for sure.

"Well, I'm glad you're feeling better. Lucky for you, painting does not require the kind of musculature fighting does."

"No, it doesn't." Dalhu grimaced.

"Listen, Dalhu, I think you should start charging for these portraits."

Dalhu shook his head. "I can't."

"Of course, you can. Who is paying for the supplies? Amanda, right?"

Dalhu nodded.

"Don't you think you should at least make enough to pay her back? I know she doesn't need it, and she doesn't expect it either, but you do—for your own self-worth. And anyway, your warring days are over, and this is probably the only day job you're gonna get. Lucky for you, this is not only something that you enjoy doing, but you also happen to have talent. Make the most out of it."

Dalhu rubbed his hand over the back of his neck. "Even if I wanted to, I don't know how to go about it. What am I going to say to the next clansman or woman —here is your portrait and you owe me a hundred bucks?"

Andrew chuckled. "First of all, you're selling yourself too cheap. You should charge something around a thousand, not a hundred. They sure can afford it. And second, you can have Amanda do the money part. Let her be your manager."

"That's actually not a bad idea. She'll have no problem charging her relatives."

Andrew pointed to the one he liked most. "You can start with this beautiful portrait of Syssi and Kian at their wedding. It should go for several thousand."

"No, this one is a belated wedding present."

"Nice."

"Yeah, I think so too."

"When are you going to give it to them?"

"The paint needs a few more days to dry. We can't wrap it in gift paper until it does."

There was a moment of silence as they both seemed to run out of things to talk about.

Andrew cleared his throat and pushed to his feet. "Well, I'm heading to Syssi's to check out her new cappuccino machine, and I was told by Amanda to drag you away from your brushes and bring you along."

Dalhu grimaced. "You go ahead. I'd rather stay here."

"Come on, I don't think Kian is there, and even if he is, you guys need to get used to each other."

Dalhu closed his eyes and breathed in. "Yeah, you're

right. Let me change into something clean. But you don't need to wait for me, I know the way."

Aha, sure. As if I was born yesterday and believe he is going to show up.

"No, it's no problem, I'll wait." Dalhu shrugged. "As you wish."

15

AMANDA

*S*weet Andrew. He had done exactly what she'd told him to do, and brought Dalhu with him. Except, by the look on Dalhu's face, he would've preferred to stay home. Dragging him over here had probably taken some arm twisting on Andrew's part.

Figuratively speaking, of course.

Even in his weakened state, Dalhu was formidable, and human Andrew didn't stand a chance against her man. Physically. Mentally, Dalhu wasn't there yet. He seemed anxious, his eyes darting nervously toward the darkened corridor. He was no doubt expecting to see Kian and bracing himself for his thinly veiled distaste.

Her brother was trying his best—but his best, unfortunately, wasn't good enough. Not that she was harboring unrealistic expectations of Dalhu and Kian becoming best buddies. It was never going to happen, but she hoped that with time they would at least become comfortable enough with each other to share a beer maybe, or tell some dirty jokes— the kind of stuff guys did with casual friends.

91

She sauntered up to Dalhu and kissed his cheek. "You can relax, darling, he isn't here," she whispered in his ear.

Her words worked like a magic wand. Instantly, the stiffness in his shoulders disappeared, and he walked over to the bar to examine Syssi and Kian's new coffee making contraption.

"This is one hell of a gadget," he told Andrew, who joined him for the inspection.

"It's a big fucker. There is barely any counter space left." Andrew walked around to the other side, examining the machine's back.

"Do you want to see me making it?" Syssi asked hopefully.

"Sure." Andrew stuck his hands in his pockets and shrugged.

"Cappuccino or espresso?"

"Cappuccino. I had one earlier today in a coffee shop, and it was fantastic. I'm curious to taste the difference," Andrew said.

"Dalhu?"

"The same. Amanda wants me to compare it to our Nespresso."

Syssi snorted. "Nespresso is for amateurs. When you're ready to play with big boy toys, I'll give you the name of the supplier for this beauty."

For some inexplicable reason, Syssi's comment made Dalhu uncomfortable, and he looked away. Amanda wrapped her arm around his midriff and rested her head on his shoulder. "I'm happy with the simplicity of our little machine. And in my humble opinion, there isn't that much of a difference in taste."

Andrew chuckled. "You don't have an opinion that is humble. In fact, I'm not sure you know what that word means."

Syssi giggled.

Dalhu smirked.

"What? You all think I'm a show-off?"

Andrew raised his hands. "I'm going to shut up from now on."

Dalhu nodded.

"Perhaps not a show-off, but you're definitely an extrovert," Syssi patted her shoulder. "But that's part of your charm that we all love so much, so don't take offense."

Amanda harrumphed and crossed her arms over her chest. They had a point, though. "Fine, be like that."

"This is even simpler to operate than your capsule machine. I just press this one button and voila, it does everything."

It was funny, the way the four of them were standing quietly around the thing, listening to the various noises the machine was making as it produced the first cup.

"Andrew, here is yours." Syssi handed him his cappuccino and put another cup under the machine's twin spouts. They all waited until the second one was ready and she handed it to Dalhu.

"Go ahead, mix in the sugar and tell me what you think."

Andrew forwent the sweetener and brought the small cup to his mouth.

"Hmm, really good." He took a few more sips. "But I think the one I had this morning was better."

"Dalhu?" Syssi looked at him hopefully.

"It's good. But I really can't tell the difference. I think both machines are good, and given the huge cost difference, I think ours wins." He wrapped his arm around Amanda's shoulder and brought her closer to him.

"You guys have no taste buds." Syssi wasn't trying to

hide her disappointment. "Amanda? Do you want another one?"

"No, I'm all coffeed out."

"Don't stand around, take a seat." Syssi shooed them toward the couch. "I'm going to bring us something to munch on."

A moment later, she joined them and put a tray with an assortment of mismatched munchies on the coffee table. "Dig in, guys."

Amanda reached for a chunk of Brie. "How was your trip to Washington, Andrew?"

"Boring. Two weeks wasted, listening to a bunch of bureaucrats who like to hear themselves talk."

Dalhu snorted. "Yeah, I know the feeling. They all think they know better than the field guys."

"I guess pencil pushers are the same no matter which side they are on."

"Only their own, my man. Only their own. All that talk about some noble goals is nothing more than propaganda."

"And yet, you would rather fight than paint."

Dalhu shrugged. "That's what I know. It's hard to shift gears after eight hundred years of doing the same thing. But I guess I have no choice." He lifted his left arm, the one with the gleaming metal cuff on it.

"Let me see." Andrew leaned over to examine the device. "I would love to take this thing apart and see what's in it. What does it do anyway?"

"It serves dual duty; sounding the alarm if I try to leave the building, and interfering with cellular signal so I can't make cellular calls. All I can use are the landlines which are monitored by security."

"Ouch." Andrew grimaced. "I can't believe Kian still doesn't trust you. I was sure Edna's speech would do the trick."

Amanda chuckled. "I think it did, and the only reason he still insisted on the cuff was to get back at us for disobeying his orders and moving up here."

"Oh yeah? He gave you guys a hard time about it?"

"Not as bad as I thought he would," Dalhu said.

Amanda nodded. "It was just a token resistance. He came up here and informed us about the special cuff he was having William make, didn't even demand that we move back to the cell."

"Did he talk about it with you, Syssi?" Andrew asked.

"Not really. I think Amanda is right. Kian was in such a good mood after our honeymoon that he didn't want to fight with anyone. Besides, I believe that, in time, he is going to fully accept you, Dalhu. It's just that he is also an old fart who finds change difficult."

"Hey, I'm old, but not an old fart." Dalhu pretended offense.

"No, you are not. You are my handsome prince." Amanda patted his knee.

"Yes!" Dalhu pumped a fist. "I'm finally not a frog."

Amanda kissed his cheek. "You were always a prince to me, darling."

"If you say so."

16

ANDREW

"*I*'m fine, Andrew. You can go home. By now I'm used to long, lonely evenings of waiting for Kian to finish his work."

He pretended offense. "What? You're anxious to get rid of me?"

She slapped his arm. "Of course not."

"Okay then." He planted his butt back on the couch and stuffed another cracker in his mouth.

Syssi smirked. "You just don't want to go home because you miss Bridget."

Not really.

He must've grimaced because Syssi's smile vanished. "What happened? Did you guys have a fight?"

"No."

"Then what?"

Andrew reached for his tie and loosened it. Should he confide in Syssi? Normally, he didn't. After all, she was his baby sister and he often felt like a father to her, which precluded conversations of this nature. Then again, she'd confided in him when things had been strained between her and Kian.

"I've met someone..."

"When? Bridget left only today..." Scrunching her nose in a sneer, Syssi crossed her arms over her chest. "Don't tell me you cheated on her. I thought you were better than that."

He caught her nose between two knuckles and gave it a little squeeze, same way he'd done when she was a kid. "No, I didn't cheat on Bridget."

Syssi slapped his hand away. "Good."

"I met that someone only today, and nothing happened. She doesn't even know I'm interested. And as to Bridget, I told you before that it's not serious—for either of us."

Syssi uncrossed her arms and slumped onto the couch. "I guess that this new interest of yours is not an immortal, right?"

"No."

Well, not entirely true. She might be a Dormant. But he couldn't tell Syssi that—for a couple of reasons. First, he hadn't asked Bhathian if the guy wanted the thing with his daughter kept secret or not, and second, until they found Eva they wouldn't know for sure about Nathalie.

"Damn, now you're never going to attempt the transition."

He shrugged. "Nothing has changed in this regard. I'm just as undecided as I've been from the start."

"Yeah, but I hoped that if you fell in love with an immortal, you would have an incentive to go for it."

"It may still happen."

"So, do you want to break up with Bridget?"

Andrew sighed and popped the first button of his dress shirt open. "Here is my dilemma. I know that the next time

I see that someone, I'm going to flirt with her, and I'm going to feel like an ass for doing so while Bridget still thinks that we are together. On the other hand, to break up with her over the phone is not something I'm thrilled to do either."

"Can't you wait for her to come back?"

"No."

"Wow, you got hit hard, didn't you?" Syssi tilted her head and gave him an appraising look.

Andrew scratched his head. He hadn't thought of it this way, but it was true. Nathalie's impact on him was more profound than he'd realized.

"I guess you're right. Since I first saw her, which was only a few hours ago, I felt an almost obsessive need to be with her. And it's not only a physical attraction, although she has a banging body..." Damn, Bhathian had used the exact same words to describe Eva.

"So, what's her name? And what does she look like?"

"I can't tell you her name, not yet, and don't ask me why."

Syssi rolled her eyes. "Come on, Andrew, you can't pull your national security bullshit in this case, she's just a girl."

"I know. But I can't because there is another person involved and I need his permission first." He raised a palm to halt her next rebuttal. "I'm not going to say anything more on the subject. Are we clear?"

"Argh, you're such a tight-lipped meanie." Syssi pouted and crossed her arms over her chest again.

"I promise, I'll tell you the moment I'm allowed to."

"Okay." She seemed mollified. "But if you can't wait, you need to call Bridget and let her know. Just do it gently. She's a good person."

"I know. I'll do my best."

"Do it now before it gets too late. It's already near midnight where she is. Do you want to use Kian's office? You know, for privacy?"

"I thought about calling from the car on the way home, but I guess this is better. Like ripping off a bandage—get the pain over with as soon as possible."

Syssi leaned and kissed his cheek. "You're a brave guy. Now, go." She gave him a push that had him almost topple over. "Sorry, I keep forgetting how strong I've became."

"I don't feel comfortable using Kian's office. I'll just go into the bedroom I used before. If it's okay with you?"

"Sure. Want a drink to take with you?"

He chuckled. "No, I can handle an uncomfortable conversation fully sober."

She shrugged. "Suit yourself."

As Andrew closed the door behind him and pulled out his phone, he wondered whether he should go back and take Syssi up on her offer. And the need became even stronger when he brought up the last batch of messages he'd exchanged with Bridget.

Damn, this was going to be tough.

Can you talk? He sent.

Give me a moment, I'm in a noisy place. I'll call you.

Without turning on the light, he walked over to the bed and sat down, cradling the phone in his hands and staring at the small, brightly-lit screen.

Three minutes and forty-two seconds later she called.

"Hi, Andrew." She sounded breathless.

"Hi, yourself. Sounds like you're having fun."

"I am with Julian and several of his buddies in a club. I've been dancing for the past two hours. But it's so damn noisy in there that I had to step outside."

Immediately, he got worried. "I don't want you alone

on the street, in the middle of the night, in front of a club that is probably full of drunks."

There was a slight delay before she answered. "I'm not alone. One of Julian's friends was kind enough to accompany me outside."

Was he imagining it? Or was she just as uncomfortable with this conversation as he was?

"What's up, Bridget?" he asked in a tone that didn't encourage a casual answer.

"Um, I'd rather not talk about it over the phone."

So he'd been right.

"It's okay, Bridget. Did you meet someone? Is this what's bothering you? Because it's okay if you did."

"Kind of, but I can't talk about it right now."

"Is he standing next to you?"

"Yes."

Andrew closed his eyes, barely stifling a relieved breath as he let go of the tension he'd been holding in his shoulders. "Well, I kind of met someone myself. That's why I'm calling. It's not that anything happened, but I wanted to clear things up between us before anything did."

"I appreciate it."

Even though she sounded relieved, he detected a shade of sadness.

For a moment, he tried to think of what to say to make her feel better and switched the phone to his other ear. "I just wanted to tell you that you're an amazing woman, Bridget, and any guy would be extremely lucky to gain your affection. I had a great time with you. But we both felt that it wasn't meant to be, true?"

"Yeah, I know."

"I hope things will not be weird between us when you come back."

"Yeah, me too. You're a great guy, Andrew. Good luck."

"Thanks, you too."

Andrew clicked off the call and raised his eyes to the ceiling.

"Thank you, God."

17

SEBASTIAN

"How about this one?" Tom pointed to a skinny girl with long legs. A decent looking specimen, despite the red patent leather micro mini and the pair of monster platforms.

"No. She is with friends."

"So are most of them."

"Exactly. You need to search for the few that are here alone. Like this one." He pointed to a girl sitting sideways next to the bar, smiling at a guy who was using every opportunity to touch her. A hand on the knee, a pat on the hand, he was getting more brazen by the minute.

Tom raised an eyebrow. "She is with her boyfriend."

"That's not her boyfriend. A moment ago, a different guy was drooling all over her. This one just came in."

"She might be a pro."

"No, look at what she is wearing."

Tom focused on the woman. "Her skirt is short enough, and I can see part of her boob through the floppy sleeve of her blouse. That's provocative, right?"

Sebastian sighed. The kid had a lot to learn about women. "Look at her shoes."

"What about them?"

"Flats, Tom. She is wearing flats and not because she is too tall to wear heels."

Tom nodded as if he understood. "I see. And whores don't wear flat shoes?"

"No, they usually don't. Heels make a woman's ass and legs look good. They can't afford not to use every trick available to them. But that's not all. If you look closer, you'll see that her shoes are dark blue, not black."

"So?"

"Come on, Tom. I know you can't tell the finer details, yet, like the cheap quality of her clothes, or that her flats have a sticker from a discount store on the bottom. But the fact that she is wearing a black skirt and a black blouse with blue shoes that can barely pass for black is a dead giveaway. These are probably the only ones she owns, and for a girl living in the United States of America to have only one pair means that she's dirt poor."

"What is she doing in a bar, then? If she can't afford shoes, she certainly can't afford the price of drinks at this place."

"Aha, but she doesn't buy her own drinks, the men do."

"So, what do I do?"

"The guy hitting on her is getting too frisky and she is starting to look uncomfortable."

"I can see that."

"Go up to her and pretend like you're her boyfriend who is showing up late for their date. If she wants to get rid of the guy, she will cooperate. Once he leaves, you take it from there. Be nice, unassuming, and charming."

"Got it." Tom tossed back his beer, emptying the bottle.

"And, Tom…"

"Yes?"

"Keep your hands to yourself, for now."

"Yeah, I know. I'm the nice boy next door who is rescuing her from the scumbag."

"Precisely."

The good thing about Tom was that he was a quick study. And the guy could think for himself, which was a rarity among Navuh's troops.

Sebastian observed as Tom followed his instructions to the letter, getting rid of the tentacle man and dazzling the girl with his winning smile. Half an hour later, after he'd bought her two more drinks and a platter of nachos, she started laughing at his jokes. And shortly thereafter, she began touching him—a light pat on the arm, another one on his shoulder.

Tom pretended not to notice and didn't touch her in return, just as Sebastian had instructed. The best way to hook a girl was to let her think you're only marginally interested and letting her do most of the work.

A waitress approached, momentarily blocking his view. "Would you like a refill, sir?"

Nice. He liked the sir she'd tacked on at the end, much better than the honey or darling the others often used, which made him wish he was back home so he could throttle them with impunity.

He allowed himself a moment of fantasy as he looked down her impressive cleavage. Trouble was, with the amount of silicone she had in these super-sized breasts, he doubted she could feel any of the things he imagined doing to them.

"Sure, the same."

She picked up his empty glass and Tom's empty beer bottle and put them on her tray. "And for your friend?"

He waved his hand, "Nothing for now."

"Very well." She straightened, taking her huge breasts with her as she walked away.

Tom and the girl were no longer at the bar. With a quick scan, he found them on the dance floor, swaying with the rest of the cattle to the beat of the impossibly loud music.

The girl was taller than he'd first assumed, and given Tom's modest height, it was good that she was wearing flats. Long black hair cascaded in thick waves down her back, stopping short of her ample behind. Somewhat on the plump side, she was nevertheless very attractive—in an earthy kind of way. Her bright smile revealed a set of straight white teeth that contrasted pleasantly with her dark skin tone. And her large mouth, framed by a pair of lush, fleshy lips, looked like it was custom made to accommodate his shaft.

He wouldn't mind commandeering her for himself. In fact, he was getting hard just from imagining her on her knees, naked, with her hands tied behind her back, and him pumping in and out of that lush mouth of hers.

Sebastian sincerely hoped she fit the profile.

He couldn't wait to find out, but the couple kept dancing and he was getting impatient. A few minutes later he signaled Tom to bring her over.

"Sebastian, this is Letty," Tom introduced her.

"*Hola, señor.*" She offered her hand.

"It's a pleasure to meet you, Letty." He cast her a smoldering look as he took her hand and brought it to his lips for a kiss.

Even with her dark complexion and the club's dim interior, her blush was visible, and she lifted the corners of her fleshy lips in a tight, embarrassed smile.

"Please, sit down. What would you like to drink?"

She turned to Tom. "*Qué?*"

"Letty speaks very little English, and when she gets nervous she speaks even less," Tom explained before repeating Sebastian's question slowly, while using hand gestures.

She nodded and whispered in Tom's ear, "Cola."

As they sat down, Sebastian waved the waitress over and ordered a coke for Letty and another beer for Tom.

The guy leaned in, supposedly so Sebastian could hear him, not that there was any need for it with an exceptional hearing like his, but Tom seemed excited about the information he wished to share. "Letty is new here, only a couple of months. She came from Guatemala to find work so she could help out her family back home. She cleans houses for money, and also this bar."

Sebastian's smile must've been as broad as the wolf's in the fairytale about the girl with a red coat. "This is perfect because I was just looking for a pretty, young maid like you, Letty."

18

NATHALIE

*F*unny, getting used to good things, like having a new powerful appliance in her kitchen, was easy—not so to the things that sucked, like waking up at four o'clock in the morning.

Six days a week. Month after month. Year after year.

Nathalie hated it with a passion.

It was still night outside, and even though the window of her second-floor bedroom was tightly closed, it was cold, and she knew it would stay this way for at least four more hours. Usually, by eight, the California sun would get strong enough to bake away the last vestiges of the fog shrouding her sleepy neighborhood. From then on, it would get progressively warmer until at about two in the afternoon it would become uncomfortably hot.

After all, this used to be a desert, and without the planting and constant artificial irrigation it would still be one. The nearby Pacific Ocean did little to moderate the weather extremes.

Okay, no more stalling, one, two, three... She threw off the duvet and jumped out before her soft, warm bed succeeded in luring her back to sleep.

The pastries, breads, and bagels were not going to bake themselves.

Her regulars were expecting her to open shop at eight sharp. Like Mr. Chen, the owner of the dry cleaners down the street, who had a habit of getting there even before opening time—standing outside the door with his hands in his pockets and waiting impatiently for his morning coffee and a butter croissant.

She'd better rush.

Nathalie had hacked her morning routine so it now took her under fifteen minutes to get ready, including getting dressed and making the bed. The trick was to shower quickly, weave her wet hair into a tight braid and not bother with makeup or clothing selection. Imitating Steve Jobs's style, everything in her closet looked basically the same, jeans for bottoms and black for tops, so any combination matched.

But today she wanted to look pretty because a certain handsome guy with a sexy scar on his chin had said he would be there for breakfast.

Before leaving the bathroom, she hastily rummaged inside the vanity's top drawer until she found the black eyeliner pencil and mascara she was looking for and stuffed them in her jeans pocket. Once the first batch went into the oven, she could spare a minute or two to apply makeup in the coffee shop's bathroom.

Heading down, she stopped by her father's room to check on him. He was still sleeping.

Good.

The old building housing her shop and upstairs living quarters was perfect for their needs. After her father's condition had become such that he needed constant supervision, she'd sold their family home and closed the Studio City café so she could buy this forties era small house. It was a step down even from their modest home, but it served them well.

What used to be the living and dining room had been converted into the sitting area of the café, and the old kitchen had been renovated with modern equipment. The upstairs had three little bedrooms, which all shared a single bathroom. She turned one of them into a living room for her and her father. There was just enough room for a couch, a bookcase, and a TV. It didn't matter. After all, they were spending most of their time downstairs.

But the best part was the single interior staircase leading directly from their upstairs living quarters to the downstairs shop. This configuration made life so much easier on her. Her father had no way of wandering off without her noticing it, and the fact that she didn't need to go out at such ungodly hours of the morning, or rather night, was definitely a bonus for a single woman who for all intents and purposes was alone.

After all, the ghost living in her head and her elderly, mentally impaired father wouldn't be much help if someone attacked her.

Hey, not true, I can give advice, Tut said.

"So you decided to come back. I was hoping that this time you were gone for good."

It's true that I have to wander around in search of some action because your life is so boring, but I always come back. You missed me, admit it.

"No, I didn't, go away." Nathalie put on her apron.

Why? There are no customers—no one to see you talking to yourself.

"Fine, stay if you want to, but promise that you'll leave as soon as I flip the sign on the door to open."

I will, promise, now tell me everything that happened while I was away.

Right, as if she was going to.

"You said my life was boring, and you were right. So, how about you entertain me with tales of your many adventures?"

You know I can't.

"You see, that is how I know you're not real. If you were really a separate entity, you could tell me stuff I don't know about. But because you are nothing but a figment of my imagination, you know no more than I do."

Nathalie pulled out several batches of the dough she'd prepared yesterday from the fridge and placed them on the shelf above her work table. Next out were the slabs of butter she'd pounded into nice big squares inside ziplock bags and refrigerated overnight. Croissants were the most time-consuming pastry, and she always started with them.

I'm not a figment.

"Then prove it."

She unwrapped one of the square-shaped dough packages and dropped it on her work table, then reached for her rolling pin.

I can tell you a fascinating story.

"Humph, as if my brain isn't capable of making up tales. We've been over this before. Unless you can tell me something that can be verified by an external source, and that I have no way of knowing about, I'll keep maintaining that you are imaginary."

To shape the dough into a rectangle, she rolled her pin over it, back and forth several times to make it ready for the butter.

Damn! Her braid fell forward, but she couldn't use her

hands to push it back because they were covered with flour. Instead, she tried to flip it into place by shaking and wiggling. Sporting a dusting of white powder was one thing, having a braid covered in clumps of gooey yellow substance was another.

You look ridiculous. And anyway, that braid of yours should be wrapped around your head and covered with a kerchief or a hat. What you're doing isn't sanitary. If a health inspector catches you working like this, you'll get a citation.

"Hats are not mandatory."

Maybe, but I'm sure hair is not an acceptable ingredient in croissants either.

"And who is going to tell on me? You?"

That shut him up. Nathalie placed a slab of butter in the middle of her rectangle, then folded the flaps over the butter. One more roll and it was ready for the dough sheeter.

You're getting meaner as you get older. Maybe I should look for a more amiable host.

Nathalie sprinkled more flour on her work table and unwrapped the second package of dough. "Go ahead, what are you waiting for?"

Tsk-tsk, so ungrateful. Did you already forget what life was like for you before me?

No, she didn't forget. But she hoped that after all these years of living with only one voice in her head the others were gone for good. She shuddered thinking what would happen if they came back, flooding her brain with their whining voices, their demands...

Tut had been a godsend when he'd come and closed the gate.

However, if Tut and the voices that had come before him were indeed a product of her malfunctioning brain, which was the most likely explanation, then having only him for so many years must mean that she was at least partially cured. If she managed to somehow get rid of him as well, she might be free of the voices for good.

Dream on, Nattie, without me you're guaranteed to go nutty.

Tut laughed, his nasty cackling slowly fading away.

19

ANDREW

"Good morning, partner," Bhathian greeted Andrew with a handshake as he exited his car. With the perpetual frown practically gone, the guy's face looked almost friendly this morning.

Andrew clicked the little red button on his key and locked the car, the thing doing the double chirp in confirmation. "Is there a reason why you are waiting for me on the street?"

Even this early in the morning, the only available parking spot was a few hundred feet away from Nathalie's shop, and that was where the guy had been standing.

Bhathian rubbed his palm over the back of his neck. "I'm not good with small talk. What would I have said to her?"

"How about, a coffee and a croissant, please?"

He shrugged his big shoulders and pushed his hands into his pockets. "Maybe next time. For now, I prefer for you to do the talking."

Andrew chuckled. "I'm not sure you're gonna like it much. My small talk skills are of the flirting variety." He clapped Bhathian's back, amazed anew by the amount of hard muscle on the guy's body. "What are you training with? Railroad cars? One on each side?"

That pulled a rare smile out of the guy. "Come to the gym with me, and I'll show you my routine." He appraised Andrew's slender physique with a critical eye. "You look like you're in good shape, but you need to bulk up."

As they reached Nathalie's café, the sign on the door was already flipped to open, and Bhathian opened the way. "After you." He motioned for Andrew to precede him.

Fighting the urge to check out his reflection in the window, Andrew stepped in and looked around. The place was packed, and Nathalie wasn't up front. With a quick glance, he found her serving coffee to one of the booths.

Damn, the woman had a fine ass.

Bhathian got in his face, blocking the view. "You said flirting, not ogling," he hissed menacingly, all traces of good humor gone.

"Give me a break, will you? I mean no disrespect. She is a fine woman, that's all."

Bhathian frowned for a moment longer before showing a set of scary teeth in what was supposed to be a smile. "Just messing with you." The clap he delivered to Andrew's back sent him toppling forward, making him wonder whether he should head out to the hospital to have the thing X-rayed.

Andrew regained his balance and leveled a hard stare at his companion. "You know, my sister will be very angry if you maim me. And what makes Syssi angry, makes her husband furious, you feel me, my man?"

Bhathian's face lost some of its color. "Sorry, I keep forgetting you're just a human."

"Shh, keep your voice down."

"Sorry," he whispered.

"Andrew, Bhathian," Nathalie called from behind the guy's wide back, then walked around him. "I'm so glad you made it."

"Good morning, Nathalie." Bhathian offered his hand.

She placed her small palm in his large one, but her eyes were trained on Andrew. "So, how did the guys in the office enjoy my croissants?"

As Bhathian held on to her hand, she made no move to pull it away. It didn't seem to bother her.

"Everything was devoured in minutes. I'm telling you, hearing all those groans of pleasure, someone standing outside the room would've gotten a very wrong impression—considering that they were all male."

She laughed. "Really? Or are you just saying it to make me feel good?"

Bhathian put his free hand over his heart. "I swear."

She tilted her head. "Is it true, Andrew?"

"I wasn't there, but it sounds right. Piranhas, that's what those guys are. And your croissants are out of this world."

She blushed. "Thank you, it's so sweet of you to say so."

"It's the honest to God truth." Andrew put his hand over his heart as well.

Nathalie giggled. "You guys look like you're ready to recite the National Anthem."

He winked. "Perhaps we should compose one in honor of your baked goods."

She slapped his arm. "Oh, you guys."

Nathalie looked so pleased that Andrew wanted to say more, but it would have been too much, and besides, he would've just ruined the effect, sounding insincere. He needed to gather more material.

"It looks like you're busy this morning. Do you think you can find us a booth?"

She looked back, appraising her customers. "Give me a

minute. Mrs. Goldberg over there is a schoolteacher, and she's already running late. I'm going to give her a nudge."

Nathalie hurried back and stopped by the second booth to the right, bending at the waist to say something to the occupant, who must've been Mrs. Goldberg. It was hard to tell who was sitting behind the newspaper.

"Oh, dear," Mrs. Goldberg exclaimed, folding her paper and stuffing it into her large satchel. "Thank you for telling me. I was so absorbed in this article that I didn't notice the time fly. I must run." She scooted out of the booth and kissed Nathalie on the cheek. "I'll see you tomorrow, dear."

"Goodbye, Mrs. Goldberg," Nathalie called after her, then quickly collected whatever was left over from the woman's breakfast. Next, she produced a rag from her apron's pocket and wiped the table.

"Here you go, All ready."

"Thank you." Bhathian chose the seat Mrs. Goldberg had vacated, and Andrew took the one across from him.

"What would you like? Same as yesterday?" she asked.

"Yes. Coffee for both of us, and whatever pastries you think we should try."

"Perfect." She beamed. "You are my kind of customers. I'll be back as soon as I can with your order."

On her way back, Nathalie collected dishes from another booth, piling one thing on top of the other in a precarious heap while doing acrobatics with the rag to wipe the table without disturbing its balance.

"She works too hard." Bhathian frowned.

"Yeah, I wonder why she doesn't have help. She obviously needs it."

"And to think that she has already put in several hours of work to bake everything."

"I'll ask her when she comes back with our order."

Bhathian nodded and pulled out his phone.

"Are you going to call someone?"

"No, just checking the schedule of my classes."

"What are you studying?"

"Teaching."

"What?" It was hard to imagine the guy teaching anything. With the exception of combat fighting, that is.

Bhathian shifted in his seat. "Sex education to our young men."

Andrew couldn't help a snort. "You? Of all people? Why?"

The guy's lip twitched. "Why do you think? To scare the shit out of them, of course. After a class with me, the ramifications of inappropriate behavior are very clear."

"I bet, and I guess it's not about the birds and bees kind of class."

"I have no idea what birds and insects you're talking about, but the class is about consent and gentlemanly conduct."

"Okay… Is this a problem for you guys?"

Bhathian smirked. "Not anymore. But what surprised me was that the kids asked for one more class. I think it's a lark."

Might be. Or a bet between the guys to see who would have the guts to ask the ogre for one more. "What will you do if it is?"

"I'll think of something to get back at them. Perhaps force them to attend my next gig. I'm going to teach a self-defense class. Since we've started with them, the demand has been steadily increasing, and Kian asked me to join the effort."

"Here are your coffees, guys, and I brought an assortment for you to try." Balancing the tray on her hip, Nathalie pointed a finger at the plate. "There will be a test later. Make sure you're prepared."

"Yes, ma'am." Bhathian saluted.

Andrew glanced at the tray she was holding. After unloading their order, the thing still held two cups of coffee and a teapot, as well as three sandwiches and two plates of pastries. "Can I ask you a question, Nathalie?"

She looked uncomfortable but nodded anyway. "Sure."

"How come you have no help here? The place looks like it's doing well. You shouldn't be doing everything by yourself."

Nathalie sighed. "This tray weighs a ton. Let me just deliver these and I'll come back and tell you."

Glancing at his watch after she'd left, Andrew realized that it had taken longer than he'd anticipated for their order to arrive, and if he stayed to talk to Nathalie, he would be late for work.

"You have to leave?" Bhathian asked.

"I should, but I won't. I need to find out what's going on. Given her heavy sigh, there is a story here."

"Yeah, my thoughts exactly."

20

NATHALIE

*O*nce she'd delivered everything on her tray, Nathalie put it on top of the counter. It was a quarter to nine, and since most of her morning customers had already been served, she expected to have a quiet hour or so before the next wave started at around ten o'clock.

Perhaps she could even sit down with Andrew and Bhathian while telling them about Tiffany. After all, yesterday, they had all but admitted to being some secret branch of law enforcement. They might be able to help her.

Yeah, right. As if this was the only motivation to sit down next to Andrew. Thank God, Tut hadn't come back yet. Maybe she'd be able to flirt a little.

And why would you? The voice in her head was her own.

As a soft sigh escaped her lips, Nathalie let her head drop. She might be able to have a little chat with Andrew, nothing else. Working as she did from four in the morning until eight in the evening, she was in bed by nine-thirty. Not a schedule that allowed for any social activity. And she wasn't free even during the little time she wasn't working either. Her father needed constant supervision.

Before Tiffany's disappearance, she used to leave the girl in charge and take a nap after the lunch crowd had come and gone. It had allowed her to stay open later. Sometimes, she'd even run out to take care of an errand while Tiffany had kept an eye on her father.

Now, Nathalie had reworked her schedule so she could do everything by herself.

Her only day off was Saturday, and she used it to go to the bank and purchase supplies for the coming week. God knew that doing it while dragging her father along was a nightmare. But what choice did she have?

It wasn't as if she could call a babysitter for him.

There were the adult daycare facilities she could use in case of emergency—leave him there for a couple of hours. But it would be too confusing and disturbing for him, and she was afraid of doing anything that might worsen his condition.

It was ironic, she thought as she walked over to Andrew's table, despite being surrounded by people all day long, she felt like a hermit.

"You mind if I sit next to you?" she asked Bhathian.

"Sure." He scooted to make room for her, trying to push his bulk into the corner, but still taking up most of the space on the bench. And yet, sitting so close to him that their thighs were touching felt surprisingly comfortable— the way she imagined sitting next to a brother would've felt if she had one.

On the other hand, she knew that the same proximity to Andrew would've been electrifying, even without the touching—too intense to handle. She couldn't remember having ever been so attracted to a guy.

It was better like this. Sitting across from him allowed her to see his face, look into his beautiful eyes…

"I had a waitress," she began. "Tiffany, and things were

much easier with her around. But less than a month ago she disappeared. At first, I thought she was flaking out on me. She was always on the lookout for auditions, and I was sure that she was skipping work to go on some. She dreamed of a career in movies. Later, when she still didn't show up, I thought that maybe she managed to score a small role. But as I kept calling and calling and she never answered, I began worrying. I even tried calling from someone else's phone in case she was ignoring my calls on purpose, but she still didn't answer."

"Did you call the police? Maybe something has happened to her," Andrew offered.

Nathalie grimaced. "I didn't."

"Because you're not family?"

"No, that wasn't the reason. I was afraid they'd think I had something to do with it."

"Why on earth would they think that?"

"Because a few years ago my mother went missing and I filed a report with the police. What are the chances of two unrelated people disappearing on the same person?" She arched a brow and raised her hand, holding two fingers up. "I'm like a black hole or a freaking Bermuda Triangle."

Andrew seemed to contemplate the information she'd just shared, his brows taking a dip. "Perhaps I can help you with that."

Nathalie sighed. "I was hoping you would. Being a detective... or something like that."

He smiled. "Something like that. I'll look into it, but I need some more information about Tiffany."

"Sure, anything I can do. I have her address..." Nathalie lowered her eyes. "But going to check on her with my father in tow would have been extremely difficult. He has dementia, and I can't leave him alone even for a minute."

Bhathian patted her hand. "Is he the older gentleman

that was sitting here last evening?" He pointed to the booth Fernando had occupied.

"Yes. He is upstairs now, still sleeping. He had an episode earlier, his hallucinations turned violent, and he was shouting, scaring off the customers. I had no choice but to give him a mild sedative so he could sleep. Hopefully, when he wakes up, he'll be better."

Andrew shook his head. "You don't have it easy, do you, Nathalie?"

"Nope. But I deal. I just need to find someone to help me out here. Someone cheap and part time because I can't afford more than that. I should've put a help-wanted sign in the window after the first couple of days, but I was hoping that she'd show up. Looking for someone to replace Tiffany felt like admitting that I've given up. I should, though. It's pointless to wait any longer, hoping for a miracle that is not going to happen."

"I'll try to find you someone," Bhathian said with another pat on her hand.

"You know someone who is willing to work mostly for tips?"

"I'll ask around."

A good feeling flitted through her, raising her spirits and lifting some of the weight that had been sitting on her shoulders since settling there the day her father had been diagnosed. She hadn't felt this particular sensation for so long that it took her a second or two to comprehend it.

By offering to help her, these two men made her feel like she wasn't alone in the world. The last two years had been the most difficult. With her father's condition worsening to the point where she'd been forced to shoulder the entire operation because he'd become more of a hindrance than help in the kitchen, it had taken all she had just to keep afloat while dragging him behind.

She wouldn't admit it, not even to herself, but she was exhausted, physically and mentally. Was it a wonder then that she'd clung to the first shard of hope she'd been offered?

So it might have been silly, assigning so much importance to Bhathian and Andrew's offer of help. After all, they were just a couple of kind strangers. And yet, the hope they had given her was precious. No one had done it for her before.

"Thank you." She covered Bhathian's hand with hers, closing her fingers in a light squeeze. "I welcome any help I can get."

21

ANANDUR

"Ahoy! Anybody out there?" Anandur switched the bucket of sudsy water to his other hand and reached back for the rag that was hanging out of his shorts' ass pocket to wipe the sweat off his forehead.

For his *disguise*, he'd cut off the legs of an old pair of jeans, putting them through a couple of wash and dry cycles to produce the frayed effect. Unfortunately, he wasn't all that good with scissors, and the result of his repeated attempts to get both sides to the same length was that the inside pockets were sticking from below what was a ridiculously short pair of shorts.

It was all good, though. His muscular thighs were getting a lot of attention, as was his bare chest. The shirt he had on was a short-sleeved button-down, left unbuttoned, and the gentle breeze was doing an excellent job of blowing the light fabric away from his body for maximum exposure.

He'd just finished spiffing the deck of a yacht that hadn't really needed cleaning, his physique delighting its two female occupants whose husbands had been conveniently absent. Now that his assumed occupation had been established, he was ready to take on the infamous crew of the *Anna*.

"Hello!" Anandur called out again.

A dark-haired, muscular woman walked over to the railing of the upper deck and leaned down, appraising him with a pair of suspicious gray eyes. "What do you want?"

He flashed her one of his well-practiced charming smiles and lifted the bucket. "Do you need a deck boy? I work cheap."

"No." Apparently not in a hurry to get back inside, she kept checking him out, fleshy lips pursed in disapproval.

A leggy blonde, just as muscular, joined the brunette at the railing and gave him an unabashed once-over before asking, "How much?"

"Fifty bucks for all exterior decks, two hundred for everything."

The blonde raised a brow and smirked. "Everything?"

He winked. "Everything."

A hushed back-and-forth in Russian ensued, which, unfortunately, he didn't understand. A big disadvantage for someone who was supposed to spy on a bunch of Russians. On the other hand, he had no problem reading their body language and hand gestures.

The brunette, who he assumed was the captain, Geneva, was shaking her head from side to side, while the blonde, who must've been the bitchy Lana, was trying to convince her boss to hire him. With her hungry eyes flicking over to his body every other word, he had a good idea why she was being so adamant, and helped out by flexing whatever he could without striking a pose.

Lana was practically drooling.

Perhaps he should rethink his strategy, and instead of trying to seduce the captain, who looked like a particularly tough cookie, or Marta, who was quite homely according to Amanda, he could go after Lana. The woman was easy on the eyes, and he had no problem with bitches. After all, sometimes all that was needed to cure this nasty, female affliction was a good shag or two.

The doctor is in the house, sweetheart, Anandur smirked, *and he has all the medicine you need right here.* He swiveled his hips suggestively, just in time for Lana to catch the move.

The arguing intensified and finally it seemed that the captain was capitulating.

Lana leaned over the railing, her large breasts resting on her crossed arms. "Hundred fifty, no more."

"Throw in a couple of beers and lunch, and you got yourself a deal."

"How about vodka and steak?"

He raised two fingers, then added one more. "Make it three. Do I look like a guy who can be satisfied with only one piece of meat?"

Lana laughed, a throaty, sexy sound. The corners of Geneva's lips lifted a little.

"Half bottle vodka, three steaks, one hundred and fifty dollars." Lana spelled out the conditions of the deal.

Anandur gave her the thumbs up.

"Okay, deck boy, you have permission to come aboard," Geneva pressed a button on a remote, extending the hydraulic side boarding stairs.

"Thanks." Anandur saluted. He waited until the staircase locked in place, then bounded up, careful to keep his bucket level.

"Where are you going so fast?" Geneva stopped him. "Start with the stairs. They need a good scrubbing."

"Yes, ma'am!" He turned around and started from the bottom.

"Fucking hell, I really hate cleaning," Anandur murmured as he pulled out a scrubbing brush from his bucket.

There was a little dirt trapped between the furrows of the rubberized runner covering the teakwood stairs, and he carefully scrubbed each step before going in reverse up to the next one.

All along, Lana, who'd taken a seat on one of the lounges on the lower deck, was watching his ass. Which was good for his ego, but prevented him from planting William's tiny listening device.

"Like what you see?" He glanced back.

"*Da*, you work body good."

What did she mean by that? He cast her a quizzical glance.

She mimed holding a bar and doing a chest press. "How long each day you work gymnasium?"

Aha, okay, now I get it.

"Weight lifting and other muscle work, two hours each morning. And if I have someone to spar with, I can put in a couple more."

That piqued her interest, and she sat up straight. "What you spar? Wrestling? Judo?"

Anandur dropped the brush in his bucket and sauntered toward her.

"That depends." He stood so close that her face was only a few inches away from his crotch.

For a moment, her nostrils flared as she inhaled his scent, then she cranked her head up to look at his face. "On what?"

Lana was one of those blondes who were so devoid of pigmentation that they looked almost like an albinos. Her hair, as well as her skin, was incredibly white, her eyes were a pale, watered-down blue, and her lips, although big and puffy, were only a shade pinker than the rest of her.

Not to say that she was unattractive

On the contrary, the combination of long, powerful legs with boobs that rivaled some of the best enhancement jobs he'd seen, but in Lana's case were real, and the uncommonly fair coloring was both interesting and sexy.

He ran his knuckles over the smooth skin of her cheek. "On who's my partner. I can do wrestling..." he slurred a little as his fangs filled his mouth. "I also do mixed martial arts." He caressed her other cheek.

Lana's lush lips parted and her eyes hooded. "I do wrestling," she breathed.

Anandur chuckled. "I'm game to do some wrestling with you..." he leaned to whisper in her ear. "In bed."

"You want?" She smiled, but he deduced a challenge in her eyes.

"I do."

"Why I do with a deck boy? Ha?"

"Because I'm sexy." Anandur turned around in slow motion. "And because I'll give you multiple orgasms so good that you'll be screaming my name."

"Humph, all you men think you so good." She crossed her arms under her impressive breasts, turning her cleavage into something that belonged in a porn movie.

"Ah, but I really am." He leaned and kissed her cheek, using the opportunity to stick a bug to the chair's underside, then straightened up and grabbed his bucket.

It wasn't the best of places—somewhere inside would've been better—but there were plenty more where this one came from. Next time he'd find somewhere strategically more advantageous. "If you'll excuse me. I have work to do." He spun around and began walking.

"How I know?"

He turned only his head and smiled. "How do you know that I'm the real deal? There is only one way to find out, isn't there?" He winked and walked away.

"What's your name, deck boy?"

"Anandur."

"A Scot?"

"Aye."

She grinned. "I hear Scots are very good lovers."

"As I said before, only one way to find out."

The hook had been cast, and Lana had bitten. Next step would be to reel her in.

Easy.

He was going to have so much fun with the hot Russian.

22

ANDREW

*A*ndrew glanced at the big white clock hanging on the wall above Agent Kravitz's head, willing the arms to move faster. His work day was dragging on like a stink behind a port-a-potty. Every fucking minute felt like an hour.

It had something to do with a craving for coffee. But not the watery thing brewing in the break room. Andrew wanted a good, hot cappuccino, served by a sexy lady with big brown eyes. Eyes that looked tired but full of life, hardened by experience but innocent.

Sweet Nathalie.

The moment he'd left her shop, he'd decided to go back straight after work. Without Bhathian this time. He wanted to pursue the thing that was going on between them sans her father's intimidating presence.

Problem was, Nathalie had more than one daddy.

True, her adoptive one suffered from dementia, but nevertheless, he hung around the place, and pretending like he wasn't there while flirting with his daughter would no doubt feel awkward.

Poor Nathalie, how was she supposed to have a love life while working such long hours in the café and caring for her adoptive father? It was quite likely that the last time she'd seen any action had been in college because Andrew couldn't imagine her grabbing a quickie in the kitchen, which given the circumstances was the only way she could've gotten busy with a guy.

That reminded him that he'd promised to check on her missing waitress, but staying after work to investigate would mean less time with Nathalie.

Fuck it, he could do a quick search while on the clock.

The address Tiffany had given her boss had no phone number attached to it. No big surprise there. Her generation didn't bother with landlines anymore. Everyone was using their cellphones for everything. The only information Andrew found pertaining to that address was the name of the landlord—a corporation owning hundreds of rental units all over the country.

He emailed the main office in Seattle, asking for the phone number of the manager of Tiffany's building.

The best thing would've been to drive up there, knock on the door, and question the girl's roommates. But it would've meant more time wasted between now and finally getting to see Nathalie. Given that her café closed at eight, and the earliest he could get there was five-thirty, he wasn't about to shorten the little time he could have with her even further.

At a quarter to five, Andrew closed his computer, pocketed his keys and his access card, and said goodbye to the agents sharing his office without bothering to come up with an excuse for why he was leaving early. He'd skipped lunch so he could leave at five instead of five-thirty, and cutting an additional fifteen minutes to leave even earlier didn't require explanation.

If his boss had a problem with this, he could find another monkey to do Andrew's job.

The drive to Glendale that would've taken him twenty minutes without the damned traffic took forty-five, which wasn't too bad for L.A.'s rush hour. Thankfully, there were no accidents to bring the congested freeway to a complete standstill, and slogging along with the rest of the workplace refugees he got there, as planned, at five-thirty.

"Andrew, what a nice surprise." Nathalie's face lit up as he came in. "Where is your friend?" She tilted her head to look behind him. Funny girl, as if someone as big as Bhathian could've been hidden by Andrew's body.

He leaned his elbow on the counter to get closer. "I wanted you all to myself." He winked.

"Oh…" Nathalie blushed. "Would you like some coffee? A sandwich? I can make a custom ordered one for you. What would you like in it? There is tuna, salami, or perhaps the vegetarian, my favorite, with eggplant and roasted bell peppers. Or perhaps something else?" By the time she finished reciting the options, she was out of breath.

Sweet, her response had taken him all the way back to junior high when girls had still gotten flustered when he'd hit on them. Was she so unused to getting attention? Not likely. Nathalie was pretty and sexy and seemed like a genuinely nice person.

She was probably fending off guys all day long.

So, was it him? Was he making her nervous? Perhaps his scars were to blame, or his stupid comment from yesterday—the one about having to kill her if he told her about his and Bhathian's *secret project*. Or both.

He smiled, trying to go for friendly. But given his pose and proximity, it must've come out wrong. He probably ended up looking as if he were leering.

Her face got a shade redder, and she started chewing her lower lip as she waited for him to answer.

To give her space, Andrew straightened up and took a step back. "Surprise me," he said.

Nathalie's chest expanded as she took in her first deep breath since he'd come in. No wonder. He'd been hitting on her with the tact and finesse of an adolescent.

"Sure thing. Take a seat anywhere you like. I'll make you something that I hope you are going to like."

"No pressure. I'm going to like whatever you make."

The only vacant booth was the one at the very end of the café, and as he glanced in the direction of the one across the aisle from it, Andrew confirmed his suspicion that its occupant was indeed Fernando.

Bummer. He'd hoped to sit as far as possible from Nathalie's daddy. Grabbing a newspaper from the stand, he tucked it under his arm and headed for the back. Perhaps he'd erect a shelter using the thing.

As Andrew slid inside the booth so he could sit by the window, Fernando raised his head from his own newspaper and gave him a curt nod.

Surprised, Andrew nodded back. Did the old guy remember him from yesterday? Or did he nod at everyone who happened to be seated across the aisle from him?

He was going to ask Nathalie about it. Perhaps Fernando remembering him was a good sign. His dementia couldn't be too bad if he remembered someone he had seen only once. True, it had been just yesterday, but from what Andrew knew about the disease, short-term memory was the first to go.

Busying himself with flipping through the *New York Times* pages, reading mostly headlines, Andrew waited for his food to be served, or more to the point, for the one serving it to arrive at his table. A couple of times he lifted his head to check on her, but the place was full, and she had other customers to take care of.

It seemed like everyone had gotten their food before she finally arrived with his.

"Sorry it took me so long, but I wanted to get all the other orders done first so I could sit with you for a little while."

Now, wasn't that music to his ears. "I'm glad you did. For the pleasure of your company, I don't mind waiting."

Nathalie smiled, removing two cups of cappuccino, two tall glasses of water, and a plate heaped with mixed greens and a sandwich cut diagonally into two triangular pieces.

"Just a moment," she excused herself, turning to her dad. "Are you okay, Papi?" She put her palm on his shoulder. "Do you need anything?"

"No, sweetheart, I'm fine. You go ahead and sit with your guy."

"My…" She turned her head and cast Andrew an apologetic glance. "He is not my guy, Papi, he is just a friend."

Fernando smiled and patted her hand on his shoulder. "If you say so."

"Sorry about that," Nathalie said as she sat down across from Andrew. "I don't know why he would say something like that. It's probably his dementia."

Andrew hesitated for a moment before mustering the guts to say what he wanted to say. "I don't want to be just your friend, Nathalie. I want to be your guy."

Nathalie's cheeks got red like a couple of ripe tomatoes, and she opened and closed her mouth, then opened it again, but no words came out.

"Do I frighten you? Is that why my advances are making you so uncomfortable? I'm a nice guy, I swear. And that stupid comment I made yesterday was just a bad joke."

"I know," she whispered, then reached for the water

glass with a shaky hand and gulped down half of it before returning it to the table. "I'm not scared of you. I know you're a nice guy, it's just that I like you too."

Was there a sheen of tears in her eyes?

Andrew reached across the table and took her hand. "Is it a bad thing? Liking me?"

She nodded, dropping her eyes.

"Why? Is there someone else?"

Nothing about Nathalie suggested that she had a boyfriend, but that didn't mean that there hadn't been one in the past. Someone who had either hurt her so badly that she was afraid of getting hurt again, or someone who still exerted influence or control over her despite her breaking up with him.

God knew there were enough jerks like this.

"Is anybody threatening you, Nathalie?"

She shook her head. But Andrew wasn't going to leave it at that. She might be afraid of involving him in her problems or some other crap like that.

"Because if anyone is, you need to tell me. I'll never let anyone hurt you, and these are not empty words. I'm perfectly capable of taking care of, like in eliminating, whatever and whoever is giving you trouble."

She chuckled, but the sound was devoid of mirth. "Oh, Andrew. This is the sweetest thing anyone has ever said to me. But unless you know how to cure dementia, there is nothing you can do to help me."

That was unfortunately true, but Andrew failed to see how her father's disease had anything to do with him.

"No, regrettably, my various talents don't include miracle working. But I don't understand why your father's condition would influence the way you feel about me."

With a heavy sigh, she pulled out her hand from his grasp, and he let her, sensing she needed the distance. "I can't leave my father alone even for a moment." She whispered so quietly he had to lean forward to hear her. "He wanders off, looking for our old house—the one we sold years ago—and gets lost. Every time he manages to escape, I lose a year of my life until he is found. He has dog tags and a bracelet with my phone number on them, so I usually get calls from the nice people who find him, telling me that they have him. But not everybody is nice, and I'm afraid that one of these days he'll escape and never come back."

"That must be tough."

"It is, but I can deal with it. The problem is that I can't have a relationship, not even a friendship. I can't go out, ever. Not to a movie, not to a restaurant, not to visit someone's home. It's just my dad and me. There is no one else to step in and give me room to breathe."

"Now, there is. I'm here, and I don't care if the only way I can be with you is sitting here in this booth and waiting for you to have a few moments to spare, or hanging out at your place. I don't care about going out to movies or restaurants. All I care about is being with you and getting to know you."

"Why? You're a handsome man, you can get any woman you want. Why me and my baggage? Why settle for less?"

Her questions and her self-deprecation were starting to annoy him. "Let's get one thing straight. I don't want to ever hear you say that you're someone to settle for. You're a unicorn, Nathalie. You are rare and special, and I'm one lucky bastard to have not only found you, but to have, for some inexplicable reason, piqued your interest or even won your affection."

The shy smile that bloomed on her face was priceless. "Okay." She squared her shoulders. "So, given the limitations, how do we proceed?"

23

NATHALIE

It must be a dream, Nathalie thought, a very nice dream, and at any moment she was going to wake up. Things like this just didn't happen to her. A sexy guy, one who'd been starring in her very naughty fantasies last night, just offered to accept her with all her limitations because she was so fabulous that he couldn't stay away.

Right.

But if this is a dream, please don't wake me up.

"You close at eight, true?"

"Yes."

"Do you need to stay and clean up?"

Oh, God, if she had to do this too, she would've jumped off the nearest bridge. "No, I have a service that comes and cleans the place at night."

"Good, so after eight you're free, other than babysitting your father, that is."

"Yeah?"

"Are you in the mood for Chinese?"

"I'm not hungry, but maybe later. Do you want to order takeout?"

It could be nice. She was a little sick of her own pastries and sandwiches. But was she being careless? Inviting a guy she'd only met yesterday up to her apartment?

Nathalie had a good feeling about Andrew, but that didn't mean much. He was attractive and she was so lonely that she would've probably ignored any troubling signs, even if subconsciously. And anyway, with her lack of experience, she wouldn't have known what to look for.

Where was Tut when she actually needed him?

Whenever a guy would show interest in her, the ghost in her head would issue warnings or nasty comments or both, making it impossible for her to conduct a friendly conversation with anyone she found even remotely attractive, let alone anything else.

"I'll go and get us some from the Golden Palace. As far as I know they don't deliver. And I'll get a movie from the supermarket's vending machine. Anything in particular that you like?"

"Perhaps that latest *Star Wars*? I'm a big fan."

Andrew smiled broadly. "Ah, my kind of girl. I was afraid you'd go for something sappy and romantic."

"Nah, a romantic comedy yes, but I hate sad stories. I want to be entertained, not depressed."

"My thoughts exactly."

She glanced at his uneaten sandwich, and the cappuccino that was most likely cold. "Finish your food before you go."

"Yes, ma'am." He dutifully lifted the sandwich she'd made for him and took a bite, rolling his eyes as he chewed. "Delicious," he said after swallowing his first bite.

Nathalie could've gladly spent the next few minutes watching Andrew eat, but the jingle of bells announced new customers and she had to get up. "Would you like me to make you a new cup? This one is probably barely tepid."

"Thank you, but no. This is perfectly fine." He grabbed the small porcelain cup and emptied it on a oner.

"I have to go." She cast him an apologetic look as she scooted out of the booth.

"It's okay, go, take care of your customers." He waved her away.

As she rushed to the front, Nathalie sneaked a quick peek behind her at her father. He seemed absorbed in the newspaper spread out on the table before him, but the small smirk on his kind face hinted that he'd been eavesdropping on her conversation with Andrew, and that he approved.

It made her feel good, even though God only knew what scenario Papi's dementia had painted for him. He might have imagined that Andrew was her husband, or that she was someone else altogether. He had gotten confused before, thinking she was Eva. Except, she doubted he would've been happy to see his ex-wife flirting with a man.

"I'll be back shortly," Andrew said over the head of a customer who was ordering coffee and blew her an air kiss before leaving.

Wasn't a real kiss supposed to come before a pretend one? She thought it was kind of funny.

An excited flutter started in her belly, and she struggled to school her face for the sake of the older lady, who was done fumbling in her purse after having found the exact change to hand over. Never having to fake a smile for a customer before, Nathalie hoped she was doing it right and not looking like one of those plastic store mannequins.

Later, when the last customer had left, and she flipped the sign on the door to closed, the enormity of what she'd agreed to hit her hard.

God, was she nervous. Thirty years old and clueless, how embarrassing.

Everyone assumed that only the painfully unattractive or the severely socially-awkward people remained alone, never having experienced a relationship with the opposite sex. The truth was, though, that she wasn't a rare exception. Like many others—some even famous, like Jane Austen—she was a victim of circumstances. One thing had led to the next, and before she knew it, she was entering her third decade as a virgin.

And it wasn't even Tut's fault, not completely, even though she liked to blame him for it.

It might have been true in high school, but by the time she'd entered college, she'd learned to hide her *crazy*—a Bluetooth earpiece providing the perfect cover for whenever she'd slipped.

At first, thinking she had plenty of time ahead of her, Nathalie had taken things slowly, or rather not at all, too scared to start exploring the dating scene. How could she have known that her college days were numbered? That her good, reliable Papi would need her to step in and take care of not only his business, their only source of income, but also himself.

Since then, it had all been one big blur of work and more work. Andrew was like the first ray of light to penetrate the fog that had overtaken her life.

Wrong verb, Nathalie, oh, boy, really wrong.

Conjuring the image of Andrew doing a penetrating of a different sort, she felt like laughing hysterically, and she would've if not for her father. She should be excited, should look forward to finally experiencing what a woman her age should've been experiencing for at least a decade.

Instead, she was terrified.

Not of the act itself, but of admitting to Andrew that

she was still a virgin. Like there was something wrong with her. Like there had been no one who'd ever wanted her.

Shit.

But that was the thing, there *was* something wrong with her—she was a freaking loon—*Nutty Nattie.* And as to not being wanted? She'd never given anyone a chance to get close enough to find out.

That being said, though, Nathalie was pretty sure that upon discovering the truth about her any normal guy would've run so fast he would've left skid marks on the pavement.

As would Andrew. And it was going to hurt like hell.

Maybe she should lock the door and pretend like she wasn't there. Andrew didn't have her phone number so there wasn't much he could do other than knock.

Eventually, he'd give up and leave.

24

ANDREW

"Nathalie, open up, it's me, Andrew." Paper bags under each arm, Andrew had no choice but to tap the door with his shoe instead of knocking.

Had she gone upstairs and couldn't hear him?

It was damn embarrassing to stand outside her shop and call her name, but there was no doorbell. And in his stupidity he'd forgotten to ask for her phone number. True, he had it written down in the file he'd compiled about her, but the thing was in the office. And anyway, receiving a call from him, when she hadn't given it, would've creeped her out.

Worse, she would've suspected him of being a stalker.

He kicked the door again, more forcefully this time, the bells hanging on the inside jingling as it rattled. She must've heard those.

"Nathalie! Open up!" he called again when another minute passed.

"Coming!"

Hearing her finally answer him, Andrew let out a relieved breath. For a moment there, a disconcerting thought had flitted through his mind that she wasn't going to let him in.

He must've been nervous. Or perhaps excited.

It was, after all, their first date, so to speak. It wasn't that he lacked confidence, or feared making a fool of himself. At his age, after having been on the dating scene for so long, Andrew had accumulated countless first dates under his belt and had it down to a fail-proof formula. He could charm the pants off a woman in less than an hour, two tops.

But there was something about Nathalie that made him feel like a teenager again. A freshness. An innocence. Which was peculiar since she was a grown woman of thirty, living in one of the largest metropolitan areas in the world, and not some young, small town girl.

Perhaps it was her character.

He'd met a few people like that over the years—the eternal Peter Pans and Pollyannas, who somehow retained their youthful disposition regardless of the date of birth listed on their driver licenses and in spite of the hardships life had thrown at them.

No, on further reflection, this wasn't it either.

True, Nathalie didn't let her troubles bring her down, but she wasn't overly cheerful either.

In any case, it was too early for him to form an opinion about her, one way or another. This was what people were supposed to do on dates, learn about each other. Although these days, it seemed as if dating was more about finding the shortest route to bed than building rapport.

Not this time.

With Nathalie, Andrew intended to be the perfect gentleman and focus on learning as much as he could about her. The exploration of her smoking hot body would have to wait for another time.

The bells on the door chimed as Nathalie threw it open. A guilty look washed over her face when she saw the paper bags under his arms. "I'm so sorry that I kept you waiting outside. I was in the bathroom and didn't hear you knocking."

A lie.

Not a biggie, it had happened to him before on other dates. Wanting to make a good impression on him, she'd probably been hard at work, straightening things upstairs in a hurry. No girl wanted a guy to know that she was messy, and that her place wasn't immaculate at all times.

"No problem." He smiled and waited for her to open the door all the way to make room for him.

For some reason, she hesitated for a moment before doing so. Was she still afraid of him?

Yeah, probably.

He didn't fault her hesitancy. A woman, who for all intents and purposes was living alone, should be wary of inviting strange men to her home.

One man, just one.

Whoa, where has that come from? Jealous, some?

Andrew shook his head. This was new.

He had no idea that there was a secret caveman living inside him. One who had been biding his time, evidently, and just waiting for Andrew to develop some sort of feelings for a woman before raising up his stupid head at the mere thought of another male with her.

Andrew used to mock his friends for this sort of thing, thinking it would never happen to him.

"Follow me." Nathalie circled the counter to get to the kitchen. "You can put the Chinese in the fridge over there."

He did as she'd instructed, taking out the various containers and putting them on a shelf inside her commercial fridge.

"This one is for upstairs." He motioned to the last bag which contained a movie, two bottles of wine, and a small box of chocolates.

"What's in there?" She peeked. "Oh, wine and chocolates..." She cast him a glance that seemed two parts worried to one part excited.

He'd better put on his most friendly, unthreatening, boy-next-door face.

Andrew shrugged and smiled broadly. "Those are just to emphasize that this is a date. If I can't take you out to dine you and wine you, I want to at least provide the second part."

"Oh... that's very sweet of you," she said in a small voice.

What is it with the sweet again? He wanted to roll his eyes. In his opinion, he was as far from sweet as a mostly good guy got.

"I got *Star Wars*." He pulled out the movie to show her.

Nathalie's eyes brightened, and she clapped her hands. "Oh, goodie, I've wanted to see it forever. Follow me." She crossed the kitchen, going toward the back door, where a small corridor led up to a narrow staircase.

Andrew had been wondering where it was hidden, assuming that it must be at the back of the building but speculating that it was attached to its exterior. He was relieved to see that the staircase to the second floor was inside the structure, so Nathalie and her dad weren't risking late night forays into the secluded alley just to go up to their apartment or down to their café.

The advanced age of the building was more evident in the back where less care had been given to appearances. The back door was small, its white paint cracked and faded, and the stairs they were climbing would not have been permitted by today's standards. For one, they were too narrow, and second, too steep—each step about a foot tall. The climb must be really hard on Fernando's old knees.

The stairs terminated at a small landing. From there, parallel to the staircase, a narrow corridor led to four doors. The last one was open, and by the intermittent sounds of laughter, Andrew guessed that Fernando was watching a sitcom.

"That's our TV room." Her smile was embarrassed. "I'll move Papi to watch his shows in his room."

Awkward.

Even though Andrew wasn't planning on any hanky panky, it wouldn't be much of a date with her father around. On the other hand, kicking Fernando out of his TV room wasn't something that sat well with him either. "I don't want to make the man uncomfortable in his own house. Perhaps he would like to watch *Star Wars* with us?"

Nathalie blushed, a pretty pink shade spreading over her high cheekbones. "It's okay, he won't mind. There's only one couch in there, and I don't think it could sit the three of us comfortably. It's rather on the smaller side."

"Okay then, lead the way." He waved his hand and followed her into the room.

Before Nathalie had converted it into a den, it must've been a bedroom, and a small one at that. Smack across from the door, he could see the back alley through its only window, and under it, two folded tray tables were leaning against the cream-colored wall—their dark cherry wood contrasting with the soft earth tones of everything else in the room. On one side was the couch she'd mentioned, and across from it a thirty-five-inch flat screen stood on its own built-in stand, and seemed much larger in the cramped space. In between, there were no more than six or seven feet of floor space.

The couch looked inviting, though, upholstered in some velvety fabric with large fluffy cushions at its back. A throw blanket was draped over one arm, and a soft rug covered the old hardwood floor. All in all, not bad.

Nathalie's den was tiny, but it exuded warmth and comfort.

Seated on the couch, Fernando lifted his head as Nathalie entered, a smile spreading across his wrinkled face.

"Papi, this is Andrew, my friend." She rested her hand on Andrew's arm and extended the other toward her father. "Andrew, meet my father, Fernando Vega."

Andrew walked over to the old man and extended his hand. "It's a pleasure to meet you, sir."

Fernando shook what he offered, his old calloused hand surprisingly strong for a man who looked quite feeble. "Yes, nice of you to come visit Nathalie, young man. She missed you, you know, while you were away."

Okay… what was he supposed to say to that? Andrew cast Nathalie a sidelong glance.

"Just roll with it," she mouthed.

"I'm here now, sir, and I'm not planning on going anywhere anytime soon."

"Good." Fernando nodded and squeezed Andrew's hand harder.

"Papi, would you mind watching your shows in your bedroom? Andrew and I are going to put on the new *Star Wars* movie in the DVD player."

"Of course, sweetheart, you know I don't like all those futuristic movies with all those robots running around." With difficulty, Fernando pushed off the couch. Nathalie offered him a hand up, and he took it, though it was clear that he was embarrassed.

"Thank you, dear. These old bones are not what they

used to be. Enjoy your movie." He kissed her cheek and shuffled out of the room.

"That was easy. Weird, but easy." Andrew walked over to the flat screen, unwrapping the DVD case on the way. "Who do you think he thought I was?"

"I have no idea." Nathalie unfolded one of the tray tables and put it in front of the couch.

"Was there someone you were dating in the past that he liked? Maybe he thought I was that guy?"

Nathalie snorted. "Nope, this is purely his dementia at work."

Interesting. Fernando had either never met Nathalie's ex-boyfriends or hadn't liked any of them.

Andrew wondered why. Had Fernando been one of those overprotective fathers who believed their daughters were too good for mere mortals?

Except, in Nathalie's case, it was true.

But if Fernando imagined Andrew was that special one, he was mistaken. Regrettably, Andrew was just another nothing-special, ordinary guy.

NATHALIE

*T*hey were alone. At last. For the first time.

Stealing a glance at Andrew's back, Nathalie hoped to get a peek at his behind while he was still turned around, busy fiddling with the DVD.

She smirked. Instead of *Nutty Nattie*, her new nickname should be *Naughty Nattie*.

Regrettably, Andrew had come straight from work, wearing the slacks, tie, and jacket his job evidently mandated, so his assets were hidden beneath the back flaps of his blazer. At the moment, the only parts of him she could appreciate, other than his handsome face and capable hands, were his strong thigh muscles as they flexed under the thin fabric of his slacks. But then, as he bent down to insert the disc into the player, she finally got to glimpse a little more.

God, he was such a handsome man.

Were his chest and arms as muscular and defined as his lower half?

She wished he'd take off his jacket.

Bad girl, you're ogling the man like a stallion.

She didn't need Tut to feel guilty about the way she was objectifying Andrew. Go figure, apparently women could be just as bad as men when checking out the opposite sex.

Nathalie let out a soft sigh and reached into the paper bag Andrew had brought, pulling out one of the wine bottles. What had Andrew been thinking, bringing two? Was he planning on getting her drunk?

Somehow, she knew he wasn't the type. Maybe the second bottle was for him. She cast him a sidelong glance. "I don't have wine glasses."

"Do you have some downstairs? I'll go and get them." Andrew straightened up from where he was crouching.

She pulled out the box of chocolates and put them on the tray next to the wine. "No, the only thing I have we can use are tall juice tumblers."

"Perfect." He smiled, a friendly smile that at first put her at ease but on second thought worried her.

She didn't want friendly, platonic. She wanted steamy, exciting.

Nathalie wanted a hot kiss—an epic one like in the movies or in the romance novels she liked reading, one that would make her toes curl.

Last night, in bed, she'd fantasized about it... and much more...

As her cheeks heated up, she turned around to hide the telltale blush. "I'll go get them. I have some in my room." She ran out of there as if her tail was on fire.

God, she was usually so good at pushing carnal thoughts away, precisely because of the damn blushing, but she just couldn't help herself around Andrew. He was so profoundly masculine—not a boy, not a guy, but a real man. The kind every woman wished for. Strong and confident, commanding yet accommodating, respectful...

Oh, boy, hopefully, he wouldn't respect her too much.

Nathalie was desperate for that kiss she'd been fantasizing about for ages, and it was about bloody time she got it.

Even if the initiative would have to come from her.

Did she have the guts, though?

The sight greeting her upon her return had her drooling, and she almost dropped the tumblers she was holding. Andrew had not only removed his jacket but had already rolled up one of his shirt sleeves and was finishing rolling the other. For some reason, his exposed forearms—strong, tanned, and sprinkled with a smattering of dark hair—were incredibly sexy.

With a hard swallow, Nathalie clenched her thighs together to relieve the sudden tingling that had started at their junction.

Lifting his head to look at her, Andrew paused the folding and frowned. "Does this bother you? I can put the jacket back on."

Shit, she must've been gaping like an idiot. "No, of course not. Um... I was just admiring how precise your folds are. Papi could never manage this, even when he was still okay. I used to always undo what he'd done and roll his sleeves for him because he never got it right."

Okay, saved, blabbering like a silly valley girl, but at least not visibly drooling.

Andrew cocked one brow and finished the last fold he'd been working on. "How did I do?" He extended both arms, bringing his wrists together so the bottoms aligned.

"Perfect." Her voice sounded breathy even to herself. Great, next she'd be singing *Happy Birthday Mr. President* in a throaty Marilyn Monroe voice.

"Good, we are almost ready for the movie. I'll just get rid of this fu..., excuse me, tie."

Oh, good, so she wasn't the only one walking on

eggshells. "It's fine. I don't mind." She waved a hand that was still holding a tumbler. "I'd better put these down."

Andrew took off his tie and added it to his jacket, which he'd draped over the other folded tray table, then grabbed the remote and joined her on the couch.

"My lady." He handed her the device.

"You're giving me control of the remote? I heard that no guy would relinquish it without a fight."

Damn, had she just said *heard*? Like she'd never watched television with a guy before?

Other than her Papi, that is.

Andrew glossed over her slip. "You heard right, but when wine uncorking is involved, it takes precedence. We Neanderthals have our priorities."

Remote in hand, she watched his biceps as he unscrewed the cork and pulled it out, then poured wine into the two tumblers and handed her one.

Leaning forward, he raised his glass and clinked it with hers. "Cheers."

Up close, the smell of his cologne was doing a number on her, and she had the urge to bring her nose to where his shirt was unbuttoned and take a good sniff.

"Cheers," she said and looked away. "Is it time to press play?"

"Yes, ma'am."

Nathalie skipped over the commercials and the credits to the beginning of the movie.

She'd wanted to see this one since the first commercial she'd seen for it. But being so painfully aware of Andrew, sitting just a few inches from her, she wasn't paying attention to what was happening on the screen—it was an effort just to breathe—and if anyone had asked her what the movie was about, she wouldn't know.

Perhaps she should just turn and kiss him, get it over

with so she could take a full breath again. It was too intense, this pretending to be watching because they were supposed to be on their first date and it was too soon for kissing. Nerve-racking.

"Are you okay?" He turned a pair of concerned eyes on her.

"Yes, why would you think I'm not?" She forced a smile and lifted the wine to her lips. Thank God, her hand only felt like it was shaking but didn't.

Apparently, Andrew didn't find her answer satisfactory, and as he regarded her for a long moment, she was so hyperconscious of his scrutiny that her palms turned clammy.

"I'm making you uncomfortable." It was a statement, not a question.

How the hell was she supposed to respond? Say yes? But then he'd ask why, and she'd be forced to admit things she absolutely, positively didn't want to disclose. But if she said no, he would know she was lying.

Nathalie opted to say neither. "It's just that it's a little stuffy in here. I'll open the window." She put her tumbler down on the tray table and got up on a pair of rubbery legs.

Pushing the window open, she discreetly wiped her sweaty palms on the sill and leaned out, breathing in the cool night air. Outside, a possum was grunting as it rummaged through refuse spilled from an over-turned trashcan, defending its territory from other denizens of the alley. And further down, two cats were engaged in a fierce battle, probably over a similar treasure.

The scent of rotting organic matter, or perhaps it was the stink of the possum, wafted up, and she contemplated closing the window. But the truth was that her small den was indeed stuffy, and regardless of the stench, the cool air was helping calm her frayed nerves.

Suddenly, Andrew was behind her, caging her between his outstretched arms as he braced them on the window frame on each side. She hadn't even heard him approach. He leaned closer, the heat of his body warming her back and his masculine cologne scrambling her brain. Without making contact, he dipped his head so his cheek was almost touching hers. "Tell me what's wrong," he demanded in a tone that brooked no argument.

Nathalie closed her eyes and turned around. Shielded behind her own eyelids, she gathered her courage and lifted her face to his. "Kiss me."

26

ANDREW

"*K*iss me," she said in that beautiful, sexy voice of hers—her lids closed and her lips parted as she waited for him to deliver what she'd asked for.

Fuck his promise not to touch her tonight. After all, she'd asked, hadn't she? And he wasn't going to say no. Nathalie seemed like she needed this with a desperation he couldn't decipher but welcomed enthusiastically. The why of it wasn't something he was about to dwell on while she was waiting for him to make his move.

She wanted to be kissed. He wanted to kiss her. End of story.

Tentatively, still bracing against the window frame, Andrew held his chest a scant inch away from her heaving breasts as he leaned into her and dipped his head. Feeling his breath on her face, Nathalie parted her lips a little more, inviting, coaxing him to plunder. But he was in no rush, and touching his lips to hers, his kiss was soft, gentle, almost chaste.

Nathalie's lids popped open, her eyes blazing with

pent-up desire. A second later, her hands shot up, plowing into his hair as she smashed her lips against his.

Who knew that sweet Nathalie was a lustful little minx? And it seemed that she needed a real kiss, not a tease.

A soft moan escaped her throat as he dropped his hands to her waist and gathered her into his arms, bringing her tight against his body. Andrew didn't plunge in right away, even though she obviously wanted him to. Instead, he licked at her lips, first the bottom one, then the top, exploring, discovering her treasures one at a time.

Sometimes, delaying pleasure made it more intense.

He half expected Nathalie to take over, but she sagged into him, boneless, and let her lids drop down again. When he finally breached her mouth, it was his turn to moan, and as his hands wandered down to cup her luscious butt cheeks, he couldn't help himself and gently kneaded the firm yet giving flesh.

When he squeezed a little harder, Nathalie jerked in surprise, but then she relaxed into his palms and even pressed herself against his erection with a barely there undulation.

If she were any other woman, he would've been undressing her by now, reaching for her bra hook to release her breasts and suck on her nipples, but instinct, or maybe a subconscious hunch, was guiding him to go slow, to let her set the pace.

There was an unpracticed innocence to her enthusiasm that was giving him pause. He couldn't put his finger on it, or perhaps the clues just didn't add up. Because it was impossible that a woman Nathalie's age hadn't been kissed before. But even though his hands itched to palm her breasts, and even though he was pretty sure she would've welcomed the touch, on the remote chance that she wouldn't, he kept them down on her delectable ass as he deepened the kiss.

When he finally released her mouth, Nathalie's head dropped back on her shoulders, and Andrew had a feeling she would've crumpled to the floor if he wasn't holding her up.

"Wow, it was even better than I imagined," she said in a dreamy voice.

He chuckled. "Am I such a good kisser?"

She lifted her head and opened her eyes, her swollen lips curling up in a smile. "The best I ever had."

Now, that he didn't mind hearing. Not at all. Especially since she was telling the truth.

Still holding her close, he filled his chest with air and straightened. "Did you see that? I just got taller by an inch."

She giggled, but then shook her head and pressed her lips tight as if an unpleasant thought had just drifted through her mind.

"What's the matter, Nathalie? Talk to me."

"I wish I could," she whispered into his chest.

Andrew brought his hand to the back of her head and started caressing it gently. "I only want to know if there is something I'm doing wrong, or if there is something that you would like me to do. I'm not a mind reader, you need to tell me."

On a sigh, she closed her eyes and rested her cheek on his chest. "You're perfect, everything about you is. But I need a little more time."

Good, so it wasn't him. But what could it be? He wanted to know. The investigator in him felt a burning need to question her until she told him everything there was to know about her. But he couldn't demand it from her. After all, she wasn't a suspect, and he was still a stranger to her.

Not for long, though.

"I understand. You barely know me. Of course, you can't trust me. Yet."

"But I do. I know you. Don't ask me how, but I do, deep down in here." She pointed to her heart. "I just need more time. For me."

He cupped her cheeks in his hands and kissed her lips gently. "Whenever you're ready, sweetheart."

She nodded, but her smile looked sad, resigned.

Now he really needed to know. Perhaps he should go back to the office and dig deeper for more information about her.

Don't be a jerk, Andrew Spivak. She'll tell you when she's ready.

27

NATHALIE

*W*as she really going to tell Andrew all of her shameful secrets?

Like that she'd never even been kissed before?

Nathalie felt bitter anger bubble up from deep down in her tummy—toward her mother, her father, the cruel fate that had her loose so many years' worth of kisses like this.

Not that there was a chance in hell any other guy could've been as good of a kisser as Andrew.

But still, she could've been enjoying this for many, many years, this and much more. If not for the damn voices in her head; if not for her mother divorcing her father and then disappearing from their lives altogether; if not for the dementia that had been stealing the pillar of strength that used to be her father away from her—one piece at a time.

For years, she'd been keeping the resentment bottled up inside, convincing everyone, including herself, that she was fine, that she was strong—a survivor. When in fact, she was lonely and scared of spending the rest of her life alone. With no one but Tut to keep her company.

Where is he anyway?

For a moment, panic gripped her. Had he abandoned her as he'd threatened he would? As annoying as Tut was, Nathalie couldn't imagine life without him. She'd be completely alone.

Lifting her head, she looked into Andrew's concerned blue eyes. Small wrinkles fanned around them, evidence of not only his age but also his propensity to smile. He was definitely a keeper, and if she had any brains at all, she'd reel him in and do everything in her power to win his heart. A chance like this wouldn't present itself ever again.

Kind of like Scheherazade, she needed to tempt him with a thousand tales, one for every night, until he would fall in love with her, or at least get so accustomed to her company that he wouldn't be able to imagine life without her.

This was so unlike her, this plotting of entrapping a hapless guy, weaving a net like some spider woman. But just like the legendary Scheherazade, Nathalie was a survivor, and survivors seized opportunities—unlike victims who let good fortune slip through their fingers while they were busy wallowing in self-pity.

She stroked a finger over the old scar on Andrew's chin. "I'll make you a deal. Every evening, you'll tell me the story behind one of these, and I'll tell you one of mine."

His broad grin was something between wolfish and boyish, adorable and dangerous. It sent tingles straight to her core.

"So, I get to come back?"

"Sure you do. You think I'm going to let you get away so easy?"

"Who said I want to get away? On the contrary, you'll find it very difficult to get rid of me. I'm a stubborn guy, and once I set my eyes on something I like, I go for it, all out."

She tilted her head a little. "Did you just tell me that you like me?"

"I more than like you. I want you." He ran his finger over her lips. "These are addictive, I could spend hours kissing you," he husked. Reaching for her braid, he brought it forward and draped it over her breast. "I'm dying to see all this beautiful hair free of the braid, cascading over your shoulders and down your back. Preferably, while you're wearing nothing, but for now I will settle for the first part."

Oh, wow, Andrew was moving fast. They were on their first so-called date, and he was already talking about wanting to see her naked. Not that she didn't want him to, but not just yet.

Don't wait too long; you've already waited long enough. The new voice in her head startled her, and she jerked away from Andrew. *Who are you?* Luckily, she retained enough presence of mind to think it rather than say it out loud.

"I was just joking." Andrew misinterpreted her sudden move.

Shit, she'd better come up with something fast before this lovely romantic moment deteriorated into an embarrassing fiasco. "I know, it's not that. I just thought I heard my father. I'd better go check on him." Nathalie forced an apologetic smile. "I need to make sure he is not trying to sneak out while I'm otherwise occupied." She winked at him before beating feet out into the hallway.

To give herself more time, she went through the pretense of opening Papi's door and peeking into his room. It was dark inside, his light snoring confirming that he was sleeping.

Who are you? she asked again.

I'm sorry, just ignore me and go back. The strange new

voice sounded truly remorseful, which convinced her that it wasn't Tut playing tricks on her.

Oh, God, not again. She could deal with Tut, but not with the barrage of voices that would come flooding in if he were to leave the gate unguarded. Which was what he seemed to have done.

"Tell me who you are, please," she whispered into the darkness of the room.

For a moment, she thought he wouldn't answer her, and not because he was gone—she could still feel the foreign presence in her mind.

I'm not sure.

Great, a confused ghost, a newbie. "Do you remember who you were before?"

Before what?

Should she tell him he was dead? No, it wasn't her place. And besides, she might be wrong, and the voices belonged to something other than ghosts.

"Before now, before you popped into my head."

I can't. I thought I was dreaming, or rather sharing your dream. It began when I heard you, I mean your thoughts, debating whether to open the door for Andrew. I listened, thinking that I was dreaming someone else's dream. But this conversation between us is weird, it doesn't feel like a dream. Can you help me figure it out?

"Fine, but not now. I'm trying to appear sane, and you're blowing my cover. Wait until Andrew leaves."

I'm truly sorry for ruining your date. But I still think you should jump his bones. The man is fine, a little too old for you, but a prime stud nonetheless. Besides, you said so yourself; you've already wasted too much time.

Nathalie rolled her eyes. Was she just imagining it? Or was the new stowaway hitching a ride inside her head a gay ghost? Could ghosts be gay?

"Could you please leave?"

I'll try. Oh, here it is...I can see the exit... She heard the voice fading away.

Perhaps this was the end of it, and she wouldn't hear from him again. And yet, she had to admit that this one seemed nice, not bossy and sarcastic like Tut, or whiny like the other ones who'd invaded her thoughts before Tut had taken over.

"Is he okay?" Andrew asked when she entered the den.

"He's sleeping. I must've imagined it." Damn, she hated lying, and what was worse, Andrew didn't seem like he was buying it. In fact, he looked a little disappointed. Or perhaps she was just projecting what her guilty conscience expected to see rather than what was really there.

"I think I should go." He reached for his jacket and tie, draping both over his arm. "How about we watch the movie tomorrow?"

Andrew's tone wasn't as warm as it had been before. Evidently, his disapproval was real, not conjured by her conscience. Nathalie felt like crying. Had she blown it? Was he even coming back?

"Yes, definitely. That's a great idea. I would like that. Very much." She looked down, afraid to see reproach in Andrew's eyes, or a fake smile while he promised to come back without meaning it.

Her eyes followed his shoes as he got closer and hooked a finger under her chin. As he lifted her head, she was relieved to see that his expression had softened. "It's okay, Nathalie, there is no rush." Andrew dipped his head, his lips touching hers softly for a brief kiss. "Come, walk me down."

Downstairs, he paused at the door and put his hands on her waist. "How about a kiss goodnight?"

She nodded enthusiastically.

Andrew chuckled. "Come here." He drew her close to his body, kissing her long and hard until she was left breathless. "Sweet dreams, Nathalie." He kissed her forehead and reached for the bolt, unlocking it with the key she handed him, and opened the door.

A cold gust of wind rushed inside, and she folded her arms over her breasts, hugging herself against the chill. "Goodnight, Andrew."

He smiled. "Lock the door after me."

"I will."

Only once she was sure Andrew was a few feet away did she let out a sigh and sag against the door.

God, she was exhausted. Emotionally drained.

She'd almost blown it, and yet the hot goodnight kiss he'd given her was a good sign, wasn't it?

It didn't feel like a last kiss goodbye, more like a promise of many more to come.

28

ANDREW

*S*ometimes, Andrew's *gift* felt more like a curse to him. During the drive home, he replayed in his head the events that had led up to the lie.

Why had Nathalie done it?

He'd sensed that she'd been overwhelmed by the rush of desire that had swept through her. Nathalie had practically melted in his arms. And yet, she'd done nothing to hide her reaction or try to tame it. She'd even giggled at his joke. This could not have been what had had her bolting out of the room with that lame excuse. An excuse he would've bought if not for his special *gift.*

Andrew had a niggling suspicion that Nathalie hadn't been kissed much, mainly because of the way she'd been blown away by the experience. Almost like a teenager who'd been kissed for the first time. But that couldn't be. She was too old for that to be a possibility—even a remote one.

Unless she'd been in a coma for the past fifteen years, or Amish, there was no way he'd been the first guy to kiss this beautiful, sexy woman. The thought was so preposterous that it made him uncomfortable to even consider it. Maybe other men would've found a complete innocent thrilling, excited by the idea of being a girl's first in everything, but all he could think of was the terrible loss—the loneliness that hadn't been alleviated even by fleeting hookups.

For a grown woman, who appeared to have a healthy appetite for sex, it must've been plain cruel to be denied this most basic of pleasures.

Not a stranger to loneliness—hell, she was his most ardent mistress—Andrew had at least known pleasure, intimacy, camaraderie. True, none had been lasting, but there had been plenty, most of whom he'd enjoyed and remembered fondly.

Why would Nathalie deny herself? Or be denied?

Was it for religious reasons?

When he'd shaken Fernando's hand, Andrew had noticed the small golden cross hanging from a thin gold chain around the old man's neck, but the fact that the guy was religious was a far cry from proclaiming him a fanatic who'd cloistered his daughter. There had been no other religious paraphernalia around, unless it was all in Fernando's bedroom.

Nah, it didn't add up. Nathalie didn't behave like someone who wished to save herself for marriage, or who'd been brainwashed to stay away from men. She was passionate, and not shy about it either. After all, she'd been the one who had asked to be kissed. His plan had been to keep his hands to himself and try to enjoy a platonic evening with her.

So what was it?

The only other thing that came to mind was that she'd been sick. Perhaps a heart condition? Diabetes? Parkinson's?

He'd seen a movie once about a young woman afflicted with that disease. Parkinson's wasn't exclusively an old people's thing.

This, or something like it, would explain her reluctance to share with him what had troubled her. Not something one wished to disclose on a first date.

Except, this didn't make sense either—and thank God for that. Nathalie worked insane hours while taking care of her dad. There was no way a person suffering from a life-threatening or debilitating disease could've managed that.

Damn it, what could it be?

Hell, the answer was probably simpler. It wasn't that Nathalie had never been kissed, or that she was still a virgin, but that it had been a really long time since she'd been with a man. Except, even this more plausible scenario begged the question why.

The mystery had him both excited and anxious. Excited about the unraveling of secrets, anxious about what these secrets might be.

29

BHATHIAN

"*J*ackson, would you care to share with your friends the subject of this evening's class?"

Smirking, like he was letting them in on a grand joke, Jackson exchanged looks with his three sycophants, Gordon, Chase, and Vlad.

Damn, what had this kid's mother been thinking when she'd named him Vlad? That crazy maniac had done more damage to the clan than all their enemies combined, and the woman had named her kid after him?

"I'm waiting."

"Yes, sir. The reason I asked for another class was that your previous one was incomplete. You told us about all the things we were not supposed to do with girls, but you said nothing about what we could and should do. I thought we could all benefit from your vast experience on the subject."

Aha, so that was his game.

If the boy had thought to embarrass him, Jackson had another thing coming. By the time Bhathian was done with them, they would be blushing like a bunch of

168

virgins, which he suspected at least two out of the four still were.

Not Jackson, the little prick had been quite active for some time now, and perhaps Gordon. But for sure not Vlad and Chase.

Bhathian leaned his butt against the edge of the desk and crossed his arms over his chest. "An excellent idea. Actually, I'm going to call your mother and compliment her on raising such a fine young man. To seek knowledge is a commendable trait, and not to be shy about asking questions even more so." Bhathian wished there were cameras in the classroom so he'd have a souvenir of Jackson's bewildered expression.

Unfortunately, there were none.

"So, Jackson, what is it that you find most difficult?"

The boy took only a few seconds to reevaluate the situation and come up with a new plan of action. He smiled and leaned back in his chair. "Let's say I'm alone with a girl and I want to kiss her. What do I do next?"

"I thought I was very clear on this the other evening. You ask permission."

"How?"

"A simple 'can I kiss you' will do."

Jackson grimaced. "Do you have anything more subtle than this lame approach? You don't know anything about girls today. I'll get laughed at."

Bhathian stifled a chuckle. Watching the back and forth between him and the boy, Jackson's friends were turning their heads like a trio in a synchronized swimming performance.

Still, he sensed that there was at least some truth to Jackson's statement. Perhaps this generation played by different rules.

"Very well. You can ask permission without saying a

thing. You put your hands on the girl's waist and gently draw her to you. If she resists, even a little, you let go. But if she lets you, you go to the next step and bring your lips close to hers, without touching, and wait. Nine times out of ten she will close the distance and kiss you. Problem solved."

"What about the one out of ten?"

"Then you go to the third step. You close the distance, but very slowly, giving her every opportunity to turn her head away, or step back. If she does none of those things you can proceed."

Gordon groaned. "This will make me look like a spineless wuss; like I'm not man enough to make the first move."

Jackson nodded his agreement. "Girls like guys who are confident."

Gordon snorted. "They like assholes. The worse a guy treats them the more they want him. I don't get it, but this is the way it is."

Uncrossing his arms, Bhathian sighed. "Look, boys, I'm not an expert on female psychology, but I've been around long enough, pondering the same question, and I came up with a hypothesis. But bear in mind, this is only my opinion and not a fact, and it is not scientifically backed so I might be totally off. We all know that women are impossible to understand, and smarter men than me and you have been unable to solve the mystery."

That earned him a snort from Jackson and chuckles from the other three stooges.

"You've got that right. Let's hear it, then." Jackson straightened his back, the other boys leaning forward to listen to Bhathian's words of wisdom.

"I think it's subconscious, a survivor instinct from a time when a female who succeeded in securing a strong, dominant male as a mate had better chances of survival than others, and, of course, the benefit extended to her children as well. A nice guy wasn't a priority."

Vlad harrumphed. "And I thought Jackson's pretty face was responsible for his success with girls, when all along it was his jerky attitude."

"Hey, I'm not a jerk."

Vlad folded his arms over his bony chest. "A bully then."

Jackson shrugged. "I don't let anyone get away with shit. That doesn't make me a bully. I don't terrorize the weak and the meek. Only those who pick up a fight with me."

"So good looks have nothing to do with it?" Chase asked. "I always thought that good-looking guys got away with being jerks, and hot chicks got away with being bitches, just because they could."

The kid had a point.

"Yeah, I guess being attractive doesn't hurt, and those who get enough attention from the opposite sex without having to work for it sometimes develop an entitled attitude." He looked pointedly at Jackson. "Still, you don't have to be a jerk to project confidence, and confidence makes a man seem more attractive to women. Especially when he also has a job and makes a decent living." Bhathian winked. "No girl wants a penniless loser, not even for a hookup."

"I got it. Confidence and a job. Anything else?" Gordon glanced at Jackson, whom the boys appeared to look to as an authority on everything having to do with girls.

"You got to be kidding. Nothing is ever as simple as that with chicks. Though I have to agree with Bhathian about the job thing. It feels wrong to ask my mom for money to spend on a date. But that's just one small part. There is so much more to it."

Now, this should be interesting. A seventeen-year-old's perspective on this most difficult of subjects. The boys seemed to agree, all three staring at Jackson and waiting for him to reveal the secret to his success.

"Their expectations are insane. It's like no guy can be all of that. They want you to be tough but sensitive to their feelings; to be dominant and assertive but do what they want, how they want it, and where they want it. And the worst part is that they will never tell you anything. They expect you to guess. No wonder guys end up just ignoring their bullshit and behave like jerks."

If he weren't the teacher of this class, Bhathian would have clapped, applauding the boy's wisdom. He couldn't have put it better himself.

Women could be so frustrating.

Jackson's succinct assessment seemed to depress his friends.

Vlad threw his hands in the air. "So how do you do it? It seems impossible to please a woman."

Gordon and Chase nodded with twin dejected expressions.

Jackson shrugged. "You don't. You do the best you can and if they are not happy with it, tough."

"Are all of them like that? And why? What do they get out of making us feel like failures?" Vlad whined.

Bhathian chuckled and raised his palm to stop Jackson, who was about to respond. "First of all, you have to realize that they don't do it on purpose. This is important to remember when you get frustrated with a girl. Gender roles have changed, but not the underlying physiology. A woman's hormones, which are a remainder from a more primitive time, might compel her to seek the best protector and provider. At the same time, though, these qualities are not as desirable in modern society, and men are expected to be more accommodating and nurturing. She may crave a dominant man in bed, but not outside of it, which is confusing to us simple-minded creatures. But women don't have it easy either. They are expected to be soft and feminine but to succeed in a world that demands the exact opposite. An assertive, bossy guy is called a leader; a woman exhibiting the same qualities is called a bitch."

"Well, I'm no smarter now than I was before. I still have no clue how to behave." Vlad pushed his chair back and got up.

Bhathian motioned for him to sit back. "We are almost done. I just want to give you boys a parting piece of advice." He raised two fingers. "Communication and respect. Internalize it and repeat it like a mantra. As long as you communicate clearly and show respect, everything else will work itself out. And if not, let it go, it's not worth it. Never compromise on these two things. And, of course, it should go both ways. You should expect the same in return."

His concluding statement must've impressed the boys. Vlad was first. He got up and walked up to Bhathian to shake his hand. "This was good. I'm still clueless, but at least no longer blind." Bhathian clapped his back. "Good, I'm glad."

Chase was next, then Gordon. Jackson waited until they cleared the room before approaching Bhathian. For a moment, he just looked down at his white Converse shoes. "I want to apologize."

"Yeah?"

Lifting his head, Jackson offered his hand. Bhathian shook it.

"None of us came here expecting to learn anything, it was supposed to be a joke. You know, getting back at you for the other class when you made us feel this small."

Jackson brought his thumb and forefinger together to illustrate. "But I was wrong. You're cool."

Bhathian smiled as he clapped Jackson's back. He had to hand it to the boy, Jackson had balls to come clean like this. Most people were too scared to even say hello to him, let alone apologize.

"Tell me, Jackson. Where are you going to college next year?"

"I'm not. I'm going to take a gap year. My mom agreed to let me dedicate this time to pursue my music career, but only if I find a job and work at least part time. She doesn't want me to spend all day sleeping while staying up all night, performing non-paying gigs with my band."

"Do you have anything lined up?"

"Yeah, a couple of clubs. But we have to bring the audience. Not a problem, since half of our high school will come to see us play."

"I meant job wise."

"No, not yet. I have no experience, and that's the first question everyone asks."

"I think I have something that might be perfect for you."

"Oh, yeah? What is it?"

"What time do you get out of school tomorrow?"

"I have a final tomorrow morning, and that's it. I should be done by ten."

"Wait for me outside. I'm going to pick you up."

"Where are we going?"

"It's a surprise."

NATHALIE

*N*athalie had been waiting for Andrew to show up all morning, but neither he nor Bhathian had stopped by. She had a sinking feeling that yesterday evening had been the last she'd seen of Andrew.

He hadn't called either. So yeah, she'd forgotten to give him her number, but she was in the directory, or at least the coffee shop was.

Good job, Nathalie, congratulations on chasing another guy away, and you can't even blame me for it.

Tut hadn't been the culprit this time, but his absence had allowed that other voice to intrude, startling her worse than Tut could've ever done. So, at least partially, it had been his fault.

Where were you?

The morning rush was over, and the few customers remaining were sitting all the way in the back. Nevertheless, she was reluctant to risk addressing Tut out loud even though she found conducting internal conversations with him too intimate.

His presence alone was intrusive enough.

I've been checking out more interesting hosts.

Nathalie rolled her eyes. He'd been saying it for years, and yet he was still in her head.

I had a visitor while you were away. He was nice, not sarcastic like you. Perhaps I should invite him to stay. It was an empty threat since the new voice hadn't returned. And anyway, she couldn't imagine life without Tut. For better or for worse, he'd been a constant presence since she was a little girl. Annoying, but also reassuring.

Perhaps you should.

Damn, Tut sounded serious. Had she offended him?

"I was just joking," she whispered.

I know, but I can't stay forever, Nathalie. I've already stayed too long. I'm struggling to hold on because you need me to guard the gateway to your mind, but I won't be able to do it for much longer. Each day I'm being pulled away more and more. You must've noticed it.

She had. But she'd assumed that Tut was just wandering around, or perhaps that she was getting better, and one day the voices would stop altogether. But it seemed that Tut had been misleading her.

"Why didn't you tell me this before?"

You would have panicked.

"So why now?"

Because I no longer have a choice. The fact that someone else got through my defenses proves that I'm getting weaker.

Shit, this was serious. And he'd been right about her panicking.

"What am I going to do without you? Is it going to be the way it used to be? With dozens of different voices driving me crazy?"

Forgetting herself, she had switched from whispering to talking, and now some of the customers were looking at her. She smiled nervously and pretended to adjust the nonexistent Bluetooth in her ear, then turned around and fled to the kitchen.

You're older now. You should be able to control them better. Start with that new visitor you mentioned, practice blocking him.

"Yeah, right, as if I wouldn't have done it already with you if I could."

When you really didn't want me to know something, you did.

He was right. She'd managed to hide Andrew from him. "I think I learned how to keep some thoughts private, but that's just a small part of the problem. I don't know how to block the voices from talking to me, and that's the worst part."

Start practicing. I'll stay for as long as I can, but it seems that I can no longer keep the gate tightly closed, and some will manage to get through to you. Practice on those, and hopefully, by the time I'm gone for good, you'll learn how to control them.

God, this was just what she needed now. Even on the remote chance that Andrew still wanted to see her, she wouldn't be able to see him. Managing the voices while trying to appear normal wasn't going to work.

Perhaps a clean break was exactly what she needed—before she got used to having Andrew in her life.

Not fair. Really, really, not fair.

The bells on the door chimed, announcing a new customer. With a sigh, Nathalie wiped a stray tear away and left the shelter of her kitchen.

Her heart skipped a beat when she saw it was Bhathian. Tilting her head sideways, she tried to peek behind him, hoping to find Andrew. But the only one standing next to Bhathian was a handsome teenager with a killer smile. He kind of reminded her of Luke, the guy she used to have a crush on in high school. They even had similarly conceited expressions. Not that she could really blame Luke or this boy for their cockiness. It was probably impossible for a guy to remain humble when every woman, regardless of age, was checking him out.

"Hi, Nathalie, I want you to meet Jackson. Jackson, this is my d— dear friend Nathalie, the owner of this coffee shop and your future employer."

Jackson seemed just as surprised as she was by Bhathian's introduction, but he recovered first. Flashing her a gorgeous smile, he reached over the counter and offered her his hand.

"Hi, boss," he said.

The boy's smile was infectious, and she found herself smiling back as she took his hand. "It's nice to meet you, Jackson, but I haven't hired you yet."

"How about we all sit together and nail down a deal," Bhathian offered, pointing to the first booth on the right.

"Sure, go ahead, I'll be right with you."

Nathalie glanced at the customers sitting in the back. They seemed fine, but just so she wouldn't get interrupted later, she grabbed a coffee carafe in one hand and a water jug in the other and refilled everyone's drinks before joining Bhathian and Jackson at the booth.

"So, Jackson, have you waited tables before?" she asked as she sat across from the guys.

His confident smile turned into a slight grimace, and Jackson cupped the back of his head. "No, I have no work experience. But I'm a quick learner, and I'm good with people. And I'm willing to start cheap," he tacked on at the end.

Nathalie smiled. "You just said the magic words. You're hired. How many hours a day can you work? I assume that you're still in school?"

"I have only two finals left, and then I'm free. So the

only times I can't work are next Monday and Wednesday mornings."

"How about your band? Don't you need time to practice?" Bhathian asked.

Jackson shrugged. "The guys will work around my schedule, and if we get a gig, we'll worry about it then."

So the boy had dreams of becoming a rock star. Cute, but unrealistic. Then again, at his age, dreaming impossible dreams was still allowed.

"All I can pay is minimum wage. But you get to keep all of your tips, which given your charming smile, I have no doubt there will be plenty of."

The conceited expression returned full force to his handsome face, and he extended his arm for a handshake. "When do I start?"

"How about right now?"

"Sweet."

Bhathian chuckled. "You forgot something, my boy. Your car is still at school, and I'm not going to wait for you to finish work to drive you back."

"Damn, can you drive me now? I'll get it and come back. If it's okay with you, boss?"

"No problem, and you can call me Nathalie."

Jackson got up and waited for Bhathian to slide out of the booth, which considering his size wasn't an easy feat.

"I'll be back before you know it." Jackson shook her hand again.

Nathalie was amused by the boy's enthusiasm at the prospect of working for minimum wage plus tips. He was probably overestimating his potential earnings. This was a coffee shop, not an expensive steak house, and the tips weren't that big.

As she saw them to the door, Nathalie desperately

wanted to ask Bhathian about Andrew, but at the end, she chickened out.

There was just no way she could ask if Andrew had said anything to him about her. Which she imagined was something along the lines of describing how crazy he thought she was. And anyway, it wasn't as if Bhathian would have told her anything.

BHATHIAN

"Congratulations." Bhathian clapped Jackson's back as they exited the shop.

"Thanks, man, I owe you."

Bhathian clicked open the doors and got behind the wheel. "No problem. I got two birds with one stone. You needed a job, Nathalie needed help. Everyone got what they wanted."

Jackson scratched his ear. "I'm not sure I know what I'm supposed to do. Is it just waiting tables?"

"I suppose. Just do whatever Nathalie tells you to do. Perhaps she'll need you to work the register, take orders, clean the kitchen. I have no idea. But you're a smart guy, you'll figure it out."

"Yeah, how hard can it be, right?"

How hard indeed. Bhathian hoped this arrangement would work out, and Jackson would not disappoint. Problem was, the boy was a teenage immortal, and working with humans might tempt him to use his powers.

"Listen, Jackson. You need to be careful and remember never to use your powers. I'm sure there will be situations when you'll be tempted to. Like thralling a customer to give you a big tip, or worse..." He gave the boy a stern look. "You know what I'm talking about—girls. You're a good looking guy, and if your looks and charm get you laid, I have no problem with that. But if I even suspect that you thralled someone..."

Jackson raised his hands in the air, putting on an innocent face. "Never, I swear. I've never thralled a girl for that. I don't need to."

Was this a slip of a tongue? "Then what other things have you thralled them for? I mean, other than after the sex to erase the memory of your fangs and the biting."

"Nothing, I swear."

"Jackson!"

The boy sighed in resignation. "Okay, just once, and it wasn't a girl. I was failing math and thralled my math teacher to give me a passing grade." He seemed worried as he glanced at Bhathian's grim face. "I was desperate, my mom said she wouldn't allow me to practice with my band unless I passed math. I had no choice. Please, don't tell on me."

"Was it the only time?"

"Yes, I swear on my best guitar."

Bhathian chuckled. "Okay, I'll let it slide. But if I hear you've done anything of the sort while working for Nathalie, I'll personally whip you for it."

Jackson shrugged. "Trust me, I know, you have nothing to worry about."

ANDREW

*D*amn, it was after seven in the evening, and he was still at the office instead of leaving early like he'd planned. Upstairs had requested, or rather demanded, to see a progress report on his airport personnel investigation, and the fuckers wanted it by tomorrow morning.

Cutting corners left and right, he'd managed to finish it in record time, but the end product was a semi-passable thing that he would've never accepted from a subordinate. It would no doubt raise some brows—especially the ones belonging to his boss. After all, Andrew's subpar work was going to reflect poorly on him.

But to hell with it. After years of exemplary work, he was allowed one shitty report. True?

Fuck, he should call Nathalie and let her know he was running late. Not that he was afraid she would go somewhere, stuck as she was at home with her father, but she might not open the door if he arrived after eight. The coffee shop would be closed already, and she'd be upstairs.

Pulling up the file he'd compiled about her, Andrew

chose to use the shop's number instead of the residence. Less incriminating, he could always claim to have gotten it from the directory.

"Fernando's Bakery and Café, how may I help you?" Nathalie answered after one ring. She sounded breathless.

"Busy day, eh?"

"Andrew." He could tell so much from just the way she'd said his name— surprise, relief, longing.

God, he was such an insensitive dumbass. Clearly, she'd thought he wasn't coming back. He should've called her ten times by now just to let her know how much he liked her.

"I'm on my way, just wanted to tell you that I'm running a little late. I hope that it's still okay with you."

"Of course, I'm not going anywhere. Take your time and drive safely."

"I will."

Poor girl, she'd sounded so relieved. Andrew felt guilty, and yet, he couldn't help also feeling a little smug.

Nathalie wanted him.

Without further hesitation, he emailed the report. Worst case scenario, his boss would chew his ass, and he would come up with an excuse, promising to do better next time. It seemed that his days as an exemplary government employee were over. He was becoming a slacker.

Andrew shrugged. He had more important things on his mind than winning the employee-of-the-month badge. Not that his department issued them.

As he drove to Nathalie's place, he wondered whether he should stop somewhere and buy flowers. It felt awkward showing up empty-handed, especially since it was only their second date and he was going to her place. But that would introduce another delay he wanted to avoid. Still, once he got off the freeway, Andrew kept his eye out for a flower shop. If there was one on the way, he would stop by.

There was one, right on Nathalie's street, and he stopped and ran out.

"Give me a nice bouquet for fifty, something for a date," he told the girl behind the counter. Andrew wasn't an expert on flowers, but he hoped that the amount would get him a decent arrangement.

"Do you know what kind of flowers she prefers?"

Andrew shook his head.

"Okay, how about color. What's her favorite?"

"I don't know. Please, I'm in a hurry. Just pick something you would've liked to receive from a guy."

The girl shrugged and headed out to the refrigerated section of the shop. A moment later she came back with a big bouquet. Too big.

"This one is nice, but it's seventy-five."

Whatever, he didn't have time to send her back for another one.

"Fine, I'll take it."

"Do you want a card to go with it?"

"No." He handed her his credit card.

Andrew didn't know what was worse, showing up empty-handed, or with a thing that was as big as some of the centerpieces he'd seen in hotel lobbies.

Damn, he hoped she would like it. The good news was that he would be arriving after eight, which meant that there would be no one in the shop to see him walk in with the flowers.

Wrong.

True, the sign on her door said closed, and there were no customers in the café, but the door was open, and as he came in he was greeted by a young guy who was wearing an apron with the café's logo on it.

"Hi, I'm Jackson, the hired help." He offered his hand for a handshake. "And you must be Andrew."

They clasped hands, and Andrew glanced around looking for Nathalie. But the only one there, other than the new guy was her father, who was sitting in his booth, busy with a coloring book. Strange.

"Nathalie is upstairs taking a shower, and she told me to entertain you in the meantime. Can I offer you coffee? A Danish, perhaps? You've got to try the Danish, man, it's out of this world." Jackson rolled his eyes.

The kid was a good salesman, that was for sure.

"Why not. Do you know how to make a cappuccino?"

Jackson snorted. "Single? Double? Whole milk? Skim?"

"Double, skim."

"Shaken not stirred?"

Andrew chuckled. "You got it."

He walked over to Fernando, who was bent over his coloring book and concentrating hard on staying inside the lines of an intricate geometric shape.

"Good afternoon, sir, how are you doing today?"

Fernando paused with his red pencil pressed firmly into the page and looked up. There was no recognition in his eyes, but he tried to bluff his way through it. "Very well, thank you for asking. And you?"

"I'm good, thank you. Well, I'll let you go back to your"— given the guy's age, it seemed wrong to say coloring—"hobby"— much better. "It was good to see you."

"Same here," the old man smiled and waved him off, then bent back down to continue his work.

"It's good for his condition," Jackson whispered as Andrew slid into the booth he'd chosen, one that was next to a window, naturally. The boy placed a plate with a steaming Danish in front of him.

"Thanks for warming it up."

"That's the only way to eat it. I'll be back with your cappuccino."

Andrew took a bite, and his eyes rolled as well. It truly was out of this world. Nathalie had a gift.

He was halfway done with the pastry when Jackson came back with the cappuccino and slid into the booth across from Andrew with a cold can of coke in hand.

"So, Andrew, Nathalie tells me that you're Bhathian's friend." Jackson raised a brow as if to ask how Andrew knew the guy.

Had Bhathian been there today, visiting Nathalie on his own? Good for him.

"We work together."

Jackson shifted in his seat, popped the coke can open, took a sip, and cupped it between his hands. The kid was trying to say or ask something and wasn't sure how to go about it. "Bhathian is a great guy. He got me this job. I had to take a class that he teaches. That's how I met him."

Andrew smiled. Jackson was telling him who he was in a way that only someone who knew Bhathian would get. Smart.

Andrew offered Jackson his hand. "I'm Syssi's brother. Your regent's wife."

The kid's eyes popped wide open. "Damn, I should've recognized you from the wedding. You look different without a tux."

Andrew narrowed his eyes. "I didn't notice you there either."

Jackson smirked and looked both ways as if checking to see that no one was listening in, then leaned toward Andrew. "Me and my buddies swiped a bunch of bottles from the bar and snuck out. We got wasted in the gym."

"Aha, no wonder then." Andrew smirked. He'd pulled similar stunts at Jackson's age. Not being a hypocrite he had no intention of scolding the kid. "Tell me, Jackson, what did you guys tell Nathalie? She doesn't know about us."

"The truth. I was a student at a class Bhathian taught, and I told him I needed a job. That's it. She didn't ask any more questions, so I didn't have to invent any lies."

"What if she asks what kind of class it was? She thinks Bhathian and I are part of some secret arm of law enforcement."

Jackson snorted. "Well, you are, kinda. And I'll tell her the truth about the class as well. Bhathian teaching a class to juvenile delinquents fits well with what she thinks of you guys."

"True."

33

NATHALIE

*A*s she descended the stairs, Nathalie's heart was beating twice as fast as normal. She was even more nervous now than she'd been the day before.

Until Andrew had finally called, she'd thought of nothing else. She kept going over every detail of their date and analyzing every word said and every touch, to either reinforce or discard her suspicion that he wasn't coming back.

Vacillating between hope and despair, by the end of the day she'd been a nervous wreck.

Problem was, even though she'd been relieved to the point of feeling faint to hear that he was still coming to see her, her high level of anxiety hadn't gone all the way down yet.

Pausing by the doorway, she took a deep breath before leaving the kitchen's shelter and stepping into her shop.

With a quick glance, she found Andrew sitting with Jackson in one booth, and her father in the one across the aisle from them. He was still busy with the adult coloring book Jackson had bought for him.

The boy had turned out to be a godsend. The customers loved him, and he'd learned to operate the cappuccino machine in one go—which was something that had taken her previous helpers weeks to do. But all of this was not as astounding as Jackson's positive attitude toward her father. The boy had even called his mother, who happened to be an occupational therapist, to ask what would be a good activity for Fernando.

She'd suggested the adult coloring books.

Immediately, he'd volunteered to drive to the nearest bookstore that carried them. Nathalie had given him two twenties, and in less than half an hour, he'd got back with three books and a box of coloring pencils. Right there and then she'd decided to give him a raise. He was definitely worth more than minimum wage. Regrettably, she couldn't afford much more than that.

Still, she was sure it would at least make Jackson feel appreciated. And besides, the way he was charming the customers, the boy was going to earn double if not more than what she was paying him in tips.

It had been impossible not to notice the look-overs Jackson had been getting all day—mostly from women, but also from some of the men. At times, Nathalie had found it disturbing to see women old enough to be his mother or even grandmother ogle the seventeen-year-old boy.

And yet, she suspected that Jackson not only wasn't bothered by the looks but was actively encouraging them —probably to get even bigger tips.

The boy was a godsend but certainly not an angel. In a few years, he was going to leave a trail of broken hearts. Come to think of it, he probably already had.

Not that she would know anything about it. The one advantage of never having had a boyfriend was that she'd never been dumped. That being said, though, she might soon find out all about it. Because if things didn't work out with Andrew...

Damn, why did it hurt so bad to even think about it?

Well, as the saying went; nothing ventured, nothing gained. She had to take a risk. Even if it terrified her.

Nathalie took another moment to gaze at Andrew's handsome face while Jackson kept him distracted.

There was something extra sexy about a man wearing a tie and blazer, a certain air of sophistication, of authority. Or perhaps it was Andrew's personality more than his professional attire that was projecting this quiet air of command. That he was a capable, dependable man was evident just from his facial expression and the way he carried himself.

Charisma, confidence, he had all of those in spades.

And for some reason, he was interested in her, a woman who was still a virgin at thirty.

With a sigh, Nathalie shook her head. It didn't make any sense. They were not a good fit. She was probably setting herself up for a heartache.

At the same moment, Andrew sensed her presence and turned his head to look at her. His eyes popped wide in a most gratifying way, and he got up, ignoring Jackson, who was still talking to him.

Her legs refusing to move an inch, Nathalie remained glued to her spot right outside the kitchen, mute, unable to even say hello as she waited for Andrew to reach her, which he did in a few long strides.

His arm reaching around her waist, he pulled her to him, his eyes full of heat as he looked down at her.

"Did anyone ever tell you how spectacular you are?" His other hand plowed into her hair, and he combed his fingers through it. "I've told you I've been dying to see you like this, imagining how you would look with your hair cascading down your back, your front—" His fingers brushed against the side of her breast, sending a bolt of desire that made her shiver.

"But the reality is even more beautiful than the fantasy. You look like a princess."

He dipped his head, and she was powerless to deny him the kiss he took right in front of her father and Jackson.

The same thought must've crossed his mind, and he pushed her back through the doorway and into the kitchen, still kissing her like he couldn't get enough.

God, the man was setting her on fire.

Nathalie didn't care that her father was in the next room, or that Jackson was probably eavesdropping and could hear each and every one of her throaty moans. All she cared about were Andrew's hands on her, and where she needed them to be. Hell, he could've stripped her naked, right there and then, and had his way with her on the kitchen floor, and she wouldn't have protested in the slightest.

Andrew had awakened in her something that had lain dormant throughout her adult life, and she felt her body come to life with sexual hunger.

The dam that she'd erected to stifle all of her yearnings and desires—never allowing herself to acknowledge they even existed because she'd had no outlet for them save for the touch of her own hand—had been breached. With last night's earth-shattering kiss creating the first fissures, weakening the structure so today it could burst asunder.

"Andrew," she breathed when he let go of her mouth, trailing his soft lips down her neck.

"Oh, God..." She couldn't help the words escaping her

throat when he nipped her lightly where her neck met her shoulder. For some reason, she imagined him biting her there, piercing the skin, and was shocked to realize that she craved it.

What was wrong with her?

Was it the result of all those vampire romances she'd been devouring lately?

Must be, because no normal woman craved something so wicked.

"My Nathalie," he whispered before kissing her again.

Her name on his lips sounded so good, so right, and she didn't mind the 'my' either. She was all his, if only for these few stolen moments.

"I want to take you upstairs and make love to you," he mumbled against her lips, "for hours, and hours, until we both can't stand straight."

Shit, that was a splash of cold water on her raging libido. She probably wouldn't be able to stand straight after the first time, let alone hours.

She still had to either fess up to the embarrassing truth of her virginity or just let him discover it himself.

Or perhaps, she could bluff her way through it and say that it had just been a long time for her. After all, she was pretty sure that her hymen had been breached a long time ago by her first tampon.

What a nightmare that had been.

The tampon had gone in easily enough but refused to come out. She still remembered sitting on the toilet and trying to pull the damn thing out. It had taken her forever and hurt worse than pulling out a tooth. For years, she'd stayed away from tampons, using pads instead, until she'd figured out that they weren't all made the same. Some expanded in width, some in length, and the one she'd been unlucky or stupid enough to choose as her first had been probably one of those that expanded in width.

So yeah, chances were that she wasn't technically a virgin anymore, but she couldn't say so for sure.

Regardless of the state of her hymen, though, this was no way to start a relationship. What chance would they have of building trust if it started with a lie?

No, she would have to tell Andrew. She'd die of embarrassment, but at least she would go to heaven with a clear conscience.

Andrew must've noticed her body stiffen in his arms. "What's the matter? Did I go too far? I said I wanted to make love to you, but it doesn't mean that we have to tonight. There is no rush."

Great, now he thought that she was some kind of a prude or a scaredy-cat.

"No, it's not that I don't want to, I do. But we can't." She tilted her head toward the doorway.

Andrew sighed, his arms around her slackening their hold. "Yeah, you're right."

Damn, he sounded almost hopeless.

Nathalie's mind frantically searched for something to say, a plan, something that would give him enough of an incentive to keep coming back to her. She couldn't afford to lose him.

He smiled and touched his finger to her nose. "What are you thinking so hard about?"

"Trying to find a way for us to be together," she admitted.

"Easy, I take you to my place."

"I can't leave him alone."

"We'll bring a babysitter."

"He doesn't trust strangers. He will throw a tantrum."

"Okay, so we have half of a solution. That's already a step in the right direction. Now we only need to find him someone he likes."

Yeah, as if this was an easy feat. And there was still the issue of her confession.

34

ANDREW

"*Hi*, sweetheart, how is your day going?" This was the fourth time Andrew had called Nathalie today.

He just loved hearing her velvety, sexy voice. One of these days, he planned on asking her to sing something for him. Andrew had a feeling that she would be magnificent.

They were acting like a couple of lovesick teenagers.

Except, these three words were yet to be voiced by either of them.

"I miss you. When are you coming over?"

He chuckled. "Same time as every day." Since he'd met her, he'd been going to Nathalie's place every evening straight from the office. Her day started at four in the morning, so by nine she was falling asleep in his arms. The best he could hope for was to have a couple of hours with her.

The only exception had been the one evening he'd stopped by Tiffany's apartment.

Tiff's roommates had been very helpful, complaining about how she'd ditched them without notice and how they were now short on rent money. Apparently, her brother had shown up to collect her things, saying that she was going back home with him. Andrew's impression of the girl that had actually interacted with the guy was that she hadn't been suspicious. She'd said that he looked legit, knew things about Tiffany, and even had a southern accent.

She hadn't been lying.

In other words, it was a dead end. Andrew still wasn't convinced that things were as simple as they appeared, but at least it had eased Nathalie's mind.

"As soon as I can escape without getting in trouble, I'm heading to your place. I'm just going to stop by the supermarket and pick up a movie. Anything else you need from there?"

"Nope, nothing. I just want you to get here as soon as you can. I hope you're hungry. I made you something yummy for dinner."

"Starving."

"Excellent, see you at around seven?"

"You bet, goodbye, Nathalie."

Andrew had lied about being hungry. After the lunch he'd had with his boss, it would be hours before he could eat anything. But it made Nathalie happy watching him eat the special treats she was preparing for him.

Every evening, she'd have some new and exciting dish, and every time he'd put on a show for her, exaggerating wildly how much he was enjoying it and making her laugh.

He loved it, feeling a stupid sense of pride every time his shenanigans managed to get her to tear up with laughter.

Andrew sighed. Spending time with Nathalie was a pleasure, but he was suffering the worst case of blue balls since he'd reached puberty. Yesterday had been the fifth night in a row that he and Nathalie had been meeting at her place but doing nothing more than kissing. He could've taken it further, hell, Nathalie had been all but begging him to touch her, but Andrew knew that once he crossed that invisible line, he would not be able to stop.

The kissing was bad enough.

More than once, he'd been tempted to just take her on that lumpy couch in her den. But not only did he hate stealth guerrilla sex, there was something about Nathalie's fumbling inexperience that was flashing all kinds of warning signs for him to go slow and treat her with care.

So yeah, he was reliving his teenage years—of stolen kisses on the parents' sofa and achy blue balls, but also of sweet excitement and anticipation of what was still to come.

There was something to be said for delayed gratification.

Andrew wondered if the same held true for delayed orgasms. In his mind, it was a form of torture reserved for masochists, but perhaps he should give it a try, maybe it enhanced the experience the same way that delaying the whole thing did.

Although in his and Nathalie's case, it wasn't a choice or a sexual game, it was out of necessity and lack of options.

They'd contacted several agencies, but so far Fernando hadn't liked either of the two caregivers that they had invited for interviews. In fact, he'd refused to even talk to them. Maybe the old man was afraid of being fobbed off on the caregiver and losing Nathalie's constant company. To be honest, though, Andrew hadn't liked either of them.

If they were unable to locate someone both Nathalie and her father approved of, she would not be able to go out and have fun without worrying about him.

In a way, it was similar to finding a good babysitter for a kid but much worse. There were plenty of good and capable people willing to babysit a child or a baby and actually enjoy doing so. But judging by the two examples he'd seen, the same couldn't be said about caregivers for the elderly and infirm.

Since the stern reprimand he'd gotten from his boss after submitting that lousy report, Andrew didn't dare leave the office before six-fifteen. And after stopping by the supermarket and getting a movie and a bottle of wine, he'd arrived at Nathalie's a little after seven. Which meant that the shop was still open.

"Hello, my man, Andrew." Jackson was the one manning the register as he came in, and they clasped hands over the counter. The place was still full of customers even though it was nearing closing time and, curiously, Nathalie was nowhere in sight. Fernando was sitting in his usual booth at the back, still busy with the coloring books. Soon, they would need to send Jackson out to buy more.

"Where is she?"

"Taking a bath."

Andrew arched a brow. A shop full of people and she'd left Jackson alone to deal with everything? This wasn't like her.

"That's a first. How come?"

Jackson shrugged. "She finally realized that I can handle everything just fine and that she can take a breather. I told her to go relax with a bubble bath before your date." He winked suggestively.

Andrew pointed a finger at him. "Watch yourself, kid. I will not tolerate any disrespect from you. Am I clear?"

Jackson saluted. "Crystal."

Andrew relaxed his shoulders and smiled to put the boy

at ease. Though by the smug look on his too-pretty face, Jackson hadn't been impressed by his posturing.

There were four new stools next to the counter and Andrew sat on one. "When did these get here?"

"Today. Bhathian got them from that yogurt place that is closing down. You know, the one over at 3rd Street?"

Andrew had no idea what yogurt place the kid was talking about, and he still didn't understand why Nathalie needed the stools in the first place. They were cramping the already tight space next to the register. "Oh, yeah? What for?"

Jackson's grin spread wide, the smugness practically dripping from him. "You're not here during the days, so you don't know. But since I started working here, the place is filled to capacity every morning and at lunch time. Nathalie needed more seats. We even had to move Fernando to the kitchen during the busy hours so we could use his booth. Let me tell you, the dude wasn't happy about it." Jackson shook his head and made a face.

Andrew could just imagine. Since he'd been spending time with Nathalie, he'd gotten acquainted with Fernando and his habits. The old guy clung to a precise schedule and everything had to be the same. The smallest of changes threw him off, and what was worse, once he got agitated over something, he stayed like that.

"How did you get him to move without him throwing a tantrum?"

Jackson winked. "I have my ways. The dude likes me. Calls me son. Probably because I'm here every day, all day long. He thinks of me as part of the family."

"That's good to hear. Makes things easier on Nathalie."

"About that." Jackson's face got serious, and he leaned over the counter to get closer to Andrew. "You need to get her out of here. I don't know how she does it, but I know it would drive me crazy to be chained to this place like she is. I can stay and watch over Freddy, no problem. And I'll even do it for free—for her. Nathalie deserves a break."

Andrew felt like kissing the kid.

Problem was, convincing Nathalie that it was safe to leave Fernando with Jackson wasn't going to be easy.

"Thank you. I really appreciate the offer, but I don't know if she'd go for it."

Jackson shrugged. "That's your job, dude. You have to convince her."

By the time Nathalie was done with her bath and came downstairs, Jackson had escorted the last customer out and locked the door.

A quick peck on the cheek was all the greeting Andrew got, and then she walked over to Jackson and kissed him too.

It was good that Andrew wasn't the jealous type—and that Jackson was still a kid—otherwise he wouldn't have liked it. Not one bit.

"Thank you, for closing up and everything. I had a wonderful time relaxing in a bubble bath."

The kid had the audacity to kiss her back. "You're welcome, and don't worry about the cleanup. I'm going to take care of it."

"I can't ask you to do this after leaving you alone in here for so long to do everything by yourself. Go home, you've done enough."

"You're not asking. I'm volunteering." Before she had the chance to argue about it, he grabbed the rag from the counter and proceeded to the table the last customer had eaten at—the only one that still needed cleaning. All the other tables had been already cleared and wiped clean. It took him about thirty seconds to be done with it, and on the way to the kitchen with the dirty dishes, he winked at Andrew as he passed him by.

Nathalie glanced around and smiled fondly at Jackson's retreating back. "Look at him, this kid is unbelievable—on his feet since eight in the morning and still going at it full speed. I guess it's his youth. His boundless energy makes me feel old."

"That's because you haven't done anything fun for ages. I'm taking you out on a proper date. Go upstairs and put on something nice."

Nathalie looked at Andrew with incredulous eyes. "And how do you suggest I do it?"

He was about to tease her and say something like *'you lift one foot and then the other and climb'* but decided to get to the point instead. They had no time to waste. Nathalie had been up since four in the morning, and she had no more than a couple of hours left in her. After that, she wouldn't be able to keep her eyes open. He needed to get his Cinderella back to bed at nine-thirty at the latest.

"Jackson is going to stay with your father."

"Jackson. You're not serious. He's just a kid."

"Yeah, but you have to admit that he is very capable, and he gets along with your father. He says Fernando likes him, calls him son."

Nathalie's expressive face showed her inner struggle, and she hadn't dismissed the idea immediately. There was hope. But then she shook her head.

"Jackson is wonderful. He works so hard. Aside from the baking he's practically taken over my job. I can sit and read a book if I want to. He handles everything like a pro. But I just can't ask him to do it. It's not fair to him. He works eleven hours a day, and even though I tell him to get here at ten, he is here already at eight to help me with the morning crowd. It's too much for him."

"It was his idea."

"Really? What did he say?"

"I told your boyfriend that he needs to get you out of here," Jackson called from the kitchen. "Oh, and thank you for the compliments."

Nathalie closed her eyes, a blush creeping up her cheeks. "The guy has the ears of a rabbit. I don't know how he does it, but he hears everything."

Andrew knew exactly how, but it wasn't something he could share with Nathalie.

"So, how about it?"

"I don't know. And what about the lasagna I made for you?"

Andrew rolled his eyes. "I'll eat it tomorrow. Stop looking for excuses."

There was another moment of hesitation, but then she smiled. "Let's do it. We can go somewhere that isn't too far away, and if Jackson needs us we can be right back."

"That's my girl. Now go. Just don't take too long, the clock is ticking."

35

NATHALIE

*U*pstairs in her bedroom, Nathalie felt giddy like a little girl.

She was finally going on an actual date.

But as she opened her closet and stared at her practical, everyday collection of denim and black, she realized she didn't have anything nice to wear.

Shit. She'd have to improvise.

Black stretchy jeans were good for every occasion, and she pulled them on first. A fitted black T-shirt was next, but as she put it on and examined her reflection in the mirror, she didn't like how the close fitting outfit accentuated the disparity between the size of her hips and the size of her bust.

Damn, how she wished she had an hourglass figure instead of a pear shape. There was something she could do about it, though. She pulled the T-shirt off and unhooked her bra. Looking at her breasts, she had to admit that even though they were smallish, they were nicely shaped and perky. They just needed a little boost, which could be achieved with the monster bra, as she called it, from

Victoria's Secret. The thing promised to add two cup sizes, which would bring her modest B cup to a voluptuous D.

With a smirk, she put it on and reexamined her reflection. Was it too much? Now that she'd evened out her proportions, she looked sultry. Big hips, big breasts, and a tiny waist.

Perhaps the T-shirt would tame the effect.

It didn't. It kind of made it worse.

Stop fretting, you look gorgeous. You'll have all the guys drooling.

Damn, damn, damn. The new voice in her head chose a perfect timing to return. And what's worse, it was a guy, and he'd seen her naked.

"Get out," she hissed at him, trying to focus and block him like Tut had told her to.

I will. Please, don't be mad, I'm just trying to help.

He sounded so pitiful that she didn't have the heart to be mean to him. "What's your name?"

I'm still fuzzy about the details, but you can call me Sage.

"Because you're wise?"

That too, but also because I'm not sure if I'm a boy or a girl.

"You're a boy."

How do you know?

"You have a man's voice."

Can it be that you're interpreting it as masculine? I'm just a thought, I can have any voice.

He might have a point. No, it was a he, she was sure of it. "Why do you think you can be a girl?"

His masculine chuckle removed the last of her doubts. *Because I'm more excited about seeing your boyfriend shirtless than you.*

She couldn't help the giggle that escaped her throat. "Is that why you're pushing me to have sex with Andrew?

Because if you think I'll let you join the ride you have another thing coming. It's just gross."

Meanie. He sounded pouty. *But I meant what I said about the bra, keep it. Add a pair of heels if you have them, and you'll look like a knockout.*

This was exactly what she was planning to do next.

Reaching up to the top shelf of her closet, Nathalie pulled down the only pair of high-heeled pumps she owned. They were brand new and still in the box they'd arrived in.

Wow, Nathalie, you look fab. Sage ended his endorsement with a whistle.

The effect was indeed impressive. She had never looked that sexy in her life. But it was also a little scary. Would she feel awkward?

Stop it. Go on, put on a little makeup, some jewelry, and out you go. Don't let Andrew wait too long.

He was right. With a sigh, she headed to the bathroom to get her mascara and lip gloss. "Okay, but I want you to skedaddle as soon as I'm done. You're not coming along on the date."

On one condition. You let me see Andrew's reaction when he sees you like this. After that, I promise to ghost out. Sage chuckled at his own pun.

"Fine." She finished curling her long lashes and smeared a little lip gloss on her full lips. Anything more than this and she would've looked like a hooker—especially with that monster bra on. A long gold-toned pendant necklace and a few bangles completed the look.

Nathalie grabbed her purse and quickly headed downstairs. Not because she didn't want to keep Andrew waiting, but because she was afraid that given another moment in front of the mirror, she would chicken out and take off the bra and the heels and replace them with something she was more used to wearing and felt comfortable in.

But as she stepped out from the kitchen and into the shop, where Andrew was waiting for her, the smoldering look in his eyes made her glad she'd had the courage to dress up for him.

Jackson whistled, then added, "You're one lucky dude, Andrew."

"I know." Andrew's voice sounded hoarse.

I bet he's so hard his zipper is about to pop.

Nathalie smiled a broad smile for Andrew while hissing in her head at Sage. *You promised.*

Have fun, Nathalie, and bang the guy. I would if I were you.

Get lost. Or better yet, get into his head. I'm not the one who's been putting on the brakes.

I bet he won't tonight, and I want to hear all about it tomorrow.

Fat chance. Now, go away.

Sage out.

She felt him fade away and concentrated on the sensation.

Perhaps next time she would be able to force him out if he refused to leave on his own.

36

ANDREW

Fuck, she looked gorgeous.

In fact, she looked so good that he didn't feel like taking her out and having all the horny bastards ogling her amazing body.

But he'd promised.

"Aren't you going to say something?" Nathalie's eyes sparkled with excitement as she sidled up to him, sashaying those luscious hips, her high-heeled shoes clicking on the tile floor.

"I'm speechless."

She kissed his cheek. "It'll do."

"Ready to go? Or do you want to say goodbye to your father?"

"No, I'd rather sneak out without him noticing it. I don't want a tantrum."

"She's right, just get out of here already." Jackson opened the door so carefully that the bells produced only minimal sound, and waved his hand to shoo them out.

He waited for Nathalie to step out and then leaned

close to Andrew's ear and whispered, "You don't need to hurry back. I can stay the night."

Andrew clapped his shoulder. "I owe you, kid."

"And I'm going to collect." Jackson made the thumbs up sign before closing the door.

When he heard the lock engage, Andrew wrapped his arm around Nathalie's small waist and led her to his car.

"I can't believe I'm out. I feel free, like a prisoner who's just been released."

Andrew tightened his grip on her waist and turned her, bringing her flush against his body. "I need to kiss you, now." She tilted her head up to offer him her sweet mouth. With the heels on, Nathalie didn't need to stretch up on her toes, and he didn't have to bend as much to kiss her.

He licked at her lips and smiled. They were really sweet. The lip gloss she had on was strawberry flavored. "I'm going to ruin your lipstick."

"I don't care. Just kiss me already."

"Yes, ma'am." He took her mouth, licking inside it and exploring, his hands wandering down to cup her generous ass and press her against his aching shaft.

Nathalie moaned and gyrated her hips, adding to his torture.

God, he needed to fuck her so bad. He'd better stop right now before they ended up doing it in the backseat of his car.

"Why did you stop?" she breathed as he released her.

Reaching into his pocket for the car key, he pressed his thumb to the button and unlocked it. "I promised you a proper date, and I don't think a romp in the backseat of my car qualifies."

Nathalie chuckled. "I've never necked in a car before; it could be fun."

"I wasn't talking about necking." He lifted a brow. "And

how come you never had? Did you go to an all-girl school?" That might explain some of her inexperience.

A shadow crossed Nathalie's eyes, and she shook her head. "No, I went to a regular school. Private, but coed." He opened the passenger door for her, and she slid inside, pulling the seatbelt and locking it in place without looking at him.

Had he said something wrong?

Was it a touchy subject with her?

God, it was so hard to understand women sometimes. Should he ask?

Nah, she didn't look like she wanted to talk about it. Better change the subject.

"So, sweetheart, where would you like to go?"

"What are the options? You're the expert on dating, you tell me. Where do you take your other dates?"

Yeah, he'd definitely said something that had upset her. Perhaps she was the jealous type and had imagined him doing all kinds of things in the backseat, to all sorts of girls.

"We can go to a romantic restaurant, or to a movie, or a bar, or a club, or just for coffee. What's your pleasure?"

Nathalie didn't pause to think. "I want to go dancing. Food and coffee I have every day, and if I want a drink I can have it also, but dancing... Yeah. That's what I want."

"Your wish is my command. Let's see what we have here." He did a quick internet search on his phone. "I got it." He pushed the transmission to drive.

"Where are we going?" she asked as he pulled out into the street.

"It's a surprise."

"Will there be dancing?"

"Of course, I always obey a lady's wishes."

She murmured something he couldn't hear and folded

her arms over the chest—which looked suspiciously larger than usual. He stole another sideways glance. Yep, a push-up bra. Sweet Nathalie had gone all out to look sexy tonight.

Maybe she was expecting more compliments.

Yeah, that must be it.

"You look stunning, absolutely gorgeous."

She smiled and her shoulders relaxed a little. "Thank you."

Good, so he was on the right track. Perhaps a little more was needed.

"Sexy as hell."

Her cheeks reddened, and she waved her hand. "Stop it; you're making me blush."

"I like it when you blush, lets me know I have an effect on you. And anyway, it's true, you are unbelievably sexy."

She shrugged, but he could tell that she liked hearing it.

"Those stretchy pants hug your ass so perfectly that I'll be forced to dance behind you and hide these lush curves of yours from view to prevent riots."

She snorted, but her shoulders relaxed all the way.

"Is this the place?" Nathalie asked as he drove up to a valet stand with the name *Nostalgia* printed in red over its white canopy.

"Yep."

"What is it?"

"A sixties style restaurant club."

Nathalie glanced down at her jeans. "Am I dressed for a place like this?"

Andrew chuckled. "I don't think there is a dress code, but if there is, I'm going to fit in perfectly." Navy blue slacks, paired with a gray blazer, a checkered dress shirt, a tie, and brown dress shoes—yeah, a sixties club was the only place his work attire wouldn't seem inappropriate for.

"Have you been here before?" she asked as the valet opened the door for her.

Andrew joined her outside and wrapped his hand around her waist. "No, but a friend of mine from work recommended it." Andrew chuckled. "He said that it's perfect for an older crowd—like me. I hope you don't mind. If it's too staid, we can leave and find something else." He was almost ten years older than Nathalie, and her tastes might gravitate toward something more exciting.

"I'm sure it's going to be fine."

37

NATHALIE

*S*waying to the sounds of Paul Anka's *Put Your Head on My Shoulder,* with Andrew's arms wrapped tightly around her, Nathalie was hovering somewhere between heaven and hell.

It felt so good, so right to be so close to him, feeling his hard body pressed against her, smelling his aftershave and his own unique masculine scent.

She was burning for more, and yet everything was so perfect that she didn't want to cut it short.

Her first date.

Nostalgia was just the right place for a romantic outing. Dim, with little round tables for two that were covered in red and white checkered tablecloths and topped with glass jars containing short fat candles. The framed posters on the walls were of the big stars of the sixties—all clean-cut and smiling brightly. A band of six guys was playing their biggest hits. Wearing tight fitting suits and hair that was slicked back with oil, they looked like they had been plucked from an old teenage romance movie.

Kind of reminded her of the prom scene from *Back to the Future*.

Surprisingly, though, the place was full of young couples and not the old farts Andrew had told her to expect.

"Are you having fun?" he whispered in her ear.

"I love it, thank you." She lifted her head to look at his smiling eyes, and he bent a little to kiss her lips lightly.

"Would you like to sit down and order dessert?"

No, she wouldn't. The steak she'd ordered had been huge, and she was still too full to even think of taking another bite of anything, no matter how good.

"I can't, I'm too full."

"Perhaps, coffee? Another drink?"

She chuckled. "Stop trying to feed me more, at this rate, my ass is going to double in size."

"This ass?" He cupped her butt cheeks and squeezed.

"Stop it, everyone can see…" she giggled.

"I can't help myself. I've been dying to squeeze it all evening long."

"Well, you'll have to wait for when we have some privacy."

"When?"

Good point. They had nowhere to go that was private unless she wanted to take up his suggestion about necking in the back seat of his car. Not that it offered a lot of privacy, tinted windows and all.

She sighed and put her cheek on his shoulder. "I don't know."

"We could go to my place."

God, it was tempting. But it was already late, and Cinderella's clock was ticking.

"I wish I could. But I have to get home and release Jackson. It's bad enough that I had him stay so late on a Friday night. Maybe it's still early enough, though, for him to catch up with his friends and go out."

"Let me text him. I don't think he would mind missing one night with his buddies. On the contrary, I'm sure that if I offer to pay him double for staying the night, he'll jump at it."

Nathalie felt a blush engulfing her cheeks. "You can't, he'll know what we…"

"So? He's not exactly an innocent lamb."

She shook her head. "I have to work with him Sunday. I'm going to die of embarrassment."

Andrew hooked a finger under her chin and tilted her head so she would look into his eyes. "I want you, Nathalie, and that's the only way we can be together. Unless you prefer me to join you in your bedroom at home. It's either this or that. Neither is a perfect solution, but you have to choose the one that's least problematic."

She didn't need to think, her place was out of the question. She was anxious enough about revealing her secret to Andrew, not to mention having sex for the first time. The last thing she needed was to worry about her father waking up and interrupting them.

But she didn't want to wait any longer. And besides, with tomorrow being the only day of the week she didn't have to wake up early, tonight was perfect.

"Okay."

"That's my girl."

Andrew's grin was almost scary—he kind of reminded her of a hungry wolf—but all she could feel was excitement.

Finally, she was going to do it! With Andrew!

As they got back to their table and Andrew texted Jackson, Nathalie waved the waiter over and ordered another drink.

Andrew arched a brow, but she shrugged. It wasn't as if she intended to sit and sip on it. The moment it got there she was going to down it on a oner. Nathalie needed the liquid courage.

"Jackson says no problem."

Nathalie wasn't surprised. She had a feeling Jackson was aware of their situation and wanted to help. Never mind that it was beyond embarrassing to have a teenage boy concerning himself with her sex life, or lack thereof.

The waiter brought her the fancy cocktail, and she tried to gulp it down, but it was too cold and too big.

Andrew clasped her hand. "Take your time, sweetheart, we have all night."

Wasn't she the luckiest woman to have a guy that was not only handsome and sexy but also considerate and patient?

She definitely was. But the flurry of butterflies in her stomach made her too restless to take her time.

Nathalie was all out of patience.

Her glass landed on the table with a clank, and she pushed up to her feet, at the same time snatching her purse from the back of her chair. "Let's go." She swayed a little, her legs not as sturdy as they were a few moments ago.

Andrew took out his wallet and put several bills on the table, enough to cover their meal and then some.

As they walked out and waited for the valet to bring Andrew's car around, the silence between them was loaded with anticipation, with sexual tension, and in Nathalie's case, with fear.

She wondered if that was how everyone felt before their first time. Probably. It was the fear of the unknown, the stories about it being painful, other stories of it being disappointing.

Doing her homework, she'd read all she could about the

experience, and had even tried to watch porn, but it had been too awkward, and she logged out. It was a kind of voyeurism she hadn't felt comfortable with, even though the clip she'd started watching was from a movie done with professional actors. Not footage from a hidden camera with a long range lens catching some unsuspecting couple—which she'd unwittingly stumbled on during her search and quickly moved on to something else.

Her take home from all that research was that she shouldn't expect too much from her first time—that it was always awful, and those who claimed otherwise were lying.

Whatever, she needed to have this first time out of the way so she could have the second and the third and the fourth, and eventually find pleasure. Every woman went through this, and they still wanted more, so it couldn't be all bad.

38

ANDREW

"Here we are." Andrew cut the engine and clicked the garage door closed.

Nathalie seemed nervous, tense. She hadn't said much during the short ride to his house, answering his questions in monosyllables or nodding in response to the stories he'd told her. He was doing his best to put her at ease, but it wasn't working.

"Thank you," she said as he opened the passenger door and offered her his hand.

Damn, if she hadn't looked so anxious, he would've flung her into his arms and carried her straight into his bedroom. Instead, he wrapped his arm around her tensed shoulders and ushered her in, through the kitchen and into the living room.

"Your place is nice," she said, fidgeting with the long strap of her small purse.

"Thanks." He motioned to the sofa. "Please, have a seat. I'm going to get us some wine."

"Thank you."

Fuck, they were acting more like polite strangers than would-be lovers. Andrew was used to women who knew exactly what they wanted and weren't afraid to go for it. He'd walked away from those who'd exhibited even the slightest hesitation. After all, there were plenty of the other kind, and he hadn't had the time or the inclination to work so hard.

Wasn't worth it.

But Nathalie was different. He'd known since the first time he laid eyes on her that she was worth any effort. Because he had a feeling that she just might be the one.

Problem was, he didn't know how to go about making her comfortable.

Joking around had helped a little but not enough, and giving her space hadn't done much good either. On the contrary, it had only furthered the distance between them. Perhaps the exact opposite was needed. And if she balked he'd ease up a little.

As he came back with a bottle of wine and two glasses, he found Nathalie in the same position he'd left her, sitting on the edge of the sofa, the thin strap of her purse still nestled between her breasts. If she'd known the kind of attention it was drawing to her cleavage, she would've removed it right away.

Andrew put the bottle and stems down on the coffee table and sat down next to Nathalie. Wrapping his arm around her, he hooked a finger under her chin and turned her head so she would look at him. "What's the matter, sweetheart? Why are you so nervous?"

Nathalie swallowed audibly and tried to look away.

He held on, not letting her escape his scrutiny. "You can tell me anything. I'm not going to judge, I'm not going to criticize, or do any of the things that you're afraid I might do. I care for you, and I'm here for you. There is nothing you can do or say that will change the way I feel about you."

"Oh. God," she whispered. "Kiss me first, and then I'll tell you."

He pulled her closer against his body and brought his lips to hers, softly at first, stroking her mouth with his own, then teasing her lush lips with tiny flicks of his tongue.

Nathalie moaned and pressed herself closer to him, her lips parting in invitation. He slipped inside, sweeping his tongue against hers. When she moaned again, he slid his hand along the side of her breast then cupped it. But the damned padded bra she was wearing was like a chastity implement, robbing them both of sensation.

"This has to go," he murmured against her lips and reached behind her to slip his hand under her T-shirt and unhook the offending garment.

"Wait." She put a hand on his chest, and he halted his progress, but didn't take his hand out from under her shirt.

"What's the matter?"

"I need to tell you something."

She sounded so serious and so stricken that he pulled his hand out and concentrated on her face. For a moment, he had the terrible thought that maybe there was something wrong with her breasts—

Like a mastectomy—

Fuck, that would explain everything, wouldn't it...

Nathalie took a deep breath before lifting her head and looking into his eyes. *Such a brave girl.* Andrew braced for what she was about to reveal, promising himself to be as supportive as he could and not show how sorry he felt for her.

"Here goes, I've never done this before." As soon as the

words had left her lips, her courage faltered, and she looked away.

He was about to say the words he'd prepared in his head, that it was okay and that he would find her sexy and beautiful regardless, when what she'd actually told him sank in.

"What do you mean? You've never done it in a guy's home?"

She glanced up at him with a look that seemed to question his mental faculties. "I've never had sex, anywhere. I'm still a virgin." She looked down and added in a murmur, "At least I think I am."

Fucking hell! A virgin?

He'd suspected that Nathalie was inexperienced, but not as in 'never had sex before'—just not frequent or recent.

Damn, what was he supposed to do now? He'd never been with a virgin before.

"Say something." There was worry in her voice.

"How? Why? Is it religion? Were you saving yourself for marriage?"

Shit, he wasn't handling it well at all. Instead of reassuring Nathalie, he sounded as if he was accusing her of something. So what if she was a devout Catholic or something like it? "Not that it makes any difference for me, but I'm just curious, that's all."

Nathalie shrugged, and a soft sigh escaped her lips. "I wish I could say that this was the reason—that it had been my choice—even if a weird one. The truth is that it just happened." She chuckled. "Or didn't happen as is the case."

Andrew sensed that there was a long and complicated story behind her statement, and decided that it was best to get it out once and for all and put it behind them.

Anyway, his arousal had been long gone along with his

plans to finally make love to Nathalie. It had all flown out the window the moment the word *virgin* had been uttered.

He took her hand and gave it a squeeze for encouragement. "Okay, out with it, everything."

"I'm scared." There were tears in her eyes, and Andrew cursed himself for being an insensitive jerk who had no idea how to deal with this situation in a way that wouldn't make Nathalie feel even worse.

"Don't be. As I said before. I care for you, and I'm here for you. There is nothing you can do or say that will change the way I feel about you."

She snorted. "Yeah, right."

"Try me."

She looked up at him, her eyes searching his expression. He didn't look away, holding her gaze for as long as she wanted to hold his. After a long moment, she nodded.

39

NATHALIE

$\mathcal{N}$athalie had known Andrew would freak out. And she hadn't even mentioned the ghosts yet. But she was tired of hiding it from him, tired of fearing he'd run.

She was just so damn tired of it all.

In her cowardice, she hadn't been even upholding the deal she'd made with him on their first date of telling him one of her secrets in exchange for a story behind one of his scars—feeding him inconsequential little anecdotes instead.

If it ended tonight, so be it. She would cry for a month, or a year, or for the rest of her days, but if this wretched life was her fate, she had no choice but to accept it and do the best she could with it.

Screaming up to her father's God that it wasn't fair wasn't going to help her or do her any good. It was what it was, and no amount of wishing was going to change it.

"I won't blame you if, after you hear this, you want nothing to do with me."

Andrew chuckled and squeezed her hand. "Don't be so dramatic, Nathalie. It's not like virginity is a contagious disease or a handicap. It's just a temporary impediment that is easily removed." He winked.

Yeah, easy for him to say. He wasn't the one facing excruciating pain. But anyway, this was beside the point.

"That's not all. There is a reason I'm still a virgin at thirty, and it has nothing to do with religious or moral beliefs."

He nodded, but his posture revealed that he tensed in preparation for her story. God only knew what he was imagining. She'd better just spill it all out and be done with it.

"Since I was a little girl, I've been hearing voices in my head." She stole a glance at his face but was surprised to find no reaction to her statement. Encouraged, she continued.

"At first, my parents thought that I had imaginary friends, like many kids do. What they didn't realize, though, was that the voices in my head didn't belong to children, or talk about childish things. The voices belonged to ghosts, people who had died and for some reason found me a receptive channel."

She snorted. "I'm still not sure if I'm really hearing ghosts or just crazy." Andrew still looked like nothing she'd said shocked him. He was either very good at hiding his feelings or very open minded.

"It was difficult because there were so many. It felt as if they were fighting for a chance to talk to me, but all of that stopped when Tut arrived."

"Who's Tut?"

"Just one of the voices, but he somehow managed to block the others, and since then I've been hearing only him. At least until recently, but I'll get to that later. It was a huge improvement, and it allowed me to lead a semi-normal life. But not completely normal. Kids made fun of me, calling me *Nutty Nattie* because I would often talk to myself. It made me shy and withdrawn, and I didn't have friends."

She chuckled. "Except Tut, that is. But he was a sarcastic adult, not a kid. When I went to college, it was bliss. No one knew me or my damned nickname, and a Bluetooth earpiece took care of my occasional blunder. But after years of being shunned, I was shy. I figured I had time, you know, to open up, make friends, go on dates, all the normal things a girl my age was expected to do. But time flew by, and at the beginning of my third year Papi got sick, and I had to come back and help with the shop. Since then, it was one big blur of never-ending days, working, taking care of Papi."

Andrew leaned and kissed her forehead. "You're a very good daughter, Nathalie. I doubt others in your position would've done the same."

She smiled, appreciating his compliment. "I didn't have a choice. There was no one else."

He nodded.

"So that's the whole story in a nutshell. Just one thing leading to another, and here I am—a crazy, thirty-year-old virgin."

"You're not crazy." He said it with so much conviction that she was inclined to believe that he really meant it.

"So you really believe that I hear ghosts in my head?"

Andrew shrugged. "You are not the first or the only one to communicate with the beyond. Most are charlatans, but some are genuine. There is so much out there that can't be explained, or shrugged off. I keep an open mind."

Thank you, God.

This was better than she'd ever dared to hope. Andrew, a grown man who seemed as down to earth as it got, believed her and seemed to accept her weirdness as something that wasn't completely out there.

It was nothing short of a miracle.

"You have no idea how relieved I am to hear you say that. I was sure you'd make some lame excuse and take me home, then run as far and as quickly as you could."

He leaned into her and kissed her lips lightly. "You're not getting rid of me that easily. I'm here to stay."

"And the virginity?"

He chuckled. "Again, you're not the first or the only one with that condition."

"So you don't mind?"

Andrew rubbed his neck before giving her a crooked smile. "You were so brave to tell me everything that I can do no less. The truth is that I've never been with a virgin, and I'm not sure how to make it good for you. But I'm going to do my best."

Nathalie closed her eyes and released a long breath. "So we are still going to do it?"

Andrew's voice dipped half an octave. "I promise you, sweetheart, by tomorrow morning you'll be a virgin no more."

Thank God.

Andrew pushed to his feet and before she could guess his intentions, he bent and lifted her up in his arms. "I'm taking you to bed." He paused for a moment and looked into her eyes as if asking her to confirm or deny it.

She smiled and wrapped her arms around his neck. "Just promise not to drop me on the way. I'm heavy."

He grinned like the cat who was about to eat the canary. "Nonsense, you're light as a feather, sweetheart."

She wasn't, but Andrew carried her to his bedroom as if she was.

She pressed her cheek to his and sniffed his skin—aftershave and man—the scent of a promise.

40

ANDREW

*H*olding Nathalie in his arms suffused Andrew with a barrage of unfamiliar feelings.

He was humming with excitement. Her confession about the voices in her head had reinforced his belief that she was a Dormant. But his joy was tainted by a dark and unfamiliar possessiveness. Because there was only one way to find out. One that he would never allow. No male was going to touch his Nathalie but him.

Unfortunately, he was still just a mortal and didn't possess the equipment necessary to inject her with the venom she needed in order to activate her dormant genes.

Andrew wondered if it was possible to extract the venom, like from a snake, and inject it with a syringe. Problem was that even if it were possible, he still wouldn't be able to let another male's venom do the work. If anyone's essence was going into Nathalie, it was going to be his.

He would have to go through the transition first, and then turn her.

But what if she wasn't a Dormant, and he ended up squandering a chance for a normal life with her?

Or worse, what if he didn't make it?

Damn, he needed to clear his head of these thoughts because he had to deal with a more immediate concern. Bringing Nathalie pleasure while taking her virginity.

Talk about impossible goals.

Well, one thing at a time. First, he would make her climax, and only then would he dare to attempt her deflowering. And if it became too much for her to bear, he would stop and take care of his own need with the help of his own hand—same way he'd done every night since he'd gotten involved with Nathalie. And thank God that he had. He wasn't as strung up and impatient as he would've been otherwise.

Causing Nathalie anguish was out of the question. If it proved to be only a little painful, then fine, he'd continue, but he would never allow her to suffer. Not going to happen.

In his bedroom, he laid her gently on the bed and turned on the bedside lamp. It bathed the room in dim light, casting a golden glow on her perfect figure. Andrew sat down beside her and cupped her cheek. "You have nothing to fear, sweetheart. We'll go slow, one little step at a time, and if it becomes too much for you, at any point, we will stop."

She nodded on an exhale, and reached for him, wrapping her hands around his neck and pulling him down for a kiss. It started slow and gentle, a kiss meant to ease her fears, but Nathalie had other ideas. Soon she was pulling him down harder and arching her back so their bodies would touch.

He wanted her naked.

Andrew broke the kiss and smiled. "You're wearing way

too many clothes. Especially this medieval contraption." He flicked the side of her padded bra.

Nathalie giggled, blushing. "It makes my breasts look bigger."

Andrew frowned. "There's no need. They're perfect the way they are."

"How would you know?" she taunted, her tone becoming husky.

"Well, let's find out, shall we?" He tugged on the bottom of her T-shirt, and she leaned up so he could take it off, then lay back down, her breaths coming out in small, rapid puffs.

"You're beautiful," he whispered as he slid the bra straps off her shoulders, revealing just the tops of her breasts. But this was not the kind of bra that wanted to cooperate with slow seduction. Andrew got impatient and reached for the hook on Nathalie's back, snapping it open with the fingers of one hand while flinging it away with the other.

Finally, she was naked before him, even if only partially, and he hissed as his shaft kicked up, tenting his loose slacks.

"Damn." He couldn't help the word escaping his mouth. He should've worn jeans.

Nathalie was barely breathing as he watched her, drinking up her beauty.

"Touch me," she whispered.

He touched his thumb to the outline of her taut nipple, tracing it round and round.

Nathalie shivered. "You're torturing me."

Yeah, he'd teased her enough. His palm closing around one breast, he brought his mouth to the other and closed his lips around one sweet nipple, then sucked it in.

Nathalie mewled, her back arching off the bed. Her little nubs were so tight that he was sure they ached.

He wondered whether she would like having them pinched.

Only one way to find out.

Releasing the one he had been suckling, he closed his palm around it and moved to the other. When it was also wet, he cupped it with his other hand, letting her have a moment to relax before closing his fingers around both nubs, and pinching them simultaneously. Gently at first, but as her face showed more bliss than discomfort, he tugged harder, pulling her breasts up and away from her body.

Her hands shot up, but not to stop him. She laid them on top of his as if to tell him not to stop.

But he didn't want her nipples to become too tender. There was still a lot more he wanted to do to them. He eased up and then cupped her tender peaks, letting the warmth soothe them.

"Pfff…" Nathalie released a long puff of breath.

"How about we get rid of the rest of your clothes?" he asked gently

"Please." Sweet Nathalie wanted him to undress her.

"With pleasure, my lady." He popped the button of her jeans open and pulled down the zipper, then peeled the tight material off her, one leg at a time.

Nathalie seemed satisfied with letting him do the honors, only lifting her behind a little to ease the way.

Her black panties were plain cotton, and for a moment, Andrew contemplated leaving them on, thinking that she would be more comfortable with a gradual progression.

But in the end, he just couldn't help it. Andrew wanted her fully nude. With one strong tug, he divested her of the panties as well.

Nathalie didn't try to hide from him, although he could see her hands fisting the bed cover as she battled

231

against the instinct to cover the most private place on her body.

He wouldn't have allowed it.

She was his.

God, where did this come from? Andrew shook his head. He wasn't a caveman… Or maybe he was but wasn't aware of it until now.

Maybe deep down all men were still cavemen when it came to the woman they prized above all else.

As he stared at what he'd uncovered, his shaft pulsed inside his pants, begging to be released. Unlike a lot of the women he'd seen naked, Nathalie wasn't completely bare, and her nearly black, neatly trimmed pubic hair was glistening with the evidence of her desire.

"So fucking sexy."

Reassured by his compliment, she unclenched her fists and even arched her back a little.

As he traced a finger down her slit, following the wetness to its source, Nathalie gasped and jerked her thighs together.

"Sh… it's okay." He ran his palm over her thigh. "Don't be scared, I'm only going to bring you pleasure."

"I know. It was just a reflex. I couldn't help it." She tried to part her trembling legs, but they seemed to resist. "Shit, why am I such a coward? I want this, I want you, and still… it's so hard to just let it happen."

Taking a deep breath, Nathalie closed her eyes and parted her legs. Blindly, she reached for his hand. "Don't stop."

Such a brave girl, and he wasn't making it easy for her.

She was completely bare before him, while he was still wearing a blazer and a tie—his eyes roving over her magnificent body and his hands touching her in a most intimate way.

But he couldn't help himself either. There was something very satisfying in this disparity, a sense of ownership that had nothing to do with reality. And as much as his rational mind detested the idea of Nathalie still being a virgin, of all the years of pleasure she'd lost, some primitive side of him was very happy about being her first.

And if he had any say in it, her last.

41

NATHALIE

*S*ex was amazing, terrifying, exhilarating.

And they hadn't even done anything monumental yet.

Nathalie was discovering things about herself that were shockingly surprising. Like that she wasn't at all shy about her nudity. In fact, Andrew baring her one piece of clothing at a time had turned her on, especially since he was doing it while still wearing his tie and jacket.

Hot, hot, hot.

She loved his eyes on her, loved the passion in them, the smoldering desire. A girl couldn't help but feel beautiful when a guy like Andrew gazed at her nude body with such hunger.

Over her initial shock of feeling his fingers explore her wet heat, Nathalie wanted more; more of Andrew's hands, more of his mouth, more of his lips, more of his tongue. She wanted more of everything even though the emotional and physical storm bombarding her senses was so exhausting that she was afraid she wouldn't last under the onslaught.

She was on fire for him, so turned on that she felt like she could climax just from his gentle fingers caressing her folds. And if he thrust a finger inside her, she would for sure combust on the spot.

When he removed his hand, she barely stopped herself from grabbing it and returning it to where she wanted it.

But then, he got up and began stripping.

Finally, she was going to see him naked. Every time she'd felt his hard, muscular body—under her hands as she caressed his back and his chest, and against her breasts, as she pressed herself against him—she'd been imagining him naked. He was going to be magnificent.

First, he removed his jacket and draped it over the back of a chair, then his tie. His shirt was next. She loved watching him open the cuff buttons and roll the sleeves up, revealing his muscular forearms, which were covered in a smattering of dark hair. But, this time, there was no need for it, and after taking care of the cuffs he moved on to the buttons on the front of his shirt, popping each one slowly and revealing his muscular chest a little at a time.

Nathalie held her breath, waiting for the moment when he would part the two halves. But Andrew just left the shirt hanging open as he kicked off his loafers, unbuckled his belt, pulled the zipper down, and stepped out of his slacks.

She managed to get a good look at his strong thighs before he turned around and sat on the bed to remove his socks.

With the shirt still on.

Nathalie frowned as a chilling thought crossed her mind. Was Andrew embarrassed to show his chest or his back? Perhaps the scars on his face were just a small sample, and there were many more? Was he disfigured?

Not that she would find him any less sexy if he was

scarred, but it pained her that he felt the need to hide it from her.

With the socks off, he lifted a little to pull down his boxer shorts, and at last shrugged the shirt off of his shoulders.

As she'd expected, his back was peppered with scars, old bullet holes that had healed a long time ago, but it was also heavily muscled and perfectly proportioned. Andrew was even more of a hunk without clothes than he was with them—which was saying a lot since he usually wore a professional attire that tended to enhance the looks of most men, hiding their bellies while adding width to their shoulders. But in Andrew's case, it had been hiding not flaws but sheer masculine beauty.

Then he turned around.

Oh. My. God. His shaft was huge, and dark, and it was pointing at her.

Nathalie had no idea whether Andrew was particularly endowed or whether this was what most men sprouted between their legs when aroused, but in either case, she knew it wasn't going to fit. If a tampon had given her trouble, this thing was going to split her in half.

Involuntarily, a hand flew to her mouth, and she scrambled back against the headboard.

Andrew's expression turned from puzzled to embarrassed as he glanced down at the piece of his anatomy that was scaring the hell out of her.

"I should've left the boxers on, shouldn't I?"

She nodded. Maybe if he'd turned the light off and she didn't see it…

She cleared her throat. "I'm sorry, I must seem to you like some country bumpkin. It's just that you're so big… Are you? Big, I mean? I wouldn't know."

Could this be any more embarrassing?

Andrew chuckled. "I'm probably average, but no one complained one way or another, yet." He crawled on the bed and lay sideways to face her. "Go on, touch him. It will be less scary if you get to feel him."

Tentatively she reached with an extended finger, touching it lightly. "Don't you dare laugh at me," she said, feeling Andrew's big body shake with stifled chuckles. "It's not funny."

"No, I guess it's not," he choked out. "He's not going to jump and bite your hand, you know."

Oh for heaven's sake, stop being such a big coward. She rolled her eyes at herself and reached her shaking hand forward. Andrew's abdominals clenched in anticipation, his impressive six pack getting more defined. He groaned as her hand closed around his shaft which jerked as if excited to be touched.

Well, of course it is, you idiot.

Hm, he felt kind of nice. Firm yet soft, and velvety smooth, except for the big vein running under it. Curiosity won, and she leaned closer and took a sniff. Andrew's scent was even stronger there. Very nice.

In response, he inhaled sharply, and his erection pulsed in her hand, a bead of moisture arising on the broad head.

How fascinating...

She rubbed the pad of her thumb over it, spreading the viscous drop around the mushroom head.

His hand reached for her head, stroking her hair. "Well? What do you think? Not as scary anymore?" His voice was husky, strangled.

Nathalie looked up into his hooded eyes, so full of passion, of need, and felt herself grow wet between her legs. Her lips parted, and he dipped his head to kiss her, gently, even though he must've been starving for more—

such an incredible guy, giving her all the time she needed and not pressuring her at all.

"No, not scary at all. Kind of nice, actually. But I still don't think it's going to fit. In fact, I know it won't."

"We are going to try, and if he doesn't fit we are not going to force it. I told you, one little step at a time, there is nothing to fear. But I have a question."

He looked so serious that she was afraid of what he was going to ask. Though come to think of it, she had no more secrets to hide.

And wasn't that a terrific feeling? She felt at least fifty pounds lighter. "Yes?"

His eyes were smiling, the feathery wrinkles around them fanning out. "Are you going to keep calling him, *it*?"

Nathalie giggled. "What would you like me to call him? Little Andrew?"

He made a face. "I don't like the word *little* associated with my manhood."

She laughed. Even without having anything to compare it with, she was sure there was nothing little about Andrew. "Okay, how about Big Andrew?"

He shrugged. "That could work, but how about just cock? Or if you're not comfortable with that, there is dick, shaft, erection, manhood, Johnson, woody, Mr. Happy, Mr. Big, and numerous others—plenty to choose from."

She kind of liked *Mr. Happy*, but doubted Andrew would. The most common one was cock, and the least explicit one was shaft.

"I can try…" *Shit*, even this was difficult.

"Come on, go for it, say cock, be naughty," he encouraged.

It was just a word, one everyone was using, shouldn't be a big deal. "Cock," she blurted in a hurry. "Here, I said it, are you happy?"

"Yes, come here." He drew her closer to him.

"I'm really not comfortable with this word. How about shaft? Or Mr. Happy?" she tacked on.

Andrew chuckled. "Other than *Little Andrew* I'm fine with whatever."

42

ANDREW

*W*hen he'd taken off his shirt, Andrew had been worried about Nathalie's response to his scarred body, but he hadn't been prepared for her reaction to his cock.

He wasn't *that* big.

It would've been funny if Nathalie were a young girl—a disturbing thought since it would have made him a pedophile. Andrew doubted many girls reached the legal age of consent with their virginity intact.

Sixteen was probably the average age when most did away with the impediment. But not everyone. Some were left on the sidelines, getting in the game much later, and some never.

The good thing was that Nathalie seemed to have gotten over her initial hesitancy, as evident by her hand on his shaft. In fact, she seemed reluctant to let go, pressing her perky breasts against his chest and gyrating her ample hips while stroking his manhood and spreading around the drops of pre-cum gathering at its tip.

At this rate, he'd be coming in her soft little palm in no

time. Not that it was necessarily a bad plan. Nathalie could take care of him with her hand, and he'd reciprocate with his fingers and his tongue, bringing her to a climax with no pain involved.

Problem solved.

Trouble was, he was pretty sure Nathalie wanted to change her virgin status as soon as possible. She seemed embarrassed by it. And anyway, it had to be done, if not tonight then the next time. Either way, it was going to be painful for her.

He closed his hand over hers and halted her up and down strokes.

She lifted a pair of worried eyes at him. "Am I doing it wrong?"

"No, sweetheart, you're doing it perfectly—too good."

"Oh…" she smiled as understanding dawned.

Andrew gave Nathalie's shoulders a little push, helping her to her back. "It's my turn to pleasure you."

"What do you want me to do?"

"Nothing. You just lie there and focus on how it feels. I'll do the rest." He palmed one breast and kneaded, then began thumbing the nipple.

"Okay…" she breathed but seemed hesitant.

"Do you trust me?" He tugged on her stiffened peak.

"Yes." It came out as a whimper.

"Good girl." He leaned and fastened his lips around it, sucking it in and licking all around.

Her back arched, and she stretched her arms above her head, bringing more of her breast into his mouth. He rewarded her with a hand on her other breast, kneading, plucking, in sync with what he was doing with his mouth.

Nathalie's hips were restless on the mattress, going up and down and side to side, and he knew she was wet and aching to be touched. Exactly the way he wanted her to be.

Hungry for him.

Releasing her breast, he trailed his hand over her soft belly down to her needy center, slowly, teasing her.

She mewled, then bit her lower lip, trying to stifle the sounds coming out of her throat.

"Don't," he commanded. "I want your moans and your whimpers and your gasps. Don't hold anything back. Don't hide from me."

Nathalie nodded, her lip still caught between her teeth.

He lifted his hand away from where she wanted it, bringing it to her mouth, and tugged on her lip. "Let it go."

"Sorry."

Andrew chuckled softly. Nathalie was so desperate for his touch that she would've obeyed any command. Which got him thinking…

Nah, not tonight.

But some day, when she was no longer such a newbie, definitely.

He repeated the journey down her body, all along keeping his eyes on her face. She was panting, her breasts rising and falling so enticingly that he took one into his mouth as his finger reached her wet folds.

"Oh, God…" she exclaimed when he gathered her moisture and pressed his thumb to her clit, her legs falling apart of their own volition.

Nathalie was drenched and more than ready to accept his finger.

At first, he just circled her opening, keeping his thumb gently pressed to her clit. She lifted her butt in a not so subtle effort to get him to push inside her.

Sweet Nathalie, wanton, greedy, needy. It was exactly the way he wanted her. He pushed his finger inside her wet, hot sheath, just up to the first knuckle.

Her breaths were coming out in rapid puffs, and again, she wiggled her sexy ass, trying to get more of it.

"You want more, baby? You want my finger all the way inside you?"

"Yes, oh, God, yes..."

Andrew pushed as far as he could go—his thumb over her clit and his finger buried deep inside her spasming sheath.

She was going to come, and the only reason she was still hanging by a thread was that he wasn't moving his finger inside her, denying her the friction that would send her over the edge.

"Do you want to come, sweetheart?" he whispered in her ear, then licked into it.

Nathalie moaned and arched her back. "Yes, please, I'm on fire..."

One, two, three... and takeoff...

Three strokes, was all it took for Nathalie to explode, her cries loud enough to alert the neighbors.

Who cares, let them call the police...

Just from watching her come, he'd almost climaxed himself. His virgin hadn't held back. She'd taken all that he'd given her with blissful abandon and without reservation.

Magnificent. Brave. Sexy.

When her quaking subsided, he cupped her between her legs.

This is mine, he said—on the inside.

On the outside, he leaned and kissed her gently, first her lips, then her closed lids. "You're amazing."

She opened her eyes. "Me? I haven't done anything. You're the one who's amazing. This was just...wow..."

"I'm not done yet."

She blushed. "I know, you haven't had your release yet."

"We'll worry about me later. I'm not done pleasuring you."

Instinctively, she closed her legs, trapping his hand. "There is more?"

"Much more."

"I don't think I can. Not right away."

He rolled on top of her, his shaft nudging her wet entrance. He shuddered with need. She stiffened.

"Don't worry, I'm not going to push inside you." He kissed her neck then trailed his lips down to her breast.

"What if I want you to?" she husked as he swirled his tongue around her nipple.

"Patience, darling. All in good time." Andrew slid further down her body, kissing her sternum, her abdomen, and then the top of her mound.

"What are you doing?"

43

NATHALIE

*A*ndrew lifted his head and smiled. "What does it look like I'm doing?"

She'd read about it, of course. One of her favorite sci-fi romance series was all about hot aliens who loved nothing better than to go down on a woman. It had provided her with plenty of material for naughty fantasies and self-pleasuring.

She'd been yearning to experience this for so long, but now that Andrew was about to turn her fantasy into reality, she was a little apprehensive.

What if he didn't like how she tasted or smelled?

On the other hand, he knew what he was doing and must've done this plenty of times before. Chances were that she didn't taste or smell differently than the other women he'd pleasured.

Shit, thinking about Andrew with others made her angry. He was hers, whether he knew it or not.

"Do you like doing it?" she asked, hoping his answer would be the same as the aliens' in her books—that he not only loved it, but needed it, couldn't live without it…

"Of course, I do. There is nothing that turns me on more than bringing you pleasure and hearing you moan and scream my name as you climax. I love it. Now spread your beautiful legs and let me in." He applied light pressure to her knees, urging her to open for him.

This was good, not the exact same words as in her alien novels, but close enough.

Lying back on the pillows, Nathalie closed her eyes and lay back. She let her legs fall to the sides. It was so wanton and oh so naughty. But it was okay, she trusted Andrew.

"That's my girl." He slid even further down and pressed a kiss to her nether lips.

Anticipating his next move, she flooded with wetness.

Using his thumbs, he spread her wide, opening her to his eyes, his tongue. Nathalie fought the urge to clamp her knees back together and deny him access. It was too much, too soon, and yet she didn't want him to stop. She wanted this, had dreamed about it for years, and she wasn't going to chicken out. Not now, not when she was finally about to experience what was sure to be the best orgasm of her life.

"Oh…" she cried out and torqued when his tongue made contact with her wet center.

He lapped at her gently at first, just a few soft up and down swipes, then took her by surprise as he penetrated her with his tongue, thrusting in and out forcefully.

She bit her lip, trying to still her restless gyrations.

Andrew did it for her, clamping her hips as he delved deeper, fucking her with his tongue. When he withdrew and licked her throbbing clit, her head thrashed, and she heard herself mewl.

Keeping her pinned, he penetrated her with one thick finger and kept licking all around her sensitive nub. Soon, another finger joined the first. Nathalie felt stretched, uncomfortably at first, but as he kept pumping in and out of her, her sheath loosened, accommodating the extra thickness.

She was so close, and the only reason she hadn't detonated yet was that Andrew was skirting her clit, licking all around it but not touching it directly.

He added a third finger, stretching her impossibly wide. It stung, but as his velvet tongue flickered over her clit, there was an additional outpour of moisture and her sheath loosened even more. He started pumping, slowly, then faster. Greedy for those thick fingers fucking in and out of her, she moved up and down to meet each thrust.

He twisted his fingers, opening her, and as he touched a tender spot inside her, he closed his lips over her throbbing nub.

With a cry, Nathalie erupted.

He kept licking and sucking and pumping until the last of her quakes subsided. When he withdrew his fingers, a stream of wetness followed, running down her inner thighs and creating a puddle on the bed.

God, how embarrassing. Tentatively, Nathalie lifted her head and looked at Andrew.

There was a look of smug satisfaction on his face as he knelt between her legs, his massive erection fisted in his hand.

No longer concerned with the pain, she wanted to feel Andrew inside her. If her sheath had stretched for his fingers, it would do the same for his shaft. It may sting at first, but she didn't expect it to hurt as bad as everyone on the Internet claimed.

She was aching as it was, needy, empty.

"I need you."

"Do you want it inside you?" He ran his fist up and down his shaft.

"Yes."

"You don't happen to be on the pill, do you?"

Damn, she'd forgotten all about protection, though not against pregnancy. That part she had covered. "As a matter of fact, I am. I've been on the pill for years to regulate my periods."

Andrew nodded. "I'm clean. We get checked at work every three months. My last test results are from two weeks ago."

Did she trust him? Had he been with other women since they'd met? Nathalie hoped not. But she had to ask.

"Have you been with anyone since then?"

He frowned. "No, of course not." Then he smirked. "Not counting my right hand, that is. I've been with her every night, sometimes twice, fantasizing about your luscious body."

Nathalie blushed. She'd been guilty of the same. In fact, some of her fantasies about sex with Andrew had been quite shocking. She might have lacked experience, but she had one hell of an imagination.

But did she believe that he hadn't been with another woman?

He wouldn't lie about something like that, would he?

Or perhaps she wanted to believe him because she didn't want their first time together to be with a rubber membrane between them.

"Okay."

She expected Andrew to pounce on her, but instead, he bent down and resumed his tonguing. Only when he'd gotten her soaking wet and writhing again did he grip his shaft and guide it to her entrance.

"Shh... relax," he whispered as she tensed under him. "Slow and easy..." he rubbed his shaft against her wet folds, gathering her moisture and coating it with her natural lubricant.

Then he pushed, wedging in just the tip of the broad head inside, and halted.

They were both panting with the strain of it. Him—keeping still when he needed to thrust, and her—gritting her teeth against the pain.

But while the mouth of her sheath felt like a ring of fire, burning from the stretching it was forced to endure, the rest of her marveled at the feel of Andrew's big body on top of her. His sweat-slicked chest smashing her tender breasts, his rugged cheek pressed against hers, his powerful thighs cradled in between her soft ones. It felt so right. This is where he belonged—where she belonged.

"More," she breathed. "Just a little more."

As he pushed in another inch, she dug her nails into his muscular butt, not to keep him from withdrawing, but to prevent herself from bucking him off. It hurt like hell. But she wasn't going to let him stop until he was seated all the way inside her.

After tonight, she was going to be a virgin no more. Even if it meant going through hell to get there.

"A little more," she whispered again, bracing against the pain and willing her body to accept the intrusion.

He lifted his head and looked at her, his forehead beaded with sweat and his brows drawn with worry. "You're crying."

Now that he said it, she felt hot tears sliding down her temples. "It hurts, but I don't want to stop."

"Are you sure? I hate to see you in so much pain. I don't have to finish inside you. We can do this in stages, continue some another day."

This was so sweet of him, but she wanted it over and done with so the next time would be all about pleasure.

"I'm sure."

He nodded, his harsh features soft with some indescribable feeling.

Lifting his hand, he cupped her cheek and kissed her. The taste of her own juices on his tongue was for some reason incredibly erotic, naughty, and she grew wetter in a rush. The pain ebbed, turning from a burning ring of fire into a dull ache.

When he was done kissing, Andrew brought his finger to her mouth, first gently rubbing at her lips and then pushing it inside. With another outpour of wetness, she closed her eyes and sucked on it, imagining it was his shaft.

He pulled his finger out of her moist mouth with a pop, and brought it down to her clit, gently rubbing it as he pushed another inch inside.

Why was it so difficult? It no longer hurt as bad, and she would've loved for Andrew to just shove all the way in in one powerful thrust. But her inner muscles weren't cooperating, and every little push was a struggle just to get it a little deeper.

And where the hell was that barrier everyone was talking about? Was it hiding all the way at the end of her channel? But it was supposed to be near the opening and Andrew's shaft was already past that point... Perhaps it had really been that first tampon that had done away with her hymen.

For some reason, the thought relaxed her. Part of her anxiety must've been a subconscious anticipation of the tearing and the added pain it would entail. But now that she suspected that the barrier was no longer there, she felt her channel loosen a bit more.

Andrew pushed a little further. He was halfway there.

"You're so brave, sweetheart." There was tenderness in his gaze, but also something else. A possessiveness that she welcomed wholeheartedly because she felt exactly the same.

She wasn't brave enough, though, to say what was on the tip of her tongue. That he was hers as much as she was his, and she was never letting him go.

He kissed her again, deeply, passionately, and as she melted into the kiss, he drew back his hips and with one forceful thrust plunged all the way in.

She cried out from the pain, but at the same time, having him seated so deeply inside her, his shaft touching the end of her channel, felt like a victory.

They were joined.

They were one.

She wrapped her arms around him and pressed herself up against his chest.

"Are you okay?" he whispered in her ear.

"I'm great."

He lifted his head and looked at her. When he was satisfied that she'd meant it and that her eyes were dry, he withdrew and thrust again, and again, and with each subsequent push there was a little less pain and a little more pleasure.

She moaned, and lifted her hips to meet the next thrust, and the next, and the one after that.

Her enthusiastic response melted away the last of Andrew's restraint, and he turned rougher, more demanding. Grabbing her ass cheeks in both hands, he lifted her and held her in place as he drove harder, deeper, growling and groaning like an animal.

God, she loved how mindless he'd become—for her. Seeing him lose himself to the passion with such abandon sent her spiraling toward another orgasm.

His neck and chest flexing, his face contorted, he roared as he threw his head back and erupted inside her.

Fiery and wet, the climax crashed over her, and she screamed his name.

Andrew collapsed on top of her, his powerful heart thundering against her chest and his ragged breaths feathering her sweat-slicked neck.

Now that it was over, and the level of endorphins and adrenaline subsided, the burning not only returned full force but expanded. Her whole channel felt like it was on fire. She couldn't bear it even for a moment longer and pushed on Andrew's chest, but it took him a second or two to comprehend what she wanted before he withdrew.

A rush of liquid trailed after his shaft. Was it blood? Or just his semen and her own wetness? She had to know.

As Andrew rolled onto his back, she sat up and looked at the big wet spot that was left behind. But it was too dark to see colors.

"Can you turn the light up?"

He chuckled, but reached to the lamp on the nightstand and turned it up a notch.

There was no blood.

"Well, I guess it was the tampon after all," she muttered.

"Tampon?"

"Long story, but it turns out that I wasn't a virgin after all. I've always suspected that my hymen had fallen victim to a tricky tampon years ago. Now I know for sure. There was no blood."

Andrew glanced at the spot and shrugged. "Does it bother you?"

"No, not really." She plopped against the pillows.

"How do you feel?"

"Sore, but wonderful. I love sex." She smiled at him. "I could use a bath, though."

"Coming right up, sweetheart." He rolled out of bed and padded away to the bathroom.

She heard him turn the water on.

A moment later he came back, holding a couple of wet washcloths, and sat on the bed.

"May I?' he asked as he brought one between her legs.

Should she let him?

Hell, why not. "Go ahead, just be gentle."

"Of course." He dabbed the warm washcloth to her sore opening.

She couldn't stifle the relieved sigh.

Andrew winced. "That bad, eh?"

She shrugged. "It was worth it."

Andrew replaced the washcloth with the other one, and just draped it over her mound. He then climbed carefully on the bed, as if afraid to disturb the mattress, and lay on his side next to her. Gently, he cuddled up to her, draping an arm around her waist.

Nathalie turned her face to him. There was worry and guilt in his eyes as if he was blaming himself for her pain.

She cupped his cheek and leaned to kiss his lips. "You were wonderful, Andrew. And I'm glad I've waited for you to be my first. I doubt any other man would've been so careful with me and so focused on ensuring I had the best experience possible."

The worry in his eyes ebbed, replaced by some tender feeling that looked a lot like love.

Could she dare to hope?

Did she feel the same?

44

ANDREW

I'm falling in love with this beautiful, fascinating, passionate, courageous, and kind woman.

Or perhaps he'd already been in love with her, but had just realized it now.

And yet, he had to consider that it might've been the result of post-coital bliss combined with awe and gratitude to Nathalie for entrusting him with such an important milestone in her life.

Caressing her soft, flushed cheek, he leaned over and kissed it. "You're precious to me, Nathalie."

"And you are to me, my Andrew." She smiled. "But I think you should check on the water. It sounds like the bath is overflowing."

"Fuck!" He jumped out of bed and ran to the bathroom, almost slipping on the wet floor in his rush to turn the water off and open the drain.

As the bath water drained, he grabbed a couple of towels and wiped the floor, wringing them out in the sink and repeating the process until the floor was only damp. He then took a fresh towel and wiped until everything was dry. In the meantime, the water level dropped to where he wanted it to be, and he closed the drain.

Taking the bunch of wet towels into his tiny laundry room, he stuffed them in the washer and then pulled out fresh ones from the linen closet.

Back in his bedroom, he found Nathalie in the same pose he'd left her in; back propped against the pillows, knees up-drawn and slightly parted with the washcloth covering her privates, and arms resting on her sides. The only difference was that her eyes were closed, and her breaths were slow and even.

She'd fallen asleep.

Poor girl, this was way past her bedtime, and the sex must've exhausted her. For a moment, he considered letting her sleep. But she was sore, and he knew the warm water would soothe her.

Threading one arm under her knees and the other around her back, he lifted her to him.

Nathalie rested her cheek on his chest and cracked her lids open. "What are you doing?" she murmured.

"Taking you to soak in a bathtub."

"Oh, okay." Her lids dropped back.

Until tonight, he'd had no use for the corner Jacuzzi bathtub the builder had outfitted the master bathroom with. Andrew preferred showers, and even if he were into bathing, to fill the big tub with water was wasteful. And yet, he was glad for it now—it was perfect for Nathalie to soak in.

Stepping inside, with Nathalie still cradled in his arms, he very carefully lowered himself into the water. When his butt touched the bottom, he rearranged her so she was cradled between his legs, her back resting against his chest.

She sighed. "This is heavenly."

"Feeling better?"

"I am. Is this a dream?"

He chuckled and hugged her closer, brushing his lips against her neck.

She shivered, and his shaft that was pressed against the smooth curves of her soft bottom got stiff again in complete disregard of Nathalie's condition.

Down you go, he admonished his misbehaving member, but the bad boy had a mind of his own,

"I'm sorry," he murmured in her ear.

She cranked her neck to look at him. "What for?"

"My cock getting ideas."

She kissed his chin, then tilted her head up, inviting a kiss. He complied with a light peck on her lips. Lifting her arms, she draped them behind his neck and laced her fingers, then pulled his head further down and invaded his mouth.

He groaned, his hands sliding up to cup her jutting breasts. On a moan, she arched her back, pressing her luscious ass tighter against his shaft and eliciting a corresponding sound from him. Without thinking, he pinched her nipples, rolling them between his thumbs and forefingers and tugging. Her butt muscles flexed, rubbing against his cock.

Damn, he could come just from the delicious friction. And what's more, he couldn't help imagining her bent over the rim of the bathtub as he took her from behind. He was such an ass. Nathalie was in no condition to be taken from any angle. Not tonight.

And yet, she seemed as needy as he was. He skimmed one hand down her slick body and cupped her sex, pressing the heel of his hand against her clit. With his other hand, he kept tormenting her sensitive nipples, first one, then the other. She was wet, dripping, and not from the bath water, but he was reluctant to penetrate her even with a finger.

"How can I be so horny so soon?' she breathed.

He chuckled. "With eating comes the appetite, and it's especially true regarding sex."

"Do you want to do it again?" she asked in a tone that was part hopeful and part fearful.

"Of course, I do. But you're sore, so the only appendage I'm going to use is my tongue." He lifted her off his lap. "Bend over the rim, sweetheart."

She cast him a hesitant glance but did as he asked, kneeling with her belly pressed to the bath's front and her beautiful ass facing him. It was shaped like an inverted heart, the two smooth globes flaring from her tiny waist. He palmed them, kneading lightly, then pushed her up.

"Lift for me, sweetheart."

She did, but only a fraction.

He gave another gentle push. "A little more."

"It's so embarrassing," she whispered as she lifted higher, finally bringing her glistening sex above the water level.

"You're beautiful," he breathed as he scooted down and got in position. "I want to take you like this so bad, but we're going to wait until you're all better." He thrust his tongue into her slit, and she jerked. "One day, I'm going to stand you on all fours, and pound into you from behind until we both see stars." She shivered, and he ran his tongue over her sex.

One hand stroking his shaft, he looped his other arm around Nathalie's ass and pressed his thumb to her clit. He tongued her trembling slit, licking all around, and then spearing it in and out of her. As he licked faster and thrust deeper, her frantic gyrations were grinding her ass into his nose, and he tightened the fist on his cock, moving it up and down to the rhythm Nathalie's luscious ass was dictating.

When she cried out, lifting up and away from his invading tongue, his seed erupted, coating her behind in thick spurts of semen.

Damn, he was quite impressed with himself, coming so hard twice in a row.

Breathing hard, Nathalie slumped over the rim, providing Andrew with the perfect angle to caress her ass cheeks under the pretense of cleaning her up.

She shook her head. "I can't stop thinking about it."

"About what?"

"What you said before about taking me from behind—it's so hot."

Andrew chuckled and playfully slapped one of her round globes. "Oh, no, I've created a monster!"

45

ANANDUR

"*O*h, baby, you look so sexy. All the guys on the dance floor and around it are lusting after you. They are so jealous of me." Anandur shouted into Lana's ear as he put his hands on her hips, drawing her against his body as they swayed in sync to the loud techno music.

It hadn't taken much to convince her to go out with him, and she sure as hell had gotten all dolled up for the occasion. Her legs looked a mile long in the sequined micro mini and spiky heeled sandals she'd donned, and her braless breasts looked firm and taut under the halter top that left her back exposed—which was Lana's one wardrobe mistake. If he wasn't counting the slutty effect of the rest of her getup, that is.

Her back and arms were heavily muscled, but while her arms looked just fine, her back was corded like a body-builder's.

From behind, Lana looked like a drag queen.

Whatever, her front was all woman, even with the short boyish haircut. Gone was the nearly albino complexion, covered with a heavy layer of makeup, and dark eyeliner outlined her pale blue eyes. Her lids were painted in several shades of sparkly blues and silvers, and her lips in glossy pink. She must've sprayed her body with a self-tanner, or something like it because her skin was shiny like it was made from gold. The outfit and the paint job made her look like a hooker, but he didn't mind. She was hot.

With an expression even smugger than usual, Lana scanned the aforementioned males and wrapped her arms around his neck. Tall to begin with, with her high heels she was only a couple of inches shorter than him. It made kissing her easy. For a change, he didn't have to bend like a pretzel for a woman.

Fuck, the pretzel analogy got him thinking of Lana's pert butt cradled in his hands while he had her pushed against the wall—her long legs wrapped around his waist and her heels digging into his naked ass while he drove in and out of her like a battering ram.

"You like other men watch me? It makes you hot for me?" she shouted and rubbed herself against his erection, her sequined skirt catching on his zipper.

He shrugged and tried to release the fabric, but it was stuck. "Look what you've done, now we are stuck like this."

Lana swung her hips to the side, unconcerned with damaging her skirt and the sequins which went flying. "You buy me new, I don't care."

He raised a brow. As if it was his fault, but whatever, it wasn't as if he couldn't afford to buy her a new skirt. "You got it, baby."

His response made her happy, and a big grin split her face.

She sure had a big mouth, and with those fleshy lips… oh, boy, she could do some damage with those.

"You good man. You not ask how much it cost. But I tell

you so you not to worry. Only twenty dollars. Even you can pay."

That's right, she was under the impression that he was a lowly deck boy. He should be more mindful of his cover story and act accordingly.

"For you, baby, anything."

"You want we sit? I need drink."

He nodded and wrapped his arm around her waist as he led her back to their table. She felt so different from other women, it was almost like having his arm around a guy, the only difference was her proportions, which were definitely feminine. Small waist, slightly flaring hips, and a butt that was small width wise but nicely rounded.

"More of the same?" he asked before heading to the bar.

"Da." She nodded.

Anandur shook his head. Vodka, and more vodka. It seemed it was true that Russians didn't consider anything else as alcohol.

Waiting for the bartender to pour their drinks, he thought about how to go about his investigation. So he had Lana interested in him, and he was sure that their date would end up in bed, but he still had no idea how to extract information from her. Or even what questions to ask without being too conspicuous. Another problem was her English, which was limited to the basics. Lana might be a great lay, but she sure as hell wasn't a great conversationalist. And he doubted she was any better in her mother tongue.

She wasn't stupid, but she wasn't the sharpest tool in the shed either. Which should've made his job easy, and perhaps it could've if not for the language barrier.

Damn, he should've asked Andrew for pointers. Not that the thought hadn't crossed his mind before he'd gone out with Lana, but he'd been too damn proud and cocky to ask for instructions—especially from a human.

Perhaps he should just thrall her. He wasn't particularly good at it, but combined with the amount of alcohol she was consuming and, hopefully, post-coital bliss he might be able to get something out of her. It wasn't ethical, but he could chuck it together with the thralling that he was not only allowed to, but forced to do. After all, there was the inevitable biting that had to be erased from her memories.

He wondered how many times that scumbag Alex had already thralled Lana, as well as the rest of the crew, and what was the extent of the damage he had already done. Who knew, perhaps Lana had been a highly intelligent girl before Alex had messed with her brain.

And now Anandur was about to do the same.

Damn, this was a bad idea. The one who should've been assigned to this task was Andrew. Rumor had it that he and Bridget had broken off their whatever they had, so Andrew was a free agent again. And as a human and an expert investigator he could get things out of Lana without causing her more irreversible damage.

Fuck, he should call Kian and ask him what to do.

46

NATHALIE

"*L*et's go around the back," Nathalie said as Andrew parked the car in front of her shop. It was past one in the morning, and chances were that Jackson had fallen asleep in the den. She didn't want the bells hanging over her front door to wake him up. If she were alone, she would've never dared using the back door from the alley in the middle of the night, but with Andrew by her side, she felt safe.

Andrew nodded and followed her into the narrow passageway between her shop and the adjacent house to the back alley. She'd been holding the key out since they exited the car and made a quick work of opening things and getting them inside.

Andrew frowned as she flicked on the light switch next to the door. "You really should have an alarm system here. It's not safe."

"Shh, not so loud," she whispered. "If Jackson is sleeping, I don't want to wake him up."

"I'm going to have one installed first thing Monday

morning," he said in a whisper that was almost as loud as his normal voice.

"Keep your voice down. And fine, I'm not going to say no. I've been planning on installing one since I bought the place, but as with everything else, I've never gotten around to actually doing it."

"Consider it done." He followed her up the stairs.

"Thank you, but I'm paying for it." She cast him a look over her shoulder.

He shrugged. "The installation is free, and you only pay a small monthly fee."

She stopped and turned to face him. "Really? Or you just saying it to trick me?"

He rolled his eyes and grabbed her hand, bringing it to his lips and kissing the back of it. "Really. I'm not going to lie to you about something like this."

She frowned and pulled her hand back. "Oh, yeah? So what are you going to lie to me about?"

He chuckled. "Nothing."

"You better not." She pointed her finger at him.

He grabbed her hips and turned her around, then smacked her bottom. "Keep going, missy. Apparently sleep deprivation makes you cranky."

Was it?

Maybe.

She wasn't a suspicious person by nature, but she had a feeling that there was something Andrew was hiding from her, and it hadn't started tonight. It's just that until now she'd been so busy fretting about her own secrets that she hadn't stopped to think about what was it about Andrew's demeanor that had been bothering her.

It was dark on the second floor, and as Nathalie entered the den, she couldn't see if Jackson was sleeping on the couch but assumed that he was.

"I think that he's asleep," she whispered. "I'm going to check on my father."

"I'm not sleeping."

She jumped, bumping into Andrew, who was standing behind her.

"Shit, Jackson, you scared me."

"Sorry about that, didn't mean to. But Fernando is fine. I've just checked on him like about twenty minutes ago."

Nathalie fumbled for the light switch, but Jackson beat her to it, turning on the floor lamp next to the couch.

Even that dim light was hurting her pupils, that had been fully dilated ever since she'd climbed up the stairs and reached the second floor that had been steeped in darkness.

Jackson reached for his sneakers and pushed his feet inside, not bothering with the laces.

"How was he?" she asked, afraid to hear the answer. "Did he give you any trouble?"

"Nah, he was fine, we had a great time together." Jackson got up.

"Really?"

She found it hard to believe—a seventeen-year-old hotshot having a good time with an old-timer who suffered from dementia wasn't a likely scenario.

Jackson was probably just being nice. She was curious, though.

"What did you guys do all this time?"

Jackson smirked. "He asked me if I was seeing any young ladies, and we spent most of the time with me telling him stories about my various conquests, and him laughing in disbelief. I'm afraid that I'm guilty of contributing to the delinquency of an elder."

She didn't know how she felt about Jackson's admission. Mostly, though, she was glad that her father had had a good time. And as far as Jackson's stories went, Fernando would probably forget everything by tomorrow morning.

"Thank you. I appreciate what you've done tremendously, and I promise to reward you handsomely. But I think you should stay the night. It's late, and I don't want you driving home alone at this time of the night."

Jackson snorted and so did Andrew. "This is early for me. And don't worry for me, Nathalie, I can take care of myself."

"You're just a kid. You think you're invincible, but you're not. Right, Andrew?"

Andrew shrugged. "In his case, I'm not worried. Jackson could probably bench two fifty and punch a hole in the wall with his bare fist. Right, kid?"

Jackson nodded. "Three hundred."

Men and their overinflated egos. But maybe she was being overprotective. Jackson was a big boy, and despite his oozing charm, she'd sensed something dangerous in him—not towards her but as a potential. When fully grown, he would be a force to contend with.

"Fine, but be careful."

"Yes, ma'am." Jackson saluted and hugged her briefly.

"I'll walk you down and lock up after you." Andrew offered.

"Goodnight, Nathalie, see you Sunday."

"Goodnight, and thank you again."

"You're welcome."

With the guys gone, Nathalie walked over to the couch and plopped down. She was exhausted, but she didn't think she could sleep. She hated the idea of Andrew going home and her sleeping alone in her bed. Maybe he could stay, and she'd sneak him out in the morning before her father woke up. Then he could come back pretending as if he just got there.

She wondered whether she was going about it all wrong. A thirty-year-old woman shouldn't have to sneak her boyfriend into her room, and if Fernando weren't sick, she wouldn't have. But she was convinced that the routine kept Fernando from getting worse, and any big changes would affect him negatively.

On the other hand, Jackson was new in Fernando's life and yet her father seemed perfectly fine with him, embracing the boy as if he was part of the family.

Maybe she should give it a try with Andrew. If her father threw a fit because he found Andrew in her room, they would reevaluate. But it was worth the risk.

By the time Andrew came back, she had made up her mind. Reaching for his hand, she pulled him down to sit beside her on the couch. "Could you stay with me tonight?"

"I would love to, but are you sure? What about your father?"

"Let's give it a shot. If he throws a tantrum, we will rethink our strategy."

Andrew smiled and leaned to kiss her lightly on the lips. "Do you have a spare toothbrush?"

"I certainly do."

"Okay then. I hope you don't mind me sleeping in the nude."

"Not at all. But my father will if he finds you in my room. It might be too much of a shock for him."

"How about we just cuddle on the couch, then?"

That sounded wonderful. "You don't mind?"

"Are you kidding me? I would love to."

47

ANDREW

*A*s Nathalie got busy taking the big back cushions off the couch to make room for them to lie down together, Andrew went downstairs to brew them some coffee.

His girl was in the mood for cuddling, and he didn't want to disappoint her by falling asleep.

After brewing a full thermal carafe, he put it on a tray and added two cups, sugar, creamer, and a couple of left-over brownies Nathalie had put in the fridge instead of throwing away—for energy.

When he came back upstairs, the couch was ready, outfitted with two pillows and a woven blanket Nathalie must've brought from her room.

"This looks very inviting." Andrew put down the tray on the coffee table and kicked off his shoes.

"Coffee, Madame?"

"Yes, please."

He filled the two cups, leaving his own black and mixing in a little creamer and one packet of sugar in Nathalie's.

"Thank you, it's just what I need."

He wrapped his free arm around her and pulled her closer. "What you really need is to get some sleep."

"I can't."

"Want me to sing you a lullaby?"

She chuckled. "Do you know any?"

"Not any that are suitable for children. But I know an obscene one."

"Oh, yeah? Who taught you that?"

"My grandfather."

She laughed. "Get out of here, really? Your grandpa taught you a lewd song? How old were you?"

"He came to babysit me one time by himself without Nana. I was thirteen and deeply wounded that my parents still thought I needed a babysitter. My granddaddy agreed that I was too old and that they were babying me. That's when he sang me that song. He said I was old enough to have some fun, but to never let Nana or my mother know about it."

"Do you still remember it?"

"Vaguely. But it's one of my fondest memories of my grandfather. He was such a hoot."

"Did you ever tell your mother?"

"No, my father and I had a good laugh about it, but we decided that it was too crude for her. It was kind of vulgar. She wouldn't have liked it."

"Is she the prim and proper type?"

Was she? Andrew couldn't remember his mother ever cussing, not even something as innocent as *shit* or *darn*. But she had never made a big deal out of someone else cussing once in a while or telling a dirty joke.

"I guess you can say that she is proper but not prim. My Nanna, on the other hand, was definitely both prim and proper, God bless her soul. But this was how women of her generation had been raised, ladylike."

Talking about his mother presented him with the perfect opportunity to ask Nathalie about Eva. She never talked about her mother, only her father. If he hadn't known better, he would've thought that she'd been raised by Fernando alone.

"How about your mother? You never talk about her."

Nathalie sighed and lay back, scooting sideways and patting the space beside her. He lay down, threading his arm under her and bringing her head to rest on his chest.

"It's complicated. I was very close to her when I was little, and she spoiled the hell out of me, but the older I got, the more distant we became. For some reason, I was more comfortable with Papi. Perhaps it had something to do with the baking. My mom couldn't bake if her life depended on it. She could only waitress or work the register."

Nathalie chuckled. "Which was probably the only reason we made any money at all. She was so beautiful that I'm sure most of the male customers became regulars only because of her and not the tasty pastries. Once she and Papi got divorced many of them stopped coming."

Andrew ran his hand up and down Nathalie's back as he thought about what she'd told him. "Was your mother jealous of your relationship with your dad?"

Nathalie shook her head. "No. It was mostly my fault. My dad was an open book—easygoing, always smiling, and it was fun to be around him and do things together. His love for me was unconditional. My mom, on the other hand, was aloof. I always felt as if she was keeping secrets from my father and me. And the way she looked—it was kind of disturbing, to me at least."

"What do you mean?"

Nathalie snorted. "Besides making me feel like an ugly duckling? But that was only part of it. Not only was she striking, but she looked like my older sister, not my mother. Which wouldn't have been so strange if she'd had me when she was very young, but she'd been freaking forty-six when I was born and yet looked no older than thirty when I was fifteen. If not for the unmistakable resemblance between us, I would've suspected that I was adopted. Papi was younger than her by two years but looked like he was her father. It didn't make sense."

"Did you ask her about it?"

"I did, and so did others. She would say it was good genes, artful makeup, even admitting to having done plastic surgery."

"Well, perhaps that was it?"

"Trouble was, I knew she didn't. She had never even been to a dentist let alone undergone surgery. And the makeup? I think she was putting it on to make herself look older, not younger. She used to wear those long skirts and puffy blouses that made her look thirty pounds heavier. When I asked her about it, she said she liked the style and that it was comfortable."

Andrew had trouble stifling his excitement.

The evidence for Eva being an immortal was circumstantial, but it was strong. How had it happened? And why? Those were still a mystery. But immortality was the only plausible explanation for Nathalie's description of her mother.

"What do you think it was? Do you have a hypothesis?

Nathalie shrugged. "The only thing that comes to my mind is that she'd been somehow genetically altered, probably by the government as some secret scientific project. Before she met Papi, she'd worked as an agent for the drug enforcement agency, or so she said. She might have been a Bond style assassin for all I know."

Nathalie had come up with a pretty imaginative scenario. Funny how the real explanation was even stranger.

"Do you know why they split up?"

"I have no idea. When I asked her, she said it was between her and Fernando. I've gotten the same answer from him. It almost sounded like she was implying that he'd cheated on her. And the guilty look on his face when I asked him why they were splitting reinforced that impression. But it didn't make sense. Who in his right mind would cheat on a woman that looked like her? Especially since Papi was an overweight, balding, middle-aged guy."

Andrew smoothed his palm over Nathalie's soft hair, winding a long strand around his finger. "I wouldn't be surprised if that was exactly what happened."

With a frown, she turned her face to look up at him. "Why would you think that?"

"Men have egos, even your father. And being married to a goddess who everyone is drooling over can be challenging. Especially if he perceived himself as not worthy of her, or if she implied it in some way. From your story, I gather that he was a charming and friendly guy, so it's not like he couldn't attract anyone despite his looks. He might have had a need to prove to himself that he still had it. You know what I mean?"

Nathalie's face had doubt written all over it. "I don't know. Maybe. Anyway, it's water under the bridge. I know that he loved her and was devastated when she left. The onset of his dementia happened shortly after that."

"Do you blame her for it?"

"Yeah, I do. I know that the disease must've been in his system for years prior to manifesting, but I think that it would've remained dormant for many more if not for the shock of her leaving him. And it was right at the same time I was leaving for college. He was left all alone."

Nathalie had gotten all tense, her body feeling rigid in his arms. Andrew hooked a finger under her chin and kissed her lips until he felt her muscles loosening. "I bet that part of your resentment toward her is guilt over also leaving him."

"You're right. I was so mad at her that I never called, and during breaks, I stayed with Papi, not her."

"What did she do after the divorce?"

"She worked at Nordstrom's in the men's department, and I guess dated a lot. In the beginning, she tried to maintain contact and called me every day. I would talk to her, but I'd end the call as soon as I could with the first excuse that came to mind. After a while, she got the message, and her calls became less and less frequent. Then one day she just disappeared from the face of the earth."

"Any ideas about what happened to her?"

Nathalie sighed and brought the blanket up to her neck. It was getting cold, and Andrew tucked it around them.

"God knows. She might have gone back to work for the government on some secret mission. At least I hope that this was what happened. When I hadn't heard from her for over a month, I called, but the line was disconnected. I went to look for her at the apartment she was renting at the time, but it was already rented out to someone else. She left all of her furniture behind but took her personal stuff. So I know she wasn't taken by force. Still, she might have gone on a vacation, and something happened to her then."

"Would you like me to look into it?"

"What can you do? The police never found anything."

"I'm not the police. I work for a different government

agency, and I have access to information." This was as much as he dared to tell her.

"I guess it wouldn't hurt. But I'm not holding my breath. I'm tired of waiting for her to come back and hoping that she still cares for me. After all, if I find out that something happened to her, it will mean that I've lost her forever. And if I find out that she is fine but didn't bother to let me know she's alive, then it will mean that I've lost her forever anyway, because she doesn't deserve to be called my mother. Not knowing allows me to hover between the two options. I'm almost afraid to find out, so it's no longer a priority for me."

Oh, but it was, Nathalie just didn't know it. Finding Eva would provide the only definite answer to whether Nathalie was a Dormant or not. Because the other option wasn't on the table for her. There was no way in hell he would allow one of the immortals to attempt her transformation. If anyone was going to do it, it was him.

But unless he knew for sure that she was indeed a Dormant, he wouldn't risk going through the transformation. The only reason for him to put his life on the line was to facilitate Nathalie's immortality.

And if he died in the process?

Then someone else would do it for her, but at least he wouldn't be there to witness it.

48

ANANDUR

We can't switch players in the middle, and we don't have the luxury of playing nice. Go for it.

Anandur shook his head as he read Kian's text message again. This was so uncharacteristic of the guy. It seemed that Dalhu's take-no-prisoners attitude was rubbing off on their do-gooder leader.

Kian was telling him to thrall Lana.

Damn, he really didn't want to.

There must be a way to extract information from her without the help of fangs and venom. Problem was, Lana was expecting him to deliver on his promise of mind-blowing sex. Tough to pull off without biting.

Though not impossible...

Leaning against the wall outside the ladies' room, Anandur wondered what was taking her so long. Was she taking a shower in there? More than fifteen minutes had passed since she'd said she needed to pee, told him to hold her purse, and wait for her.

Bossy Russian.

In a way, it was a refreshing change from the overly

polite American women. She was direct. There was no *if-you-please-could*, or *if-it's-not-too-much-trouble*. With Lana, it was *do this* or *don't do that*.

And language deficiency wasn't the problem. It was just her attitude.

A short brunette in monster platforms wobbled out of the ladies' room and sidled up to him. "Hello, gorgeous…" She gave him a once-over. "You, I want to take home with me." Leaning into him, she pressed her large boobs to his arm and lifted a long-nailed finger to touch his face.

He patted her shoulder and gave a little push. "Not tonight, dove, I'm here with someone." He lifted Lana's purse level with her face.

She pouted but refused to budge. "If she's hot, I don't mind a threesome…"

Damn, how was he going to peel her off him without shoving her? One hard push and she would fall on her ass, probably twisting her ankle on those ridiculous platforms.

He was about to say something when Lana emerged from the bathroom, her face contorted with rage. In one swift move, she yanked the brunette by the hair and shoved her against the wall. Towering over the woman, she kept a hold on her hair as she spat, "No putting your filthy hands on my man, *kurva*, you understand?" She forced the woman's head up and down in a parody of a nod.

He knew that word—it meant whore.

Lana shot the brunette one last angry scowl before threading her hand through his arm. "Let's go."

"What took you so long?" he asked as they headed out of the club.

She snorted. "If I know you in trouble I go out before."

They exited through the back door out into the club's parking lot. "I wouldn't call it trouble, baby." He opened the pickup's passenger door for Lana. "The poor things just can't help themselves, and I try to let them down gently. There is no reason to be mean when I reject them."

Lana harrumphed and crossed her arms over her chest. "Not all, I'm sure."

Anandur circled the old truck and got behind the wheel. "Of course, not. I only keep the pretty ones." He winked at her as he turned the key in the ignition and shifted the gear to drive.

The old clunker belonged to one of the maintenance guys, Rupert, and Anandur had swapped cars with him for the week. After all, he was supposed to be a lowly deck boy of little means.

His classic Thunderbird didn't fit the bill. It was one of the original Thunderbirds, and he'd had her since he'd bought her brand new in 1956. He'd been keeping her in mint condition.

Hopefully, Rupert was treating his baby well.

"By the way, I'm flattered by your impressive display of jealousy, but you didn't need to be so rough with her. She was just drunk."

Lana shrugged. "I see her hands on you, and I get angry. And it is not important that she is a woman because I am a woman too. If another man touch me, you do the same."

She had a point. Not because he was jealous, Lana didn't inspire that kind of feeling in him, but because it was his job as her date to defend her against unwanted advances. Not that Lana needed him to fend off the jerks—most human males didn't stand a chance against her—but it was a matter of honor.

"I guess you're right. It's just that I'm not used to a woman being so aggressive."

Casting him a worried sidelong glance, she asked, "You not like?"

Poor thing, she was afraid that her display of violence

had turned him off. But he wasn't one of those guys who was intimidated by a strong woman, or who preferred the soft and timid types.

The truth was that he wasn't picky, and decent looks and several years of sexual experience were his only requirements. Other than that, there was little else that had any impact on his appetite.

"Oh, I like." He patted her knee, then smoothed his palm up her inner thigh and under her short skirt. When he found her little panties already moist, his shaft swelled and throbbed in response.

Lana's breath hitched, and she parted her legs to allow him better access. He pushed the panties aside and stroked her wet folds, gathering moisture and bringing it up to circle her engorged clit.

"We go to your place?" she breathed with a hopeful glint in her hooded eyes.

"Sorry, baby, no can do. I sleep on a couch at a friend's apartment. We will have to go to yours." He removed his hand and rearranged her skirt.

She grimaced. "My boss say no bring men on boat."

"Fuck. What are we going to do?"

She cast him a sidelong grin. "Many boats in marina are empty. We can go in no problem."

Driving one-handed, he reached for her and pulled her against his side. This was another advantage of driving the old truck over his Thunderbird—the front seat was one long bench. "Lana, you're a genius." He kissed the top of her head.

She put her hand on his inner thigh, her legs parting in invitation as she caressed her way up to his hard bulge. Hell, at this rate they would get each other off before ever getting to the marina.

Oh well, it was a good problem to have.

With a smirk, Anandur returned his hand to where she wanted it and tugged on her panties. He was tempted to give the lacy little thing a hard yank and tear it off her, but such a display of strength wouldn't go unnoticed, and the small thrill wasn't worth getting Lana suspicious.

"How about you take these off?"

She smiled, swinging her long legs up and stretching them, so her feet rested on the dashboard as she lifted her butt and pushed the panties down. Slowly.

"Fuck me..." he groaned and reached to cup her heated, wet flesh.

"Yes, I do, now. Stop where is dark."

It had been ages since he'd fucked a woman in a car. Not his favorite to say the least. He was just too big and wasn't into all the contorting. Doing the horizontal folded like a pretzel wasn't fun. But he was willing to make an exception for Lana, or rather for his cock that wanted out of the tight confinement of his jeans and into Lana's wet and welcoming sheath.

Anandur pulled into the dark parking lot of a small strip mall. The stores were closed for the night, and a waist-tall hedge formed a natural fence between the street and the parking area—hopefully providing enough privacy for their quickie.

"Can you move chair back?" Lana asked as he cut the engine.

"Sorry, baby, that's as far as it goes."

"Is okay." Lana hiked her skirt up and straddled him, reaching for his zipper. A moment later she had his jeans pushed down his hips. Pulling his shaft free out of his briefs, she gripped him in her strong hand.

His breath hissed out between clenched teeth as her fingers tightened around it. Normally, he loved the feel of a soft feminine palm on his sensitive skin, but there was definitely something to be said for a powerful grip.

"You so thick." Her eyes sparkled with excitement. "And so long," she marveled as her hand traveled the length of him.

Anandur smirked. "You no like?" He teased her with her own words.

"Oh, I like, *ya lyublyu mnogo*, I like a lot."

She lifted onto her knees and brushed his shaft against her wetness, coating it in her juices.

He groaned. "You're so wet for me, baby."

"Da." Lana agreed and began lowering herself on his shaft.

His hands shot to her hips, and he held her up, not letting her impale herself the way she intended. She was dripping wet, and not a small or fragile female, but he was large, and experience had taught him that a few extra moments made a big difference not only for his partner but for him as well.

"Let me. I want you inside," Lana hissed in her impatience.

His grip on her hips tightened, and she winced as his fingers dug into her flesh. "We do it my way, or not at all. Understood?"

The look of surprise on her face was almost comical.

Until now, Anandur had played the role of the easygoing bum, so she wasn't expecting him to take charge. Still, as far as he could tell, she didn't mind the switch. In fact, judging by the wetness that coated the tip of his shaft, she liked it.

"Okay, big boy. You the boss. Tell me what you want."

Hm, perhaps he could torture her for information by withholding sex...

Nah, he was so horny that he wouldn't last more than a minute before burying himself in her to the hilt.

"Just go slow, I don't want to hurt you."

An unfamiliar tenderness flitted through Lana's pale blue eyes and she brushed the back of her fingers over his cheek. "You're a good man, Anandur."

Not really, sweetheart.

49

BHATHIAN

*P*acing around his apartment, Bhathian stopped next to Patricia's portrait, the one Tim had drawn for him. He'd pinned it to the wall of his living room, next to the flat screen, so he could gaze at it from time to time while sitting on the couch and watching the dumb tube.

Eva, not Patricia, he reminded himself for the umpteenth time.

Ever since he'd gotten Andrew involved, the memories that over the years had finally dimmed and loosened some of their grip on him resurfaced full force, tormenting him anew.

He couldn't take his mind off her.

Instead of clubbing, he'd spent Friday night brooding alone in his apartment. he'd hardly gotten any sleep, and had awoken this morning before the sun came out.

Finding Nathalie had been a blessing that he still had trouble believing had been bestowed on him. Seeing her every day, spending time with her, talking with her—even though she had no idea who he was to her—had been the highlight of his every day. He lived for those mornings he was getting to spend with Nathalie at her café.

Problem was, she looked so much like her mother, he was constantly reminded of what he'd lost. And imagining what could've been was torture. If only he hadn't been such a coward, he could've had a family for all these years. He could've been raising his own daughter—not Fernando.

It wasn't that he harbored ill feeling toward the man, on the contrary. The love and dedication she was showing her adoptive father with every look and gesture, the sacrifices she was making for him, all reflected on the kind of father Fernando had been to her prior to his disease.

And for that Bhathian was grateful to him beyond measure.

He touched his finger to Eva's picture, caressing her cheek. *You must be so proud of her. Why did you leave her, though? What happened to you?*

He was losing sleep over these questions. They were going on a never-ending loop in his head.

And there was the most disturbing one—was she even alive?

In his gut, he knew she was, and what's more, he knew he had to find her. For Nathalie's sake as much or even more than his own. And he needed to do it sooner than later.

It was possible that Nathalie was already too old to attempt the transition and survive. Syssi almost hadn't made it, and she was only twenty-five...

The thought was so painful that he felt bile rise up his throat. He'd just found her, and he couldn't fathom watching her getting old and eventually dying.

He wouldn't want to go on without her.

Perhaps this was the reason Eva had fled and severed all contact with her daughter. If she had been turned without her or her partner realizing it, it meant that she had no idea how she'd become immortal and why she wasn't aging. And besides not wanting to see her own child age and die, she must've gone into hiding out of sheer fear of someone discovering her secret.

Just as the rest of them, she must've realized that once exposed she would be locked up in some secret lab at a facility that wasn't supposed to exist—living out her life as a test bunny.

Where are you hiding, my love?

He was a fool for calling Eva his love, but he was convinced that once he found her, he'd be able to make her his. After all, they already shared a child, were already a family.

For weeks now, he and Andrew had kept the story to themselves, and he was hoping Andrew would find Eva's trail. But the guy had too much on his plate as it was. Between his government job, the things he was doing for the clan, and spending every free moment with Nathalie, there wasn't much more he could take on.

Bhathian smiled at Eva's portrait. *You would like Andrew, Eva. He is the kind of son-in-law every parent wishes for.*

This was a bigger job than he and Andrew could handle themselves, and as much as he hated exposing his private life for everyone to see, it was time to get Kian and the rest of the Guardians involved. Especially if he wanted to take some time off to go looking for Eva.

Pulling his phone out of his pocket, he texted Andrew. *I want to set a meeting with Kian and tell him about Eva and Nathalie. Later this afternoon work for you?*

A moment later his phone rang.

"Why today? Shouldn't we wait for Monday to talk to him?"

"No, I'd rather have an informal meeting with him at

his place than schedule one for the office. For me, it's not business as usual."

"Yeah, I get what you mean. It's just that this is Nathalie's only day off, and I'd rather not cut it short."

Bhathian chuckled. "Give her a break, she probably needs to have a breather away from you."

"You think?" Andrew sounded doubtful.

"I know that I'm not much of a ladies' man, but if Nathalie is anything like me, constant company drains her."

"Fine, text me the time, and I'll be there."

"I will."

After ending the call, Bhathian texted Kian.

Are you busy? Or can I call you about a private matter?

His phone rang a few seconds later. "What's up, Bhathian?" Kian sounded worried.

"Nothing bad, boss. If you're free this afternoon, Andrew and I have a personal matter we would like to discuss with you."

"Andrew and you?"

"Yes, sir."

"Well, you whetted my curiosity. I can't wait to hear what this is all about. How about my place, four in the afternoon?"

"Perfect. We will be there."

Bhathian let out the breath he'd been holding and texted Andrew.

Kian's, at four.

50

ANDREW

"Come in." Syssi opened the door for Bhathian and him. "Hi, stranger." She kissed Andrew's cheek after shaking Bhathian's hand.

Okay, he deserved it. Ever since he started seeing Nathalie he hadn't visited or even called his sister. Shame on him.

"Sorry." He pulled her into a hug and kissed her cheek.

"It's okay, you're going to make it up to me by telling me all about this new lady friend of yours."

He followed her inside and took a seat next to Bhathian on the couch. "Actually, that is exactly why we are here."

Syssi perked up, but then glanced at Bhathian and frowned. "And this lady friend of yours has something to do with Bhathian?"

Andrew nodded. "Where is Kian? I don't want to tell the story twice."

"He's coming." She waved her hand in the direction of the hallway. "As always, he had to take a phone call about some disaster. It's as if no one in this entire organization can make executive decisions and take care of business.

They are like kids, calling daddy whenever something doesn't work out."

"You know that it's his fault. They are used to him micro-managing everything. He needs to let go."

"I know." Syssi sighed and pushed toward them a tray loaded with an assortment of small containers. "Help yourselves." The selection included roasted peanuts, almonds, olives and other munchies, along with several bottles of beer.

"Everyone is sick of me pushing cappuccinos at them, so I decided to serve beer instead. But if you guys want coffee, I can make it in a jiffy."

"Not for me, thank you." Bhathian reached for a bottle, popped the lid, and gulped half of it on a oner.

"Sorry for keeping you waiting." Kian walked in barefoot, comfortable in his weekend attire of faded T-shirt and pair of old, well-worn jeans. He looked younger and more relaxed than Andrew remembered ever seeing him.

Marriage apparently agreed with the nearly two-thousand-year-old geezer who looked like he was in his early thirties.

Kian motioned for Syssi to get up from her chair, then took her place and pulled her down to sit in his lap. She didn't object in the least, leaning back against him and resting her head on his shoulder.

It was obvious that Syssi was happy, she looked so content.

Andrew's heart swelled in a very unmanly manner, and he felt like kissing his brother-in-law on both cheeks, or at least bro-hug-and-clap him. These two belonged together, and although there would no doubt be many fights in their long future, over matters small and large, their love for each other was unshakable.

Bhathian took another swig of his beer and glanced at Andrew.

Andrew shook his head. "It's your story to tell, not mine."

He nodded. "I'm not good at this, so bear with me."

"Take your time, Bhathian," Syssi said.

"Over thirty years ago, I hooked up with a stewardess who turned out to be resistant to thralling. I somehow managed to refrain from biting her and thought it was the last I'd seen of her. A month later she found me at the same bar we'd first met at and invited me again to her hotel room. She informed me that she was pregnant and that I was the father, saying that she hadn't been with anyone else for months. I suggested an abortion, but she refused." Bhathian rubbed his hand over the back of his neck, then emptied what was left in his bottle.

The only response from their audience had been a stifled gasp from Syssi when Bhathian had gotten to the pregnancy part.

"She said she was forty-five and had given up hope of ever conceiving—which was unbelievable because she looked to be in her mid-twenties. She wanted the baby regardless of my involvement. I offered her the only thing I could, financial support. She thanked me, but that was all. She never contacted me again and never came back to the club. I went to that damned club every night hoping she'd be there, but after weeks of waiting, I knew she wouldn't and went searching for her. All I had to go on was her name and the airline she worked for. I found out that she quit her job shortly after talking to me, and moved out from the address listed in her file. I also got her social from that same file and tried to find her using it but got nowhere with it. Other than that, I had nothing else to go on."

"Why were you searching for her? She didn't want your money, and there was nothing else you could've offered her."

Syssi cast her husband an incredulous look.

"What? Did I say something wrong?"

She shook her head. "Oh, my God, Kian, sometimes I wonder about you. Think! She was pregnant with his child! If it were you, wouldn't you want to know if you had a son or a daughter? Try to help him or her in any way you could?"

Kian grimaced. "You're right. I would've."

Syssi patted his cheek as if he was a child who had learned his lesson, then turned to Bhathian. "Please continue."

"You nailed it Syssi. The not knowing has been tormenting me throughout the years. So when I heard about Andrew's access to government information, I asked him to help me find her."

He glanced at Andrew. "Perhaps you should tell this part of the story?"

"No problem." Bhathian needed a breather, and Andrew didn't mind taking over at this point.

"To make a long story short. Bhathian's stewardess, Patricia Evans, was a drug enforcement agent named Eva Paterson, who at the time was part of a long-term investigation regarding airline personnel who were suspected of drug trafficking. Following her meeting with Bhathian, she quit the agency, married a guy named Fernando Vega, and seven months later Nathalie was born. Bhathian's daughter."

"That's amazing, Andrew, do you know where they are?" Syssi sat up straight and leaned forward as if eager to hear more good news.

"We know where Nathalie and Fernando are, right here

in Glendale, but Eva has been missing for the last six years. No one knows what happened to her."

Syssi cast Bhathian a sympathetic look. "Well, at least you finally found your daughter."

A mixture of pride and love shone in Bhathian's eyes as he nodded.

"Now to the reason we are here. We suspect that Eva is an immortal."

Kian harrumphed. "Impossible."

"Here are the facts." Andrew raised a finger. "One. Eva hasn't changed a bit over the years. She looked exactly the same in the composite the forensic artist drew of her from Bhathian's memories, and the picture Nathalie provided the police when she filed the missing person's report. A woman who was supposed to be in her seventies still looked to be no more than thirty."

Kian still looked skeptical, and Andrew raised a second finger. "Two. When Bhathian met her, he also thought she looked much younger than her real age. I know of no woman over the legal drinking age who would lie about being older than she actually is."

He raised a third finger. "Three. Bhathian couldn't thrall her."

"Some humans are immune." Kian waved a dismissive hand.

"Four. Nathalie talks with ghosts in her head."

"What!?" Bhathian almost choked on the olive in his mouth.

Syssi gaped, and Kian lost his dismissive expression.

Andrew smirked. "I've been seeing Nathalie, basically every day, since Bhathian and I went to the coffee shop she owns. But she only confided in me recently about the voices in her head. She isn't sure if they are real or imagined, and has tried to keep it a secret so people won't think her crazy."

"Your mystery woman…" Syssi said quietly.

"Yes."

Kian turned to look at Bhathian, who shrugged and clapped Andrew's back. "I owe him, and I like him. Andrew is a stand-up guy, couldn't have asked for a better man for my daughter."

"Oh, wow," Syssi exclaimed. "This is serious."

Yeah, it was.

Andrew raised a hand with all five fingers splayed. "Five. Nathalie confirmed that her mother looked eerily young, despite her best efforts to make herself look older with the help of makeup and unflattering clothing."

Kian moved Syssi to sit sideways on his lap. "I agree with you that the circumstantial evidence is strong. But how on earth could Eva have been immortal if Bhathian didn't bite her? And even if he did, and she happened to be a Dormant, which in itself is extremely unlikely, the transformation would've been fatal—considering her age at the time. Not to mention what it would've done to her unborn child."

Kian had been following the same string of logic as Andrew. He was going to shorten the process for the guy. "We have to assume that she was already an immortal then, but wasn't aware of it."

"There are no immortal females unaccounted for."

"Yeah, I know. Bhathian told me as much. That's why I think the only possible scenario is that she had sex with an immortal male long before meeting Bhathian, and was unknowingly turned. It must have happened when she was very young, and for years she must've assumed that she was just one of the lucky ones who were incredibly healthy and aged slowly. But as she got even older and still remained unchanged she probably freaked out and eventually ran when it became impossible to hide it any longer."

"What does Nathalie think?"

Andrew chuckled. "That during her time as a government agent, her mother participated in some secret genetic experiment, and that her disappearance has something to do with this as well. Nathalie thinks Eva returned to her old job as an agent."

Syssi pushed up from Kian's lap and grabbed one of the beers. "Her take on it is less far-fetched than Eva being turned by one of us or a Doomer, going through the transition without realizing what's happening to her, and then getting pregnant from a random hookup with another immortal."

In the silence that followed, Andrew mulled over his sister's succinct summary, and given the deep frown on Kian's face, so did he.

Bhathian popped the lid off another bottle and let it swing from between his fingers as he shook his head. "I hate to give them credit, but it must've been the Fates. The statistical chance of this unlikely sequence of events happening is so infinitesimal it's practically nonexistent."

Kian got up and grabbed a beer for himself. "What's next? I know you guys didn't come here just to share this incredible story." He arched a brow at Bhathian.

"I want to go searching for Eva."

"And I guess you came here to ask for an extended leave of absence?"

"Not yet, but I will once I know where to start looking. Andrew is going to do some research for me, but I will probably need additional resources."

Kian nodded. "Whatever you need, it's yours. But a leave of absence is problematic. You know how thinly stretched we are. We don't have enough Guardians."

"That's why I came to you before even having the first clue to follow. We need to call in some of those who left the force, and at the same time step up the training of new recruits."

"Yeah, I was thinking along the same lines, but for a different reason. There is a large contingent of Doomers somewhere nearby, and they've certainly had enough time to get organized. I expect shitloads of trouble, and soon."

51

SEBASTIAN

"*L*etty, Letty, Letty, I told you, if you won't hold position your punishment doubles."

The sobs got louder, but the girl lowered herself back to the bench.

Testing her progress, he hadn't tied her down this time. She wasn't doing too well even though this beating was mild in comparison to the previous ones.

Stupid girl. By now she should've known that the more obedience she showed, the more submissive and compliant she was, the sooner her torment would be over, and she'd be rewarded with a bite—the pain ceasing immediately. But apparently her brain capacity was even less than that of the famous Pavlov's dogs.

Letty was trembling all over.

At this rate, she would pass out before he got his fill.

Her screams and her begging were adequate. And even though he didn't speak Spanish, yet, the sounds she was producing were lovely.

He wasn't hitting her all that hard, and the pale welts on her ass would've faded by tomorrow even without the benefit of his venom. But the girl had a tolerance for pain of a toddler.

Damn, he hadn't even gotten hard.

Swish, with a flick of his wrist the cane landed on target.

Letty cried out but held on.

Her obedience brought a small twitch to his member. "Good girl. Just one more."

She whimpered, and he delivered the last one quickly before she lost her nerve and he would've been forced to give her more.

Sebastian was tired of her.

The problem was, she hadn't gotten him aroused enough for his fangs to elongate and for his glands to produce venom. Sebastian wanted out of this room and away from this poor excuse of a sub. For a moment, he considered calling Tom to finish the job for him. Except, the guy would lose all respect for him if he got a whiff of Sebastian's problem. And besides, he doubted Tom could get it up for the sobbing mess still bent over the whipping bench.

The guy was plain vanilla.

Reluctantly, he walked up to the girl, lifted her trembling body in his arms and sat on the bench. Cradling her, he stroked her hair and praised her although she didn't deserve it. This was an important part of her training, and he had to resort to faking tenderness.

Rocking Letty back and forth, Sebastian closed his eyes and brought up the image of his attorney. Now, that was a worthy sub. Recalling their last session did the trick, and he felt himself getting harder, his fangs elongating. Imagining that the woman in his arms was plump, short, and fair-skinned, he scraped them over her neck and then bit down.

The girl sighed, her tensed muscles going lax. He lifted

her up and carried her to her room. Unfortunately, the one minute walk had defeated his short-lived arousal. He laid Letty on her bed, put a bottle of water on her nightstand, and walked out.

The question was, should he call the club and schedule a session, or go hunting again for someone he could actually enjoy?

The club won. Finding a pleasing submissive to abscond with was proving harder than he'd anticipated, as evidenced by what he and Tom had managed to snag to date. They had fifteen girls in the basement, but none was what Sebastian was looking for, and tonight his first priority was to release some steam.

Tomorrow, he would resume the hunt.

52

NATHALIE

"*H*ey, Nathalie, come meet my friends."

Jackson poked his head into the kitchen, beckoning her to come out. Lately, this had been the new mode of operation—him up front taking care of customers, her stuck in the kitchen, baking and preparing sandwiches.

The only times she ventured out were when she had to send Jackson out to buy supplies because she was running out. Thank God that Andrew had volunteered to do it today, so she could keep on baking while Jackson tended the front. The place had been a mad house all day and she couldn't have spared him even for a short supermarket run.

Jackson was a customer magnet—and not only of the female kind.

He seemed to have an endless supply of friends, whom he'd apparently been bragging to about her pastries. More and more of them were showing up each day to check out her baking. Better yet, they were coming back for more.

More of her pastries, and more time to hang out with Jackson.

The shop was booming, there was never a place to sit, and she couldn't keep up with the demand.

Fernando had been permanently relocated to a tiny corner in the kitchen, which he didn't mind and actually preferred since she was spending most of her time in there and not up front, and besides, the crowded shop was making him nervous.

Unbelievably, she was thinking of hiring a helper for the kitchen.

Wiping her hands on a towel, Nathalie grimaced. Her poor hands were showing the rough treatment she was subjecting them to. Reddened and swollen was not an attractive look. Andrew hadn't said a word, but she was sure her touch wasn't as soft as he would've liked it to be.

"Nathalie, come on…" Jackson walked into the kitchen and grabbed a corner of her apron to drag her out.

She slapped his hand. "Let me at least take this off."

He relented, waiting for her to get rid of her flour-covered apron before coming behind her and giving her a gentle push.

Expecting Jackson's teenage crowd, she was surprised at the impressive young couple standing on the other side of the counter.

"Nathalie, these are my friends, Kri and Michael. Guys, this is the famous Nathalie."

She offered her hand to the girl. "I don't know about the famous, but it's nice to meet you, Kri."

The girl, who looked like she could play professional football, took her hand, shaking it gently as if she was handling an egg carton. "Nice to meet you too. Jackson doesn't stop talking about your pastries and we just had to come and have a taste."

Nathalie laughed. "I have no idea how he has time for all the advertising he's doing for me when he's here all the time."

Kri's boyfriend lifted his phone. "It's called Facebook, Snapchat… you name it, he used it to make you famous." He returned the phone to his pocket and offered his hand. "I'm Michael."

"Okay, now you can go back to your kitchen." Jackson *graciously* allowed her to go back to work.

She rolled her eyes. "I swear, this boy thinks he owns the place." She pointed a finger at him. "But don't forget that I can fire you anytime."

He smirked. "You wouldn't. I'm too good at this."

He was right, of course. And besides, in the short time he'd been with them, both she and her father had come to regard him as family. She wouldn't let him go even if he tried.

"You're so full of yourself." Nathalie waved a dismissive hand before ducking back into the kitchen.

Thank God it was already five in the afternoon, and that Sundays she closed at six. After this last batch of muffins went into the oven, she would finally sit down and rest. Her back and her legs were begging for a good massage.

Luckily, she had her own masseur, with strong and talented fingers. So far, only her feet and her shoulders had benefited from Andrew's incredible massage at the end of each day, but after Friday night, she hoped he'd give her a full body, sensual one.

Yesterday, she'd still been a little sore, but today she was fine—eager to find out what it would be like without the pain.

Mind blowing, no doubt.

Andrew was a skilled and generous lover, and she was

so glad he'd been her first. He'd made it wonderful for her despite the unavoidable hurt, and not only because he'd been so patient and so bent on ensuring she had pleasure first. She found it beyond admirable that he'd been willing to stop at any point, and she didn't doubt for a moment that he would've even if he were a moment away from ejaculating.

Apparently, the myth that men couldn't stop once they were too far gone was just that, a myth.

A real man, a man like Andrew, could and would stop on a dime if the woman he was with asked him to.

The buzzer on her back door went off. Probably Andrew back from the supermarket.

She rushed to open up for him, and tried to relieve him of some of the many paper bags he was carrying, but of course, being the macho guy he was, Andrew refused. "I got it, sweetheart, just lock the door after me so your father doesn't sneak out."

Having Fernando in the kitchen was like having a pet who just waited for an opportunity to make a run for it, the small difference being that the door needed to remain not only closed but locked with the help of a combination lock.

Since her work table was in use, Andrew dropped the bags on the floor next to the door.

"I'll put everything away but you'll need to tell me where."

"I'll do it." She bent over the first bag and pulled out a slab of baking chocolate.

Andrew took it out of her hands. "You have enough to do, let me help the only way I know how." He kissed her lips when she pouted. "Where does this go?" He held the chocolate up.

She pointed, and he put it away then pulled out the next

item. In minutes, he had everything stored, while she finished working on her muffins and stuck them in the oven.

"Finally, it's all done. And if we run out, we'll just turn people away. I'm done with this kitchen for today."

Andrew pulled her into a hug then turned her around, her back to his front, and started massaging her aching shoulders. "Poor baby, you're one big knot."

His hands kneaded just right, not too rough and not too gentle, and Nathalie closed her eyes, letting her body slump against his.

Someone cleared his throat, and Nathalie's eyes shot to her father, but he was still bent over his newspaper.

"What's up, Bhathian?" she heard Andrew ask and turned her head the other way to see the big guy blocking the entry into her kitchen with his bulk. His shoulders literally spanned the entire distance between the door jambs. In fact, he probably needed to turn sideways so they wouldn't get stuck.

"Do you guys want to come out?"

Nathalie chuckled. "Is there anywhere to sit?"

Bhathian grimaced. "Not really, but there is something I need to talk to you about and there is no space to sit in here either."

"How about we go upstairs?" Andrew suggested.

Not a bad idea. She needed to put her feet up.

"I'll just let Jackson know. You guys go up."

Andrew shook his head. "I'll tell him, you go and rest your cute butt on the couch."

Bhathian cleared his throat again.

"Sorry, my bad." Andrew apologized to him for some reason.

What was that all about? Did Bhathian have a problem with the word *butt*? He didn't strike her as a prude.

53

ANDREW

*A*ndrew gathered Nathalie's feet into his lap and started massaging her toes. She moaned, and Bhathian, who was sitting across from them on a chair he'd brought from her room, almost choked on his coffee.

Nathalie cast him a quizzical glance, but the guy immediately schooled his face into a mask of innocence. "So, Nathalie, Andrew and I have been talking, and we decided to use our department resources to help you search for your mother."

We did?

Nathalie seemed surprised. "You will do this for me? Why?"

He gave her big toe a hard squeeze. "Because we care about you, that's why."

"Ouch, I can see that." She made a face and pulled her foot away.

Andrew pulled it back into his lap. "I'm not done with this one, yet." He pressed his thumb to the arch and she moaned again, oblivious to Bhathian's discomfort.

"I told Bhathian some of what you've told me about

Eva, but we need more information. Anything you can tell us about her could be a potential clue. Did she have family or friends somewhere? Did she talk about visiting a particular destination? Did she talk about her favorite places in the world from her time working as an airline attendant? Any pictures, paperwork, everything—even things that you think are trivial."

Damn, he couldn't remember if Nathalie had told him her mother's name. He was screwed if she hadn't and had noticed his slip.

But she had either told him or didn't remember if she had because she just offered him her other foot to massage.

"That's a lot. I will have to make a list and rummage through what she left behind, which isn't much, but I haven't looked at it for years."

"That's a good idea. Nothing off the top of your head, though?"

Nathalie shook her head. "My parents never went on vacations. Running a café is like slavery. But she never complained about it. She said she'd traveled enough for a lifetime and was tired of it. As far as family, she never mentioned anyone other than her parents, and she was their only daughter. Paris came up as one of her favorite places to visit, she said that Venice was stinky, and the food in Germany was awful. That's all I remember, I'm sorry."

"No worries, sweetheart. We will find a lead. The fact that she used to work for the government is helpful. I might be able to find some clues in her files. Agents, in particular, have a lot of information about them stored away in the archives, even after they retire."

"When do you think you'd be able to look through her stuff?" Bhathian pushed to his feet and stretched.

"Maybe later tonight. But I can't promise. I'm exhausted."

He bent down and kissed her cheek. "Call me when you're done and I'll come over."

"I will." She made a move to get up, but he stayed her with a hand on her shoulder.

"I'll show myself out."

"Thanks, Bhathian."

He gave her a two fingered salute and walked out, his steps surprisingly light and silent on the old stairs that groaned even under Nathalie's weight that was less than half of his.

This was one of the tricks Andrew thought he should ask the Guardians to teach him. It probably had nothing to do with them being immortal—just with their training.

"It's very sweet of you to offer to look for my mother and rope Bhathian into helping."

"He volunteered."

"I hope you'll have better luck with this investigation than with Tiffany's. I still find the story about her brother picking up her stuff fishy."

"Yeah, but it's not unlikely. If you want, I can try to find her parents' phone number and call to ask about her. But that would mean searching for her birth record to find out their first names, not a big deal, but it's work."

"No, it's okay. Finding what happened to my mother is obviously more important to me. I should go and pull out the box with her things from the attic while you're still here. It's probably full of spiders." She shivered. "I hate those nasty little things."

Andrew moved over a little, dragging Nathalie's feet with him and turning her so her back was against the armrest. "I will gladly assist with the retrieval of the spider-infested box, but I have other plans for this evening."

Catching his drift, she smiled. "And what would those entail?"

He tapped his finger on his chin. "Let's see. One bottle of massage oil, one naked Nathalie, two talented hands, and lots of moaning and groaning, with some '*Oh, Andrew, you're the greatest*' thrown in."

Nathalie laughed. "This sounds amazing, but I'm afraid we'll have to settle for a half-naked Nathalie and very quiet moaning and groaning."

"Nope. I'll ask Jackson to babysit again, and I'll take you to my place." He leaned closer and whispered. "Are you still sore?"

She shook her head. "Not at all. I'm more than ready, I'm eager for more." Her foot found his crotch, giving a new meaning to the term foot massage.

A loud stomping on the stairs must've been Jackson announcing his approach. The damn immortal with his freakish hearing had probably overheard the whole conversation and was coming to tell them that he had plans for tonight and couldn't babysit Fernando.

"Hi, guys," he practically shouted from the hallway in case his stomping wasn't enough of an alert.

Nathalie retracted her foot, but Andrew's shaft formed a bulge in his jeans that was hard to hide.

Jackson's barely contained smirk confirmed Andrew's suspicions. "I just wanted to let you know that I've locked up, and I'm taking Fernando on a looong walk to the Japanese comic store."

Nathalie turned around to face Jackson. "Why on earth would you take an old man to a comic store?"

"Well, the poor guy was cooped up in here all day, he needs to get out."

"I get the walk part, but why to a comic store?" Andrew had to ask.

"Not any comic store, a Japanese one."

"And your point?"

Jackson rolled his eyes. "Duh, comic books, of course."

Andrew chuckled. "Why would you think Fernando would want to see comics?"

With a grimace that said *'you old people know nothing'*, Jackson put his hands on his hips. "First of all, at Fernando's pace the store is an hour walk away, it has places to sit, but most importantly, it has tentacle porn."

Nathalie's jaw dropped.

"What the hell is tentacle porn?"

"Just what it sounds like—porn with tentacles. Fernando is going to love it." He winked.

"You're okay with it?" Andrew looked at Nathalie.

She shrugged. "He is a big boy. But if it freaks him out, you'll have to deal with his tantrum. Not an easy feat in public."

"Don't worry. I'm sure he's going to have fun. And if he throws a tantrum, I'll just tell everyone my grandfather has dementia. Anyway, I estimate about three hours before we are back. Have fun." He winked at Andrew.

Nathalie blushed the color of beets.

"The little devil is killing me," she whispered, thinking Jackson was out of earshot.

"No, he is being a saint. Now, what I want to know is where you hide the massage oil."

54

NATHALIE

"*I*n the bathroom, the cabinet under the sink."

Andrew jumped up. "I'll be back in a moment."

"Wait…"

He turned around.

Nathalie cast him a sultry look. "I want to shower first."

"Need someone to wash your back?" His voice got husky.

"That's the idea."

He was back at her side in two quick strides. Snaking one arm under her knees and the other under her arms, he lifted her in his strong arms and held her snugly against his hard chest.

Nathalie giggled as he carried her down the hallway and into the bathroom. "I can walk, you know."

"I know, but I'm a full-service kind of guy. I carry and wash for the same price." He set her down on the vanity's counter and started unbuttoning her shirt.

"And the price is?"

"A kiss." He popped the last button and parted the two

halves, his eyes zeroing on her stiff nipples visible even through the light padding of her bra. Regrettably, it fastened in the back.

Note to self, replace all bras with the kind that fasten in the front.

It was such a delightfully naughty thought that she felt herself getting wet between her legs. The idea of making herself easily accessible to Andrew at all times was hot.

Perhaps she should add skirts to her shopping list.

Oh, goodness, what is becoming of me?

Embrace your inner slut, girl, Sage's voice sounded in her head.

I wasn't talking to you, she thought at him. *Get lost.*

Sorry, I'm going, just wanted to tell you that I'm so proud of you that I have tears in my ghostly eyes.

She giggled.

"What's so funny, sweetheart?"

She wasn't about to tell him of Sage's brief visit. It would spoil the mood. But she could tell him about her naughty musings. "I was just thinking that I'm going to replace all my bras with the kind that open in the front."

Andrew skimmed his knuckles over the tops of her breasts, sending zings of desire down to her core. "Good idea." He grabbed her bra cups and pulled them down, folding them under her breasts.

As she glanced down at her pushed up swells—topped by nipples that were stiff and distended—the sight of her smallish breasts looking so lewd aroused her, and she wiggled her butt on the countertop to relieve the itch that had started there.

She was impatient. "Don't you want to finish undressing me first?"

Andrew's thumbs strummed over her aching peaks. "In a moment."

He licked his lips, and she arched her back in anticipation of his next move. With a groan, he leaned forward—his hands slapping the counter as he braced his weight against it—and took one nipple between his lips. Nathalie gasped, thrusting her breast out and grasping his head to get him to take more of it inside his hot mouth.

Andrew hollowed his cheeks, sucking as much of her breast inside as he could, then released it with a loud pop, capturing the peak between his teeth.

"Oh, my God," she rasped, her hands pulling on his hair to hold him to her. It didn't hurt, but there was something hot about the implied vulnerability. He could hurt her, but she trusted him not to. And that was hot too.

His tongue replaced his teeth, then he repeated the whole thing with her other breast. By the time he lifted his head with a satisfied smirk on his handsome face, she was ready to skip the shower and get down to business.

Nathalie shrugged off her blouse and reached back to unhook her bra. Next, she lifted a little to pull her pants and panties down.

Andrew's eyes were smoldering as he watched her no-nonsense, quick striptease. "Impatient?"

"Very." She made a move to hop off the counter, but he caught her before her legs touched the floor and carried her into the shower, getting in with her cradled in his arms.

"Put me down, Andrew," she commanded and reluctantly he complied.

"My turn." She reached for his belt buckle, releasing it and zipping down his jeans at the same time. He helped, grabbing his T-shirt and pulling it over his head, then tossing it out on the bathroom floor, while she tugged on his pants, pulling them past his hips together with his boxer briefs.

Kneeling to get them off his legs, Nathalie found herself face to face with his erection. "Well, hello there." She gave it a little kiss, and it jerked in response. "Miss me? I think you did." She fisted the hard length, running her hand up and down on the smooth, warm skin. When she licked the crown, Andrew groaned and swayed a little, letting himself fall back against the shower's tiled wall.

Did she make him weak at the knees?

Looking up at his face, she swirled her tongue around the mushroom head and watched his lids sliding shut, his lips parting on a pant.

"You like it, don't you?"

Andrew opened his eyes, his hand reaching for the top of her head. "I love it." He caressed her hair and then cupped her cheek. "And I hate to press the pause button, but I would prefer to be freshly showered for you."

She gave the plump head one last kiss before getting up. "You smell and taste delicious. But I get it, I'd rather be freshly showered too." She winked at him.

This was another fantasy Nathalie wished to explore. She'd been thinking about it ever since reading in one of her romance novels about a couple pleasuring each other with their mouths simultaneously. It had been one of her favorites, probably because the girl in the story was also a virgin, even though it wasn't a historical romance and the girl was in her mid-twenties. Nathalie could identify with the character.

Washing each other, they took a little too long caressing and squeezing and pinching. Nathalie was afraid they would run out of time.

She was pretty sure that if Jackson came back and realized they were still in her room, and the door was locked, he would distract Fernando. Still, better to be done before Jackson brought her father back.

Andrew grabbed one of the thick towels she had stacked on the shelf by the shower and wrapped her in it, then reached for another one to dry himself.

"Come on, gorgeous." He stepped out of the shower and offered her his hand. She took it, and he led her to her small bedroom.

Her twin-sized bed wasn't meant for a couple, and Andrew eyed it for a second before striding up to it and sitting down, then pulling her down to sit in his lap.

"Sorry about the bed."

"Why? Is it lumpy?" He bounced up and down with her still cradled in his arms. "Feels solid to me."

Was he the sweetest guy, or what?

She cupped his cheeks and kissed him lightly on the lips. "I love you, Andrew Spivak," she said, feeling like everything had just shifted, her crazy world realigning because of how right it felt to say these words to him.

ANDREW

*D*ear *God Almighty*, Nathalie's words, so unexpected, so priceless, hit Andrew like Zeus's mythical thunderbolt, and the shock left him speechless for about a second. Then he crushed her to him. "I love you too, Nathalie Vega," he croaked, ashamed that compared to her steady and assured tone, his delivery sounded like that of a teenage boy whose voice was still in a flux.

"You're smushing me!" She laughed.

He let go, but just a little. "Now that I have you, I'm not letting you go, better get used to it," he whispered into her hair.

She wiggled a little, forcing him to loosen his hold and free her arms.

"Look at me, Andrew," she said in a serious tone, and for a moment, he was worried that he'd gone too far.

But as he lifted his head, he saw that her eyes were smiling through a sheen of moisture.

"Now that I have found you, I'm not letting you go either. You're mine. So *you* better get used to it, buddy." She chucked him under the chin.

Her statement was meant to reassure him, but instead, it gave him pause. He was her first, and didn't most people believe that they fell in love with their first sex partner?

Nathalie was naïve and inexperienced, and surrendering her virginity to him must've been emotionally stirring for her. And it wasn't only the sex, he was also her first romantic interest. Not to mention the hope he'd given her of finding her mother. Substitute any Joe Schmo for him and Nathalie would've most likely fallen, or believed she had, for him too.

Andrew, on the other hand, had no doubt that she was the one for him. Deep down, he'd known that he'd fallen in love with her, probably from the start. He just needed to be hit over the head with her proclamation to admit it to himself.

Nathalie's finger was tracing a path down his bare torso, and he tensed, expecting her to linger on his scars, but her finger continued its downward track until she reached the top of the towel he had wrapped around his hips and gave it a tug.

"Are you going to keep it on for long?" She smiled suggestively. "Tick, tock, tick, tock... time is not on our side."

She was right, of course. And talking about whether what she was feeling was love or just infatuation could and should wait for when they were both dressed and not so hungry for each other. Perhaps when her hormones no longer ran the show, Nathalie's head would clear, and she'd be in a better position to re-evaluate her true feelings for him.

"Come here." He hooked a finger under her chin and lifted her head. Taking her lush lips in a passionate kiss, he poured his heart into it, licking inside her mouth and tasting her sweetness. She was panting when he released her mouth. With a slow hand, he unwrapped her towel. As she was revealed to him, the steam that had been trapped there rose up from her smooth skin, and he wanted to lick her all over.

"You're so beautiful, Nathalie, you take my breath away," he told her as he lifted her off his lap and laid her on the bed. "I forgot about the lotion, I'll be right back." He kissed her belly before turning to go back to the bathroom.

"Let's leave the massage for some other time." She stopped him. "Come back here, I want to taste you again." And just like that, his shaft that had been already hard from their kiss sprung up and tented his towel.

Nathalie giggled and lifted up to her knees. "Look at this…" She reached for his towel and pulled, leaving him standing in front of her with his erection standing up at attention and ready for inspection.

Dropping the towel to the floor, she took him in hand. Gently moving up and down, she then rubbed her thumb over the tip to spread the drop of moisture that had welled there.

"I love how your shaft feels, hard on the inside but velvety on the outside." She looked up at him and smiled. "The opposite of you. You're hard on the outside but sweet on the inside."

Andrew rolled his eyes. What was with that *sweet* thing? He was as far from *sweet* as it got. His internal rumblings ceased as Nathalie extended her tongue and gave it a halting lick, and then another one, then rubbed her cheek on it like a kitten on a scratching post.

He ached to bury himself in her moist mouth, but he was letting her explore.

Mercifully, she'd gone back to licking, swirling her tongue all around the head before closing her lips around it.

"Yes, just like that," he groaned, his hips surging forward of their own accord, pushing more of his length into her mouth.

She sucked it in even deeper, and he cupped her cheek, feeling his shaft on the other side. Guided by instinct, she moved her mouth and her tongue in a way that drove him wild, and it took all he had not to thrust deeper. When she moaned around him, he almost came.

But as much fun as this was, it wasn't how he wanted to proceed. It wasn't enough for him to be pleasured, he needed to pleasure Nathalie even more.

Andrew put his hand on top of her head, stroking her hair as he pulled out of her mouth.

She looked up at him with worry in her big brown eyes. "Did I do something wrong? Wasn't it good for you?"

"No, sweetheart, you did it perfectly. But even though I'm a selfish bastard, pleasuring you gives me pleasure too." He lay on her small bed and pulled her on top of him, her knees straddling his face and her mouth hovering above his cock.

She turned her head around to look at him, a blush painting her cheeks red. "Oh, God, how did you know?"

He gave her slit a lick, getting a little taste before answering her. "Know what?" He thrust his tongue in between her wet folds, finding her entry and licking all around.

Nathalie moaned. "I've been fantasizing about doing this exactly like that," she breathed and took his shaft into her mouth, going down as far as she could before retreating.

The girl was a natural. Which meant that he needed to perform magic with his tongue to have her orgasming before he erupted in that skillful mouth of hers.

Splaying his hands over her heart-shaped ass, he held her in place, stilling her gyrating hips as he tongued her.

Damn, she was hot, wild, her tender flesh quivering on his tongue, and as he pushed a finger into her wet heat, she cried out, momentarily letting his shaft slide out of her mouth.

It was good, the cool air on his wet erection was exactly what he needed to delay his climax for just long enough to bring her off first.

He added another finger, and she took him back in her mouth, groaning around him—the vibrations bringing him close to the edge again.

Closing his lips around her clit, he sucked, and at the same time scissored his fingers, thrusting them deep inside her.

Nathalie screamed, the sound muffled by his shaft, then took him so deep that he bumped against the end of her throat. With a grunt, he pulled out before his seed erupted, finishing all over her face but at least not in her mouth.

She wasn't ready for that, yet.

Rolling off him, she grabbed one of the towels from the floor and wiped her face, then sprawled next to him on the bed.

"Sorry about that," he mumbled trying to catch his breath,

"You should be." She turned her head, pinning him with a pair of narrowed eyes. "Don't you dare pull out again like that. I told you that I wanted to taste you."

"Yes, ma'am." He saluted her, barely stifling a laugh.

Who could've known that his shy virgin would turn into a hungry cougar after her first taste of sex?

NATHALIE

*N*athalie barely stifled a giggle. Andrew could not have looked more surprised and confused if she had told him that she wanted to dance naked in the street.

Maybe she'd overdone her pretense?

Yes, she was disappointed that she didn't get to enact her fantasy to the letter, but she wasn't really mad. How could she be? Andrew had pulled out only because he'd thought she wasn't ready. No doubt he would've preferred to finish in her mouth than all over it.

Hm, she'd wiped away most of it but not all. Tentatively, Nathalie licked her lips.

Oh, yeah, there it is—Andrew's taste.

She snuggled up to him, and he wrapped his arm around her, pulling her even closer. "I wish we could stay like this."

"Yeah, me too. Unfortunately, Jackson and my father are going to be back soon."

"Do you think we have time for another shower?"

"Probably. Knowing Jackson, he will text me when they are about to come back."

"Then let's go, and take your phone with you."

This time, their shared shower was all about efficiency and not intimacy. They were out of there and fully dressed in no more than five minutes.

Nathalie took Andrew's hand and led him to the den. "Let's at least snuggle until they return."

He kicked his shoes off and lay down, then pulled her on top of him. His hands gently caressing her back and her butt.

Her cheek on Andrew's chest, Nathalie smiled. The man was obsessed with her behind—in a good way. And to think that she'd always been self-conscious about the size of her ass and her hips. Apparently Andrew counted them as assets. She giggled.

"What's funny?"

"I was thinking about my ass assets." She giggled again.

He cupped her butt cheeks and then squeezed them possessively. "I love your ass." He gave it another squeeze.

Nathalie sighed. This was so nice, and she hated that soon she would have to say goodnight to Andrew. She couldn't keep him on the couch for another night. He had to go to work tomorrow.

Evidently, he was thinking along the same lines. "We need to find a better solution for your father. Jackson is an angel, but he is just a temporary fix."

"I know. But you've seen the types that showed up for interviews. I wouldn't let them take care of a dog."

"Neither would I, but we have to keep on looking. You deserve a life, Nathalie, a full one."

"I know, but I won't sacrifice my father in order to have one, I just can't."

Not even for Andrew.

Nathalie hoped it wouldn't be a deal-breaker for him, because if he left her over this, she would just die.

"I know, baby, and I'd never ask it of you. Hell, I would've been disappointed in you if you even considered it. I'm just trying to think outside the box. Perhaps we are going about it all wrong. There must be a better solution."

With a snort, she rolled off Andrew's chest and lay beside him. "I'm open to suggestions."

"I don't have anything yet, but I'm going to give it some serious thought."

"It's easier for those who have extended family, so they can take turns. But I have no one. It's just my dad and me."

Andrew made a face. "You have me, and I have an extended family. In fact, it's a pretty big one."

"Really? You've only mentioned one sister and your parents who are in Africa."

"True, but my sister is married to a guy who has a big extended family, so in a way they are mine as well."

"That's wonderful, and I would love to meet them, but it's not as if I can ask them to help."

"Maybe not, but I can ask for their advice. Or if they know someone who they could recommend as a caretaker for your father. After all, that's how you got Jackson."

She frowned. "What do you mean? Bhathian brought him."

Andrew shifted, and she had the impression that he'd said too much. "Bhathian is a cousin of my brother-in-law, and Jackson is the son of another cousin."

That didn't sound like something that should've been kept a secret, so why had no one mentioned it before? What exactly were Andrew and Bhathian up to?

Come to think of it, it was so strange how the two of them had shown up at her shop and how quickly they had ingrained themselves in her life. Bhathian was there almost every morning, drinking his coffee and sampling all of her pastries, complimenting her each time as if it was his first time tasting them. And Andrew, hitting on her full force from the first day.

Somehow, she doubted it was all a coincidence. Still, why would anyone bother to deceive her? She had nothing of value and was no one special.

Did it have something to do with her mother's disappearance?

After all, Eva could've been more than a simple drug enforcement agent, downplaying the kind of work she'd really done before retiring.

Suddenly, Nathalie saw it all clearly.

Eva hadn't retired voluntarily, she had been forced to leave and hide because she knew something that others wanted to either get their hands on, or silence her so it would never be found. And in that context, her mother's secretiveness and aloofness made perfect sense. Then six years ago they must've discovered her, and she'd had to run again. Not keeping contact with her daughter had been necessary to keep them both safe. Or… the option that Nathalie didn't want to consider—that those mysterious *they* had gotten to her mother.

Bhathian and Andrew were looking for Eva, and she'd been stupid enough to supply them with information. Luckily, there wasn't much that she really knew, and she was going to get rid of the box with her mother's stuff as soon as Andrew left.

God, am I just being paranoid? Please, oh please make it so.

To find out that Andrew was just pretending to care for her so he could get information about her mother was going to kill her.

Nathalie wouldn't survive a disappointment of this magnitude.

Hopefully, the whole mess was just in her head.

Yeah, like there isn't enough of it in there already.

But in case it wasn't sheer paranoia, to be on the safe side, she wasn't going to tell him anything else about Eva.

"What's wrong, sweetheart?" Andrew sounded so genuinely worried.

Damn, if her suspicions were true, then the guy deserved an Oscar. "Nothing, I'm just tired."

"You're crying because you are tired?"

Was she? Nathalie swiped a finger at the corner of her eye, and sure enough—it came away wet.

ANDREW

*W*hat was wrong with her? Why had Nathalie lied about the reason for her tears? She couldn't still be mad about him pulling out, could she?

Was it the talk about her father?

Probably.

He hugged her closer and caressed her arm. "Oh, sweetheart, you're so good and so brave. Such a wonderful daughter. Don't worry about your dad. We will find a solution that will make things better for him, not worse. I promise."

Nathalie nodded into his T-shirt. "I know."

"So what is it? Are you hearing voices again? Are they bothering you?"

Andrew suspected that she wasn't telling him about most of her ghostly visits. He'd often caught her making hand gestures as if she was having a conversation with someone—an internal one. But Nathalie was so uncomfortable talking about what she believed was a mental disorder that he hadn't pushed.

She snorted. "They are always bothersome, but it has

been quiet in my head lately. Tut is basically gone, I haven't heard from him in days, but there is a new guy that calls himself Sage, who tends to pop up at the most inopportune moments."

"What do you mean?" Thinking about that ghost seeing her naked when she'd looked at herself in the mirror made Andrew see red.

Nathalie lifted her eyes to him, and a small smile bloomed on her beautiful face. "Are you jealous? Of a ghost?"

"You're damn right, I'm jealous. And the worst part is that if that ghostly pervert is sneaking up on you when you're nude in front of the mirror, I can't even beat him up."

Nathalie snorted.

Great, he was mad as hell, and she was laughing.

"You have nothing to worry about, Andrew. Sage, and I'm quoting him, is more interested in seeing you naked than me."

A gay ghost? Hell, that was something. Except, there was no reason to believe that all ghosts were straight. If the guy liked other guys when he was alive, there was no reason for his preferences to make a flip around just because he was dead.

But then, another disturbing thought occurred to him. He narrowed his eyes at Nathalie. "Don't tell me he actually got to see me naked…" because that would mean the pervert had watched them making love.

Nathalie rolled her eyes. "No, I wouldn't let him. And he is nice; when I tell him to go away he does. But he butted in a few times, giving me advice."

"About what?"

"You. He encouraged me to hurry and bang you because you're so hot. His words, not mine."

"Why? You don't think I'm hot?"

"I think you're smoldering hot, and you know it."

Yeah, he did. And now he couldn't be too mad at the ghost either. Apparently, Nathalie's forwardness was at least in part due to Sage's active encouragement.

And yet, Andrew found it strange that Nathalie's ghosts were all male. It would've bothered him less if they were female...

Was it possible that they were the product of her imagination after all? She'd been lonely, and craving male companionship. Her mind might have provided an illusion as a substitute. But now that she had a real boyfriend, the previous imaginary one was no longer needed, and she'd conjured another one who fit the role of the best friend she lacked—someone she could confide in, someone who would push her to do what she was afraid of.

Made perfect sense.

The problem with this scenario, though, was that it undermined his conviction that Nathalie was a Dormant.

Communicating with the dearly departed was a paranormal ability; making up imaginary friends at the age of thirty was a mental disability.

Damn, they really needed to find Eva.

Fast.

If Nathalie wasn't a Dormant, he would gladly spend his mortal life with her, helping her find a cure for her mental condition.

But if Nathalie was indeed a Dormant, he would have to go through the transition first in order to turn her.

And he wasn't getting any younger.

Tick, tock, tick tock... his time was running out.

The end...for now...

THE STORY CONTINUES IN
DARK WARRIOR'S PROMISE
Book 8 in The Children of the Gods Series

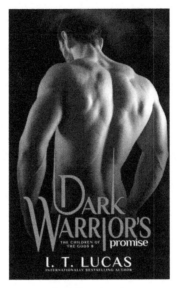

Available on Amazon

Dear reader,

Thank you for reading the ***Children of the Gods series.***

If you enjoyed the story, I would be grateful if you could leave a **review** on Amazon. (With a few words, you'll make me very happy. :-))

THE CHILDREN OF THE GODS ORIGINS

1: Goddess's Choice

When gods and immortals still ruled the ancient world, one young goddess risked everything for love.

2: Goddess's Hope

Hungry for power and infatuated with the beautiful Areana, Navuh plots his father's demise. After all, by getting rid of the insane god he would be doing the world a favor. Except, when gods and immortals conspire against each other, humanity pays the price.

But things are not what they seem, and prophecies should not to be trusted...

THE CHILDREN OF THE GODS

1: Dark Stranger The Dream

Syssi's paranormal foresight lands her a job at Dr. Amanda Dokani's neuroscience lab, but it fails to predict the thrilling yet terrifying turn her life will take. Syssi has no clue that her boss is an immortal who'll drag her into a secret, millennia-old battle over humanity's future. Nor does she realize that the professor's imposing brother is the mysterious stranger who's been starring in her dreams.

Since the dawn of human civilization, two warring factions of immortals—the descendants of the gods of old—have been secretly shaping its destiny. Leading the clandestine battle from his luxurious Los Angeles high-rise, Kian is surrounded by his clan, yet alone. Descending from a single goddess, clan members are forbidden to each other. And as the only other immortals are their hated enemies, Kian and his kin have been long resigned to a lonely existence of fleeting trysts with human partners. That is, until his sister makes a game-changing discovery—a mortal seeress who she believes is a dormant carrier of their genes. Ever the realist, Kian is skeptical and refuses Amanda's plea to attempt Syssi's activation. But when his enemies learn of the Dormant's existence, he's forced to rush her to the safety of his keep. Inexorably drawn to Syssi, Kian wrestles with his conscience as he is tempted to explore her budding interest in the darker shades of sensuality.

2: Dark Stranger Revealed

While sheltered in the clan's stronghold, Syssi is unaware that Kian and Amanda are not human, and neither are the supposedly religious fanatics that are after her. She feels a powerful connection to Kian, and as he introduces her to a world of pleasure she never dared imagine, his dominant sexuality is a revelation. Considering that she's completely out of her element, Syssi feels comfortable and safe letting go with him. That is, until she begins to suspect that all is not as it seems. Piecing the puzzle together, she draws a scary, yet wrong conclusion...

3: Dark Stranger Immortal

When Kian confesses his true nature, Syssi is not as much shocked by the revelation as she is wounded by what she perceives as his callous plans for her.

If she doesn't turn, he'll be forced to erase her memories and let her go. His family's safety demands secrecy – no one in the mortal world is allowed to know that immortals exist.

Resigned to the cruel reality that even if she stays on to never again leave the keep, she'll get old while Kian won't, Syssi is determined to enjoy what little time she has with him, one day at a time.

Can Kian let go of the mortal woman he loves? Will Syssi turn? And if she does, will she survive the dangerous transition?

4: Dark Enemy Taken

Dalhu can't believe his luck when he stumbles upon the beautiful immortal professor. Presented with a once in a lifetime opportunity to grab an immortal female for himself, he kidnaps her and runs. If he ever gets caught, either by her people or his, his life is forfeit. But for a chance of a loving mate and a family of his own, Dalhu is prepared to do everything in his power to win Amanda's heart, and that includes leaving the Doom brotherhood and his old life behind.

Amanda soon discovers that there is more to the handsome Doomer than his dark past and a hulking, sexy body. But succumbing to her enemy's seduction, or worse, developing feelings for a ruthless killer is out of the question. No man is worth life on the run, not even the one and only immortal male she could claim as her own…

Her clan and her research must come first…

5: Dark Enemy Captive

When the rescue team returns with Amanda and the chained Dalhu to the keep, Amanda is not as thrilled to be back as she thought she'd be. Between Kian's contempt for her and Dalhu's imprisonment, Amanda's budding relationship with Dalhu seems doomed. Things start to look up when Annani offers her help, and together with Syssi they resolve to find a way for Amanda to be with Dalhu. But will she still want him when she realizes that he is responsible for her nephew's murder? Could she? Will she take the easy way out and choose Andrew instead?

6: Dark Enemy Redeemed

Amanda suspects that something fishy is going on onboard the Anna. But when her investigation of the peculiar all-female Russian crew fails to uncover anything other than more speculation, she decides it's time to stop playing detective and face her real problem—a man she shouldn't want but can't live without.

6.5: My Dark Amazon

When Michael and Kri fight off a gang of humans, Michael gets stabbed. The injury to his immortal body recovers fast, but the one to his ego takes longer, putting a strain on his relationship with Kri.

7: Dark Warrior Mine

When Andrew is forced to retire from active duty, he believes that all he has to look forward to is a boring desk job. His glory days in special ops are over. But as it turns out, his thrill ride has just begun. Andrew discovers not only that immortals exist and have been manipulating global affairs since antiquity, but that he and his sister are rare possessors of the immortal genes.

Problem is, Andrew might be too old to attempt the activation process. His sister, who is fourteen years his junior, barely made it through the transition, so the odds of him coming out of it alive, let alone immortal, are slim.

But fate may force his hand.

Helping a friend find his long-lost daughter, Andrew finds a woman who's worth taking the risk for. Nathalie might be a Dormant, but the only way to find out for sure requires fangs and venom.

8: DARK WARRIOR'S PROMISE

Andrew and Nathalie's love flourishes, but the secrets they keep from each other taint their relationship with doubts and suspicions. In the meantime, Sebastian and his men are getting bolder, and the storm that's brewing will shift the balance of power in the millennia-old conflict between Annani's clan and its enemies.

9: DARK WARRIOR'S DESTINY

The new ghost in Nathalie's head remembers who he was in life, providing Andrew and her with indisputable proof that he is real and not a figment of her imagination.

Convinced that she is a Dormant, Andrew decides to go forward with his transition immediately after the rescue mission at the Doomers' HQ.

Fearing for his life, Nathalie pleads with him to reconsider. She'd rather spend the rest of her mortal days with Andrew than risk what they have for the fickle promise of immortality.

While the clan gets ready for battle, Carol gets help from an unlikely ally. Sebastian's second-in-command can no longer ignore the torment she suffers at the hands of his commander and offers to help her, but only if she agrees to his terms.

10: Dark Warrior's Legacy

Andrew's acclimation to his post-transition body isn't easy. His senses are sharper, he's bigger, stronger, and hungrier. Nathalie fears that the changes in the man she loves are more than physical. Measuring up to this new version of him is going to be a challenge.

Carol and Robert are disillusioned with each other. They are not destined mates, and love is not on the horizon. When Robert's three months are up, he might be left with nothing to show for his sacrifice.

Lana contacts Anandur with disturbing news; the yacht and its human cargo are in Mexico. Kian must find a way to apprehend Alex and rescue the women on board without causing an international incident.

11: Dark Guardian Found

What would you do if you stopped aging?

Eva runs. The ex-DEA agent doesn't know what caused her strange mutation, only that if discovered, she'll be dissected like a lab rat. What Eva doesn't know, though, is that she's a descendant of the gods, and that she is not alone. The man who rocked her world in one life-changing encounter over thirty years ago is an immortal as well.

To keep his people's existence secret, Bhathian was forced to turn his back on the only woman who ever captured his heart, but he's never forgotten and never stopped looking for her.

12: Dark Guardian Craved

Cautious after a lifetime of disappointments, Eva is mistrustful of Bhathian's professed feelings of love. She accepts him as a lover and a confidant but not as a life partner.

Jackson suspects that Tessa is his true love mate, but unless she overcomes her fears, he might never find out.

Carol gets an offer she can't refuse—a chance to prove that there is more to her than meets the eye. Robert believes she's about to commit a deadly mistake, but when he tries to dissuade her, she tells him to leave.

13: DARK GUARDIAN'S MATE

Prepare for the heart-warming culmination of Eva and Bhathian's story!

14: DARK ANGEL'S OBSESSION

The cold and stoic warrior is an enigma even to those closest to him. His secrets are about to unravel...

15: DARK ANGEL'S SEDUCTION

Brundar is fighting a losing battle. Calypso is slowly chipping away his icy armor from the outside, while his need for her is melting it from the inside.

He can't allow it to happen. Calypso is a human with none of the Dormant indicators. There is no way he can keep her for more than a few weeks.

16: DARK ANGEL'S SURRENDER

Get ready for the heart pounding conclusion to Brundar and Calypso's story.

Callie still couldn't wrap her head around it, nor could she summon even a smidgen of sorrow or regret. After all, she had some memories with him that weren't horrible. She should've felt something. But there was nothing, not even shock. Not even horror at what had transpired over the last couple of hours.

Maybe it was a typical response for survivors--feeling euphoric for the simple reason that they were alive. Especially when that survival was nothing short of miraculous.

Brundar's cold hand closed around hers, reminding her that they weren't out of the woods yet. Her injuries were superficial, and the most she had to worry about was some scarring. But, despite his and Anandur's reassurances, Brundar might never walk again.

If he ended up crippled because of her, she would never forgive herself for getting him involved in her crap.

"Are you okay, sweetling? Are you in pain?" Brundar asked.

Her injuries were nothing compared to his, and yet he was concerned about her. God, she loved this man. The thing was, if she told him that, he would run off, or crawl away as was the case.

Hey, maybe this was the perfect opportunity to spring it on him.

17: Dark Operative: A Shadow of Death

As a brilliant strategist and the only human entrusted with the secret of immortals' existence, Turner is both an asset and a liability to the clan. His request to attempt transition into immortality as an alternative to cancer treatments cannot be denied without risking the clan's exposure. On the other hand, approving it means risking his premature death. In both scenarios, the clan will lose a valuable ally.

When the decision is left to the clan's physician, Turner makes plans to manipulate her by taking advantage of her interest in him.

Will Bridget fall for the cold, calculated operative? Or will Turner fall into his own trap?

18: Dark Operative: A Glimmer of Hope

As Turner and Bridget's relationship deepens, living together seems like the right move, but to make it work both need to make concessions.

Bridget is realistic and keeps her expectations low. Turner could never be the truelove mate she yearns for, but he is as good as she's going to get. Other than his emotional limitations, he's perfect in every way.

Turner's hard shell is starting to show cracks. He wants immortality, he wants to be part of the clan, and he wants Bridget, but he doesn't want to cause her pain.

His options are either abandon his quest for immortality and give Bridget his few remaining decades, or abandon Bridget by going for the transition and most likely dying. His rational mind dictates that he chooses the former, but his gut pulls him toward the latter. Which one is he going to trust?

19: Dark Operative: The Dawn of Love

Get ready for the exciting finale of Bridget and Turner's story!

20: Dark Survivor Awakened

This was a strange new world she had awakened to.

Her memory loss must have been catastrophic because almost nothing was familiar. The language was foreign to her, with only a few words bearing some similarity to the language she thought in. Still, a full moon cycle had passed since her awakening, and little by little she was gaining basic understanding of it--only a few words and phrases, but she was learning more each day.

A week or so ago, a little girl on the street had tugged on her mother's sleeve and pointed at her. "Look, Mama, Wonder Woman!"

The mother smiled apologetically, saying something in the language these people spoke, then scurried away with the child looking behind her shoulder and grinning.

When it happened again with another child on the same day, it was settled.

Wonder Woman must have been the name of someone important in this strange world she had awoken to, and since both times it had been said with a smile it must have been a good one.

Wonder had a nice ring to it.

She just wished she knew what it meant.

21: Dark Survivor Echoes of Love

Wonder's journey continues in *Dark Survivor Echoes of Love*.

22: Dark Survivor Reunited

The exciting finale of Wonder and Anandur's story.

23: Dark Widow's Secret

Vivian and her daughter share a powerful telepathic connection, so when Ella can't be reached by conventional or psychic means, her mother fears the worst.

Help arrives from an unexpected source when Vivian gets a call from the young doctor she met at a psychic convention. Turns out Julian belongs to a private organization specializing in retrieving missing girls.

As Julian's clan mobilizes its considerable resources to rescue the daughter, Magnus is charged with keeping the gorgeous young mother safe.

Worry for Ella and the secrets Vivian and Magnus keep from each other should be enough to prevent the sparks of attraction from kindling a blaze of desire. Except, these pesky sparks have a mind of their own.

24: Dark Widow's Curse

A simple rescue operation turns into mission impossible when the Russian mafia gets involved. Bad things are supposed to come in threes, but in Vivian's case, it seems like there is no limit to bad luck. Her family and everyone who gets close to her is affected by her curse.

Will Magnus and his people prove her wrong?

25: Dark Widow's Blessing

The thrilling finale of the Dark Widow trilogy!

26: Dark Dream's Temptation

Julian has known Ella is the one for him from the moment he saw her picture, but when he finally frees her from captivity, she seems indifferent to him. Could he have been mistaken?

Ella's rescue should've ended that chapter in her life, but it seems like the road back to normalcy has just begun and it's full of obstacles. Between the pitying looks she gets and her mother's attempts to get her into therapy, Ella feels like she's typecast as a victim, when nothing could be further from the truth. She's a tough survivor, and she's going to prove it.

Strangely, the only one who seems to understand is Logan, who keeps popping up in her dreams. But then, he's a figment of her imagination—or is he?

27: Dark Dream's Unraveling

While trying to figure out a way around Logan's silencing

compulsion, Ella concocts an ambitious plan. What if instead of trying to keep him out of her dreams, she could pretend to like him and lure him into a trap?

Catching Navuh's son would be a major boon for the clan, as well as for Ella. She will have her revenge, turning the tables on another scumbag out to get her.

28: Dark Dream's Trap

The trap is set, but who is the hunter and who is the prey? Find out in this heart-pounding conclusion to the *Dark Dream* trilogy.

29: Dark Prince's Enigma

As the son of the most dangerous male on the planet, Lokan lives by three rules:

Don't trust a soul.

Don't show emotions.

And don't get attached.

Will one extraordinary woman make him break all three?

30: Dark Prince's Dilemma

Will Kian decide that the benefits of trusting Lokan outweigh the risks?

Will Lokan betray his father and brothers for the greater good of his people?

Are Carol and Lokan true-love mates, or is one of them playing the other?

So many questions, the path ahead is anything but clear.

31: Dark Prince's Agenda

While Turner and Kian work out the details of Areana's rescue plan, Carol and Lokan's tumultuous relationship hits another snag. Is it a sign of things to come?

32 : Dark Queen's Quest

A former beauty queen, a retired undercover agent, and a successful model, Mey is not the typical damsel in distress. But when her sister drops off the radar and then someone starts following her around, she panics.

Following a vague clue that Kalugal might be in New York, Kian sends a team headed by Yamanu to search for him.

As Mey and Yamanu's paths cross, he offers her his help and protection, but will that be all?

33: Dark Queen's Knight

As the only member of his clan with a godlike power over human minds, Yamanu has been shielding his people for centuries, but that power comes at a steep price. When Mey enters his life, he's faced with the most difficult choice.

The safety of his clan or a future with his fated mate.

34: Dark Queen's Army

As Mey anxiously waits for her transition to begin and for Yamanu to test whether his godlike powers are gone, the clan sets out to solve two mysteries:

Where is Jin, and is she there voluntarily?

Where is Kalugal, and what is he up to?

35: Dark Spy Conscripted

Jin possesses a unique paranormal ability. Just by touching someone, she can insert a mental hook into their psyche and tie a string of her consciousness to it, creating a tether. That doesn't make her a spy, though, not unless her talent is discovered by those seeking to exploit it.

36: Dark Spy's Mission

Jin's first spying mission is supposed to be easy. Walk into the club, touch Kalugal to tether her consciousness to him, and walk out.

Except, they should have known better.

37: Dark Spy's Resolution

The best-laid plans often go awry...

38: Dark Overlord New Horizon

Jacki has two talents that set her apart from the rest of the human race.

She has unpredictable glimpses of other people's futures, and she is immune to mind manipulation.

Unfortunately, both talents are pretty useless for finding a job other than the one she had in the government's paranormal division.

It seemed like a sweet deal, until she found out that the director planned on producing super babies by compelling the recruits into pairing up. When an opportunity to escape the program presented itself, she took it, only to find out that humans are not at the top of the food chain.

Immortals are real, and at the very top of the hierarchy is Kalugal, the most powerful, arrogant, and sexiest male she has ever met.

With one look, he sets her blood on fire, but Jacki is not a fool. A man like him will never think of her as anything more than a tasty snack, while she will never settle for anything less than his heart.

39: DARK OVERLORD'S WIFE

Jacki is still clinging to her all-or-nothing policy, but Kalugal is chipping away at her resistance. Perhaps it's time to ease up on her convictions. A little less than all is still much better than nothing, and a couple of decades with a demigod is probably worth more than a lifetime with a mere mortal.

40: DARK OVERLORD'S CLAN

As Jacki and Kalugal prepare to celebrate their union, Kian takes every precaution to safeguard his people. Except, Kalugal and his men are not his only potential adversaries, and compulsion is not the only power he should fear.

41: DARK CHOICES THE QUANDARY

When Rufsur and Edna meet, the attraction is as unexpected as it is undeniable. Except, she's the clan's judge and councilwoman, and he's Kalugal's second-in-command. Will loyalty and duty to their people keep them apart?

42: DARK CHOICES PARADIGM SHIFT

Edna and Rufsur are miserable without each other, and their two-week separation seems like an eternity. Long-distance relationships are difficult, but for immortal couples they are impossible. Unless one of them is willing to leave everything behind for the other, things are just going to get worse. Except, the cost of compromise is far greater than giving up their comfortable lives and hard-earned positions. The future of their people is on the line.

43: Dark Choices The Accord

The winds of change blowing over the village demand hard choices. For better or worse, Kian's decisions will alter the trajectory of the clan's future, and he is not ready to take the plunge. But as Edna and Rufsur's plight gains widespread support, his resistance slowly begins to erode.

44: Dark Secrets Resurgence

On a sabbatical from his Stanford teaching position, Professor David Levinson finally has time to write the sci-fi novel he's been thinking about for years.

The phenomena of past life memories and near-death experiences are too controversial to include in his formal psychiatric research, while fiction is the perfect outlet for his esoteric ideas.

Hoping that a change of pace will provide the inspiration he needs, David accepts a friend's invitation to an old Scottish castle.

45: Dark Secrets Unveiled

When Professor David Levinson accepts a friend's invitation to an old Scottish castle, what he finds there is more fantastical than his most outlandish theories. The castle is home to a clan of immortals, their leader is a stunning demigoddess, and even more shockingly, it might be precisely where he belongs.

Except, the clan founder is hiding a secret that might cast a dark shadow on David's relationship with her daughter.

Nevertheless, when offered a chance at immortality, he agrees to undergo the dangerous induction process.

Will David survive his transition into immortality? And if he does, will his relationship with Sari survive the unveiling of her mother's secret?

46: Dark Secrets Absolved

Absolution.

David had given and received it.

The few short hours since he'd emerged from the coma had felt incredible. He'd finally been free of the guilt and pain, and for the first time since Jonah's death, he had felt truly happy and optimistic about the future.

He'd survived the transition into immortality, had been accepted into the clan, and was about to marry the best woman on the face of the planet, his true love mate, his salvation, his everything.

What could have possibly gone wrong?

Just about everything.

47: Dark haven Illusion

Welcome to Safe Haven, where not everything is what it seems.

On a quest to process personal pain, Anastasia joins the Safe Haven Spiritual Retreat.

Through meditation, self-reflection, and hard work, she hopes to make peace with the voices in her head.

This is where she belongs.

Except, membership comes with a hefty price, doubts are sacrilege, and leaving is not as easy as walking out the front gate.

Is living in utopia worth the sacrifice?

Anastasia believes so until the arrival of a new acolyte changes everything.

Apparently, the gods of old were not a myth, their immortal descendants share the planet with humans, and she might be a carrier of their genes.

48: Dark Haven Unmasked

As Anastasia leaves Safe Haven for a week-long romantic vacation with Leon, she hopes to explore her newly discovered passionate side, their budding relationship, and perhaps also solve the mystery of the voices in her head. What she discovers exceeds her wildest expectations.

In the meantime, Eleanor and Peter hope to solve another mystery. Who is Emmett Haderech, and what is he up to?

―――――

THE PERFECT MATCH SERIES

PERFECT MATCH 1: VAMPIRE'S CONSORT

When Gabriel's company is ready to start beta testing, he invites his old crush to inspect its medical safety protocol.

Curious about the revolutionary technology of the *Perfect Match Virtual Fantasy-Fulfillment studios*, Brenna agrees.

Neither expects to end up partnering for its first fully immersive test run.

PERFECT MATCH 2: KING'S CHOSEN

When Lisa's nutty friends get her a gift certificate to *Perfect Match Virtual Fantasy Studios*, she has no intentions of using it. But since the only way to get a refund is if no partner can be found for her, she makes sure to request a fantasy so girly and over the top that no sane guy will pick it up.

Except, someone does.

Warning: This fantasy contains a hot, domineering crown prince, sweet insta-love, steamy love scenes painted with light shades of gray, a wedding, and a HEA in both the virtual and real worlds.

Intended for mature audience.

Perfect Match 3: Captain's Conquest

Working as a Starbucks barista, Alicia fends off flirting all day long, but none of the guys are as charming and sexy as Gregg. His frequent visits are the highlight of her day, but since he's never asked her out, she assumes he's taken. Besides, between a day job and a budding music career, she has no time to start a new relationship.

That is until Gregg makes her an offer she can't refuse —a gift certificate to the virtual fantasy fulfillment service everyone is talking about. As a huge Star Trek fan, Alicia has a perfect match in mind—the captain of the Starship Enterprise.

FOR EXCLUSIVE PEEKS AT UPCOMING RELEASES & A FREE COMPANION BOOK

Join my *VIP Club* and gain access to the VIP portal at
ITLUCAS.COM

CLICK HERE TO JOIN
(http://eepurl.com/blMTpD)

INCLUDED IN YOUR FREE MEMBERSHIP:

- **FREE** Children of the Gods companion book **1**
- **FREE** narration of Goddess's Choice—Book 1 in The Children of the Gods Origins series.
- Preview chapters of upcoming releases.
- And other exclusive content offered only to my **VIPs**.

If you're already a subscriber, you can find **your VIP password** at the bottom of each of my new release emails. If you are not getting them, your email provider is sending them to your junk folder, and you are missing out on **important updates, side characters' portraits, additional content, and other goodies.** To fix that, add isabell@ itlucas.com to your email contacts or to your email VIP list.

Also by I. T. Lucas

PERFECT MATCH

The Children of the Gods Series Sets

BOOKS 44-46: DARK SECRETS TRILOGY

MEGA SETS

THE CHILDREN OF THE GODS: BOOKS 1-6—INCLUDES CHARACTER LISTS

THE CHILDREN OF THE GODS: BOOKS 6.5-10 —INCLUDES CHARACTER LISTS

TRY THE CHILDREN OF THE GODS SERIES ON <u>AUDIBLE</u>

2 FREE audiobooks with your new Audible subscription!